The Abersoch Killings

Simon McCleave is a multi-million copy bestselling author. Before writing crime novels, he worked in television and film. He was a Script Editor at the BBC, a producer at Channel 4 and a Story Analyst in Los Angeles. He worked on films such as *The Full Monty* and television series such as the BBC Crime Drama *Between The Lines*. As a script writer he wrote on series such as *Silent Witness*, *Murder In Suburbia*, *Teachers*, *Attachments*, *The Bill*, *Eastenders* and many more.

Also by Simon McCleave

DI Ruth Hunter

The DC Ruth Hunter Murder Case Series

The Anglesey Series – DI Laura Hart

The Dark Tide
In Too Deep
Blood on the Shore
The Drowning Isle
Dead in the Water

Psychological Thrillers

Last Night at Villa Lucia
Five Days in Provence (June 2025)

Simon McCleave

THE
ABERSOCH
KILLINGS

CANELO CRIME

Penguin Random House

First published in the United Kingdom in 2025 by Stamford Publishing Ltd

This edition published in the United Kingdom in 2025 by

Canelo Crime, an imprint of
Canelo Digital Publishing Limited,
20 Vauxhall Bridge Road,
London SW1V 2SA
United Kingdom

A Penguin Random House Company
The authorised representative in the EEA is Dorling Kindersley Verlag GmbH.
Arnulfstr. 124, 80636 Munich, Germany

A CIP catalogue record for this book is available from the British Library.

Hardback ISBN 978 1 83598 282 2
Paperback ISBN 978 1 83598 176 4

Cover design by Tom Sanderson

Cover images © Shutterstock

Printed and bound in Great Britain by Clays Ltd, Elcograf S.p.A.

Look for more great books at
www.canelo.co | www.dk.com

I

PROLOGUE

August 2021

Jack looked down at his vintage Rolex. It was made in 1963, the year of his birth. The time was 11:58 p.m., and he was nicely drunk having had such a wonderful day. He stood on the immaculate lawn at the back of his vast beach-side residence in Abersoch, recently described in *The Sunday Times* as the best waterfront property in Wales. The house itself had seven bedrooms, home cinema, jacuzzi, games room, two full width terraces, breathtaking 180 degree views of Abersoch beach and a frontage that was all glass and clean lines. Jack had it recently valued at £5 million. Not bad for a boy from Birkenhead with an O level in woodwork and nothing else but a shrewd business brain, bags of charm and a fiercesome reputation that struck fear into many.

Today had been the day that Jack had walked the 'light of his life' – Sofia, his twenty-three-year-old stepdaughter – down the aisle. It had all been perfect. Even though it was the last weekend of August, the weather had been glorious and hot. Everything had gone like clockwork, mainly due to the fastidious and immaculate planning of his second wife and Sofia's mother, Lottie. The best caterers, fine wines, couture wedding dress and a stunning vintage Jaguar car. Sofia wasn't biologically his daughter.

She was Lottie's daughter from her first marriage to a failed tennis player called Pascal who had played virtually no role in Sofia's life for over a decade. So, Jack now thought of her as his daughter. And nothing was too much for his princess.

Two huge white marquees had been set up in Jack's five-acre garden that included a swimming pool, tennis court and an orchard. They'd had a hundred guests who had been catered for by exclusive film caterers that Jack had used on many occasions. He'd arranged for a free-flowing bar, celebrity DJ and even concierge parking on a nearby field. The main house was a good five-minute walk from where the wedding was being held, and Jack had made it clear that only family were allowed up there. He didn't want any drunk Tom, Dick or Harry traipsing or nosing around his beautiful home.

Cocaine. That's what I need, Jack thought to himself. *A large brandy, a Cuban cigar and a line of coke.* Remembering that he'd got some coke in his office, Jack turned to head back to the house. The guests had gone so no one was going to miss him if he was gone for half an hour. After everything he'd done today, he deserved it.

The wedding invitation had stipulated *Carriages At 11:30 p.m.* All the guests had left either in their own cars or by taxi that had been booked in advance.

'Why are you hiding out here, darling?' said a slurred voice.

It was Lottie.

Her use of the word 'darling' grated on him. It was just for show. She definitely didn't call him 'darling' when they were alone at home.

She tottered on her designer heels towards him.

'Just getting some fresh air, *darling*,' he replied with a sour tone at a barely audible volume.

Lottie wasn't listening to him.

'Jack, Jack. Now all the guests have gone, Jas wants to film us all saying a few words to Sofia,' she said in a her cut-glass accent, waving her hands around while holding a large glass of wine.

Oh, God, that sounds incredibly tacky, Jack thought but he'd better tow the line or there'd be hell to pay. He knew managing Lottie was all about picking his battles. And the wedding video wasn't one of them. Jasmine – or Jas, pronounced 'Jazz' – was his youngest daughter and at the tender age of twelve, a precocious talent. Jas was a chip off the old block and had been making her own films since she was six years old.

'I knew it had to be your idea, Jas,' Jack teased her with a proud smile.

She smiled back at him, her little braces showing on her teeth.

'Where are the boys?' Lottie asked loudly and then began to gesticulate. 'Boys? Boys?'

Jack's identical twin sons Ed and James, who were twenty-five years old and from his first marriage, appeared looking drunk but happy. Ed, the more confident of the two, had his arm around James's shoulders.

'Dad,' Ed chortled. 'We've got to do a toast to Soph. Good riddance or some bullshit like that,' he joked.

'Edward,' Lottie reprimanded him.

'Come on. You all need to stand together,' Jas groaned gesturing with her hands as she held up the video camera. 'Just there.'

Jack could feel his patience already wearing thin. Playing happy families just wasn't his thing. But if it made

3

Jas happy then he was happy to play along. Plus he didn't know if they would all be assembled like this ever again. He tried not to think about that.

'Come on, Jack,' Lottie snapped. 'Why are you standing over there?' She motioned for him to move close to them and clicked her fingers.

Jesus, she's so annoying, Jack thought through his forced smile.

'Put your arm around James,' Lottie continued. 'And for God's sake, smile properly.'

Jack gave a disgruntled groan under his breath. He didn't want to put his arm around either of his spoiled, feckless sons. To say that they were a deep disappointment to him would be the understatment of the century.

'Okay, that's great,' Jas said encouragingly. 'Do you want to say a few words?'

'I do!' Lottie cried enthusiastically as she raised her glass of champagne to the camera.

Big surprise.

'Sofia, darling. We're so incredibly happy for you and Charlie. And we all love you so much. And if you can be as happy as your father and I have been all these years, then you'll be blessed.'

Jack couldn't help but give a dark smile at his wife's brazen lies. He didn't know why she bothered. Everyone in the family knew the state of their marriage. It was no big secret.

She glanced at the others as she raised her glass. 'To Sofia, we love you, darling.'

'To Sofia,' Jack said with a smile. 'Love you, sweetheart.' For a moment, Jack found himself slightly overwhelmed with sadness. He took a breath to stop a tear coming to his eye. He'd never cried in front of his wife

4

or children before. Not even at his mother's funeral, so he wasn't about to start now. He was tougher than that. And of course, they didn't know his secret.

'Yeah, to Sofia,' Ed and James both muttered.

'Yeah, that's great,' Jas enthused and then grinned. 'And that's a wrap everyone,' she joked, mimicking the language of a Hollywood film director.

Lottie looked at Jack. 'Right, I've got to go and check that everyone has left and there are no stragglers.' She narrowed her eyes and looked at her husband. 'And if it's not too much trouble, Jack, if you could go and make sure that everyone who needs a taxi has got one. Father of the bride,' she said in a withering tone as she turned and headed back to the marquee.

There was an awkward silence between Jack and his two sons.

'Right, you heard Lottie,' Jack said. 'You'd better go and check the taxis.'

Jack had no intention of doing anything of the sort himself. They were mostly Lottie and Sofia's entitled friends from Abersoch and Cheshire. He had nothing in common with them. And he had no intention of actually conversing with them.

Jack gave Ed a surreptitious look. 'Me and you need to have a little chat before you go to bed, mate. Okay?' he said quietly.

Ed looked concerned but nodded. 'No problem.'

Jack checked that Lottie had now gone. He could see her in the empty marque.

He turned to head back to the house.

'Jack, Jack,' said a man behind him, grabbing at the sleeve of his jacket.

Now what? he thought angrily.

5

He turned to see one of Lottie's friends, Hugo, his wife Ella and their daughter Rosie.

Oh, God. Why haven't they gone yet?

'Hi there,' Jack said forcing a friendly smile. 'Couldn't you get a taxi?'

'Oh, I'm driving,' Hugo guffawed. 'Sorry, we were just heading to the car when we saw you.'

Ella touched Jack's arm. 'Aw, Sofia looked so beautiful. You and Lottie must have been incredibly proud?'

'We were. Hope you guys had a good time?' Jack said with a turn and in a tone that was designed to communicate that he wasn't stopping for a chat and they needed to go.

'Wonderful,' Ella laughed.

Right, they're not taking my bloody hint, are they?

'Jack,' Hugo said pointing to his daughter. 'This is our daugter, Rosie. She got a first in English Lit at Oxford. And she's just written a quite wonderful screenplay.'

Of course she has.

'Dad,' Rosie said pulling an embarrassed face.

'A screenplay?' Jack said looking directly at Rosie who was in her mid-twenties. She had dark hair and was very, very pretty. 'I didn't know you were a writer, Rosie,' Jack said turning on the charm. 'Send it over to me. I'll have a read and we can meet up to go through it.'

Rosie's eyes widened with excitement. 'Really? Wow. Thank you so much.'

Jack smiled to himself. Being a powerful film producer had its perks.

'You see?' Ella said to Rosie. 'I told you Jack would read it.'

'Of course. No problem,' Jack reassured them. The script would turn out to be derivative crap but Rosie might well be grateful enough to sleep with him.

Hugo pointed to the field where all the cars were parked. 'Right, we'll be off then. Looks like we're the last to leave.'

Yes you are, so off you fuck.

'See you later,' Jack mumbled as he made a beeline across the lawn, up the stone steps, across the enormous patio and through the bi-folding doors.

The house was quiet and empty.

That's nice, he thought to himself. *A bit of peace and quiet.*

He marched down the hallway and then up the vast staircase.

He finally got to his office, unlocked the doors, went in and closed the doors behind him. The room had huge floor to ceiling glass windows. The walls were adorned with framed film posters and his shelves stacked with books and scripts. The gleaming Oscar, BAFTAs and other awards sat at the far end of his desk.

Slumping down in his padded office chair, Jack gave a satisfied sigh and loosened his tie.

Right, how about a bit of me time now.

Clipping the end of his Cuban Churchill cigar, Jack popped it in his mouth. The doctor had suggested that he stopped smoking cigars immediately. *Fuck that. They're one of life's great pleasures.*

He heard voices out on the landing. Then laughter and a door closing.

As he lit the cigar and puffed, his phone rang. It didn't matter that it was his stepdaughter's wedding day. He had just finished excecutive producing a $40 million movie.

Looking at his phone, he saw that it was Alan Green, a fellow Executive Producer from September Films and Distribution in Los Angeles.

'Alan,' Jack said in a loud, friendly voice. 'If you're interrupting my stepdaughter's wedding, this better be fucking good.'

There was a moment of silence. Alan was scared of him. He knew he was.

'Shit. I thought that was yesterday. Sorry,' Alan said in a concerned voice. 'I'll call you tommorow.'

'Alan, it's fine. I'm taking the piss, mate. Anyway I'm in a very good mood tonight, and tomorrow I'll be hungover and angry about how much this fucking wedding has cost me,' Jack laughed. 'Everything okay?'

'Not really,' Alan admitted. 'It's Olivia.'

Olivia Thompson was the star of the film. But she had been tricky throughout the filming, clashing with the director Tim Shepherd whom she'd accused of being mysoginistic and inappropriate on set.

'Again?' Jack growled. He was starting to get fed up with having to walk on eggshells around Olivia. 'What is it this time?'

'She's flatly refusing to do any press with Tim,' Alan said timidly.

'Well she can't do that,' Jack groaned. 'I'll give her a call. It's time she was taken down a peg or two.'

'Be careful,' Alan said.

'Careful. I'm not going to pussyfoot around that sancti-monious little tramp any more,' Jack thundered down the phone, and he blew a plume of cigar smoke into the air. 'I'm going to remind her that I have an Oscar, two Golden Globes and five BAFTAs. She is a twenty-four-year-old actress who was waiting fucking tables in Hammersmith two years ago and doing shitty little plays above pubs. I can arrange for her to go back to all that if she doesn't toe the line.'

Silence.

'Alan?'

'I'm still here, Jack,' Alan said. 'So I can leave this with you?'

'That's why you called me isn't it? Because you don't have the balls to sort this out,' Jack said coldly. 'You always leave it with me.'

Jack ended the call, feeling a surge of self-importance. He thrived on confrontation.

Grabbing the cut-glass decanter of expensive brandy, Jack poured himself three fingers and then took a long swig.

That's better. Now where is that coke?

Opening the bottom drawer, Jack took out his 'special silver box', put it on the desk and opened it.

Then he heard a noise outside on the landing.

He stopped and listened. It sounded as if there was someone standing right outside the door to his office.

'Hello?' Jack called out. He didn't want to be disturbed.

Silence.

That's strange.

Then Jack took the clear plastic bag of highest grade cocaine.

Bingo! Straight from Columbia.

This stuff was the best. Pure. A million miles from that horrible *pub gack* that he'd been offered in some of the private members' clubs down in London.

Taking a small mirror that he kept in the same drawer, Jack tapped out the cocaine onto it. Then he pulled out his wallet, retrieved a credit card and used it to form three long lines of white powder.

Plucking a fifty-pound note from his wallet, he expertly rolled it into a tube. Placing the note in his left nostril, he leant over the mirror and in one swift movement he snorted the powder.

That smells very strange, he thought to himself as he wiped his nostril for a moment.

He'd been taking cocaine regularly for twenty-five years and had never snorted anything that smelled like that. It had an almost citrus scent. He hoped that he hadn't been given MDMA or worse, Ketamine.

Feeling moisture at the tip of his nostril, Jack touched his nose and saw that his hand was now smeared with blood.

A moment later, his nostril felt like it was on fire.

The burning sensation on the skin inside his nose was agony.

'Jesus!' he groaned, rubbing his nostrils. 'Argh. What the…'

Blood was dripping onto his hand, mouth and chin.

It felt like the skin inside his nostril was dissolving.

His head began to swim and his vision blurred.

What the hell is going on?

Then his breathing started to become laboured.

Whatever he'd just snorted, it wasn't cocaine.

Starting to panic, he tried to get up off his office chair but he was now struggling to breathe.

'Oh, God,' he gasped as he tried to suck in air. 'Help me…'

He grabbed the collar of his shirt, pulling at it.

Everything in the room was now blurred.

Using every ounce of strength he had, Jack pushed himself to his feet.

Fuck, I'm gonna need an ambulance...

He went to shout for help but the words lodged in his constricted throat.

Staggering over to the doors, he grabbed the handles and pulled them open.

But before he could go any further, his legs buckled from under him and he collapsed to the floor with a loud bang.

Managing to roll onto his back, he could feel blood trickling down the back of his throat.

Out of the corner of his eye, he saw something gold glimmering in the light.

His Best Picture Oscar.

Then everything went black.

CHAPTER 1

Detective Sergeant Jim Garrow slumped onto the sofa. It was just gone twelve p.m. He'd spent the evening making sure that his house was tidy and clean. Washed all his clothes for the coming week. He planned to start Sunday morning as he meant to go on. Getting control back in his life, which he knew would lessen the free-floating anxiety that he was experiencing.

His life had been turned upside down in recent months. His actions had resulted in a murder trial being halted and the defendant, Lucy Morgan, being released. Not only did that mean that he was going to face an employment tribunal, but he could also lose his job.

It had been a few months since Lucy Morgan had been found at the Pontcysyllte Aqueduct claiming to have amnesia on the night that her mother, Lynne Morgan, was brutally murdered at her home in Wrexham. Garrow's investigation had eventually discovered that Lucy had slashed her mother's throat after a heated argument and then faked her amnesia to cover her tracks.

However, the major spanner in the works was that Garrow and Lucy had formed a romantic attachment after Lucy had been ruled out as a suspect earlier in the investigation. Although they hadn't slept together, Garrow had been to Lucy's flat. And during the trial, she had claimed they'd had sex. Her defence team had called for a mistrial due to the allegations and the judge had agreed. It was a complete disaster.

On top of that, Lucy had started to stalk Garrow, appearing in his garden late at night. When she confronted him in a pub car park a week ago, he'd run her over on purpose.

The tail end of the local BBC news was on, and Garrow wondered what the weather was going to be like in the coming week in North Wales.

However, a photograph of a man's face came onto the screen.

Garrow recognised him, but for a moment he couldn't remember how or why.

Then he got a sinking feeling in the pit of his stomach. It was the man that he'd seen that afternoon with Lucy. The man that Lucy had said she was moving to London with.

Jasper!

The BBC newsreader said, 'North Wales Police are appealing for witnesses after a man's body was found on farmland just outside Wrexham last night. The victim, Jasper Maclean, was found in Ruabon with serious head injuries at around midnight. He died at the scene. Police have launched a murder inquiry and are appealing for anyone who saw anything suspicious in the area at that time to contact them immediately.'

Garrow sat up on the sofa. *Oh, my God, she's done it again.*

Then he made a decision to confront the problem head on. Rather than wait for Lucy to decide when, how and where she would contact him next, he was going to find her.

Grabbing his car keys, Garrow headed out, closing the front door behind him.

CHAPTER 2

Detective Inspector Ruth Hunter turned off the television and gave a yawn. They'd just watched the final episode of a very good crime drama set in Scotland with a superb twist.

'Bedtime?' asked her partner Sarah as she caught her yawn.

Ruth nodded. 'Bedtime,' she agreed. She was shattered. Now in her fifties, Ruth noticed her slowly declining energy levels as the years went on. God only knew what she'd be like by the time she reached her seventies. She knew that smoking, drinking wine and doing zero exercise probably weren't helping that, but it wasn't something she was prepared to address today.

'By the way, how come you didn't spot the twist coming in that programme?' Sarah teased her. 'Isn't that your job?'

Ruth shrugged. 'I'm not sure. Maybe I'm losing my touch. Plus the brother didn't look shifty enough to have killed two people like that.'

'Shifty?' Sarah snorted with laughter. 'Oh, God, please tell me that you don't make assumptions about suspects based on whether they look 'shifty' or not.'

'Of course not,' Ruth protested. 'But there is an element of gut instinct and first impressions.'

Sarah came over and gave Ruth a kiss and then raised an eyebrow. 'Do your colleagues know that your way of relaxing after a hard day being a detective is to sit and watch a grisly crime drama?'

'Oh, God, no,' Ruth laughed. 'They'd definitely think I was weird if they knew that.'

'Weirder, I think you mean,' Sarah quipped.

Ruth rolled her eyes. 'Very funny.' Then she took Sarah in her arms and looked at her.

'It's been a lovely weekend, hasn't it?' she said softly.

Sarah smiled and nodded. 'It really has.'

They'd had a wonderful Bank Holiday weekend at the home they shared in Bangor-on-Dee, a small picturesque village in North Wales. They'd had a barbeque that afternoon with Ruth's colleagues plus her daughter Ella. Georgie had arrived with her new boyfriend Adam, who was a paramedic, and seemed very affable.

As they left the living room, Ruth gave Sarah an enquiring look. She'd been thinking about Georgie a lot. She was over eight months pregnant, although sadly the father of her child had died. Ruth felt incredibly protective, even maternal, towards Georgie.

'Do we like Adam?' Ruth asked Sarah.

Sarah nodded. 'Oh, yes. We definitely 'like' Adam.'

Ruth rolled her eyes. 'Yeah, I know that he's good-looking. But is he a decent bloke?'

'He seeemed to be,' Sarah replied.

'Yeah, well he'd better be,' Ruth sighed as she turned off all the lights for the downstairs.

She then checked the doors were all locked before following Sarah up the stairs and onto the landing. They both instinctively stopped outside Daniel's room where he was sleeping. Sarah gently opened the door and saw that he was fast asleep.

'Aww,' Sarah whispered. 'Look at him. So cute.'

Ruth's eyes rested on his innocent little face in the darkness. She could feel her heart warm at the sight of him sleeping so soundly.

Daniel was an eleven-year-old boy who Ruth and Sarah had a temporary fostering licence to look after. They were still waiting for social services to come back to them about their application for a permanent adoption. Waiting for them to reach their conclusion was making Ruth and Sarah both a bit jittery. They couldn't imagine their lives without Daniel now.

As they closed the door, Sarah leaned over and gave Ruth a gentle kiss on the lips.

'What was that for?' Ruth asked with a bemused smile.

Sarah shrugged. 'I don't know. I just feel very happy and content with our lives together, that's all.'

Before Ruth could reply, her phone buzzed in her pocket. Taking it out, she saw that it was Detective Sergeant Nick Evans calling. He was her deputy in CID at Llancastell nick. It was definitely too late for Nick to be calling for a chat. And that could only mean bad news.

Ruth pulled a face and then glanced at Sarah. 'Yeah, you might want to hold that thought,' she said dryly.

Sarah gave a resigned expression. 'Hey, I'm used to it.'

'Nick?' Ruth said very quietly as she answered the call and went downstairs to take it so as not to wake Daniel.

'Hi, boss,' Nick said. 'Sorry for the late call.'

'What's going on?' she asked.

'Uniform have called in a death over in Abersoch,' Nick explained. 'Some big-time film producer called Jack Rush. He collapsed at home after his daughter's wedding.

Paramedics pronounced him dead at the scene,' Nick replied. 'It looks suspicious.'

'Right,' Ruth sighed. 'We'd better get over there.'

'I'll pick you up in half an hour,' Nick said.

'Okay, see you then,' Ruth said as she ended the call. Then she looked up at Sarah who was peering down from the top of the stairs. 'Sorry,' she said apologetically.

'Shame. It's Bank Holiday Monday tomorrow,' Sarah whispered.

Ruth rolled her eyes. 'Not any more it's not.'

CHAPTER 3

Georgie gazed up at the bedroom ceiling and shifted, trying to get comfortable. Her baby had kicked her twice which had woken her up. Since then, her head had been whirring with thoughts and fears.

'Can't sleep?' whispered a voice next to her.

It was Adam. She'd only known Adam for about ten days but she knew that she was already falling for him.

He was tall, handsome, athletic, with sandy blond hair and a slight Mancunian accent which Georgie thought was very cute. He was also one of the sweetest, gentlest and thoughtful men she could ever remember meeting.

They hadn't slept together yet. Adam had made it clear that Georgie needed to decide if and when she wanted to. And there was no pressure from him on that front whatsoever.

'No,' Georgie sighed. 'It's so bloody uncomfortable.' She sat up on her elbow and looked over at him as he rolled onto his side. 'Is it bad to really resent your unborn baby?' she asked with a mischevious grin.

'No, of course not,' Adam said as he glanced at his phone. Then he pointed to the screen. 'I'm just going to look for the number for social services.'

Georgie gave him a playful hit. 'I have had enough now. I know there's a couple of weeks to go but if they, the baby, decide to show themselves a little bit early, I'll be so grateful.'

Adam frowned. 'I haven't even asked if you've decided on names?'

'Elvis for a boy, Priscilla for a girl,' Georgie said with a deadpan expression. She wanted to see Adam's reaction.

'Oh, right,' Adam nodded thoughtfully. 'I didn't realise that you were such a fan.'

'Oh, yes. Big fan.' Georgie then grinned. 'I'm joking, Adam. I actually think they're cool names but I don't know how they'd go down on the playground at school.'

'No.' Adam laughed. 'Although you'd be amazed at some of the names I've come across in my line of work. Especially in Manchester. I once went to a house where a twin brother and sister were called Lazer and Awesome. I'm not joking.'

'Oh, Jesus.' Georgie chortled. 'Don't stand much of a chance, do they?'

'So? Have you got names?'

Georgie took a moment.

'Sorry,' Adam apologised. 'It's none of my bloody business, is it?'

'No, no. It's fine,' Georgie reassured him. Then she took a breath as she began to feel emotional. 'If it's a boy, then I'm going to call him Jake.'

Adam looked at her. 'Was that their father's name?'

She nodded. She'd explained that Jake had died before she'd even had a chance to tell him that she was pregnant.

'Sorry,' Georgie said as her eyes filled with tears. 'I didn't know telling you that was going to upset me. My hormones are all over the place.'

'I shouldn't have asked,' Adam sighed.

'No. I want people to know. It's important.'

'Well for what it's worth, I think it's a beautiful idea,' Adam said.

Oh, God, could he be any cuter?

'And Sylvie, if it's a girl,' Georgie explained. 'I know it's not particularly fashionable but it was my late grand-mother's name. And when I was a teenager, she was effect-ively my mum. I stayed there all the time. Mainly because my parents were arseholes.'

Adam nodded. 'Great names. I think they're lovely because they really mean something to you.'

Georgie gave Adam a bewildered look. 'Who are you?' she asked shaking her head.

Adam looked confused. 'How do you mean?'

'You hardly know me. I'm carrying another man's baby,' Georgie said as her voice trembled a little. 'And yet, here you are, saying the right things. And being... I don't know, being so kind and nice.'

Adam put his hand gently to Georgie's face. 'Because I think that you're incredibly special.'

They looked at each other and then Adam leaned in and kissed her on the mouth.

Georgie then smirked as she looked at him.

'Yeah, I often think I'm *special*,' she said with a self-effacing smile. 'But I mean it in a *special needs* kind of way.'

Adam gave her a funny look and snorted a laugh.

'Sorry. It was all getting too intense there,' Georgie laughed. 'So I had to make a joke.'

'Yeah, I could see you were struggling.'

'Could you? Really,' Georgie joked as she gave him another playful hit.

'You do know that if we're going to make a go of this, you are going to have to stop hitting me all the time. It's not appropriate,' he said with a wry smile.

'Oh. I didn't know that we were *going to make a go if it*,' Georgie said teasing him.

Adam shrugged. 'I thought that we might.'

She smiled at him.

CHAPTER 4

Garrow sat on an armchair in the darkness of Lucy's living room. He'd used a lock pick tool to open the back door. Having checked around, Garrow had seen that Lucy wasn't home. Then he'd made a surreptitious call to a CID officer he knew at Wrexham nick. Lucy had been interviewed by officers over the murder of Jasper McLean but had just been released without charge. He calculated that she would be home very soon as it was no more than a ten-minute drive.

Crossing his legs, he gazed around the shadowy living room. Slices of white light from a streetlight outside came through the closed blind and formed a jagged pattern on the floor. Most of Lucy's possessions were in boxes. After all, he'd sat watching Lucy and Jasper packing Jasper's car for their move to London about eight hours earlier. Garrow had no idea why Lucy had decided to murder Jasper. Possibly because she was a psychopath. But why go to all the palaver of packing her stuff up and loading it into his car if her intention was to kill him and dump his body? Maybe that was all part of her elaborate alibi. He wouldn't put it past her. She was both imaginative and resourceful, he'd give her that.

His eyes roamed around the room again. This is where it had all started. His foolish mistake of agreeing to have a glass of wine with Lucy while investigating her mother's murder. It had set off a series of catastrophic events that Garrow wasn't sure he was going to be able to navigate through or recover from.

Hearing the noise of a car door outside, Garrow sat up and prepared himself. The hunted had become the hunter. His presence would certainly throw Lucy. But that's what he wanted. To put her on the back foot for a change.

Then the sound of a key being pushed into the front door lock and then it opening and closing. The light in the hallway clicked on and light flooded into the living room through the open door.

Garrow's heart was thumping like a drum against his chest. He took a nervous swallow. He was starting to have doubts about his decision to break in.

Looking up to his right, he saw Lucy push the living room door open very slowly.

'Hello?' she said in a suspicious voice.

Silence.

'Hello,' Garrow replied in as casual a manner as he could muster.

Lucy smiled. 'Ah, I wondered if you'd be here when I got home,' she said casually.

For some reason, she didn't seem remotely fazed or startled by his appearance in the darkness of the room.

Well that's bullshit, Garrow thought to himself.

'I doubt that,' Garrow snorted.

Lucy then came in, clicked on a small table lamp and plonked herself down onto the sofa.

She smiled and wagged her finger at him like a scolding mother. 'I saw you watching us earlier. Sitting in your car, watching me and Jasper playing the happy couple.'

Garrow was disconcerted. He'd had no idea that she'd spotted him.

'That was of course until you murdered him,' Garrow sighed casually.

'Yes,' Lucy said. 'He had to go. Bit of a prick, if I'm honest.'

'I hear that you weren't even cautioned?'

'Checking up on me again? What are you like? You're obsessed with me,' Lucy chortled. 'No. I shed of a lot of tears and played the innocent girlfriend. I think that'll be the end of it.' Then she raised an eyebrow. 'That's unless you're going to tell them.' She pulled a face. 'You're not going to tell them, are you?'

Garrow shrugged. 'What's to tell?'

'Exactly,' Lucy agreed as she kicked off her shoes. 'So, have you come here for sex?'

'No,' Garrow replied.

'Pity. That would take the edge off. It's been a very stressful day, if I'm honest,' Lucy said blowing out her cheeks. 'Why are you here then?'

Garrow uncrossed his legs and looked over at her. 'I just wanted to know what your plan is.'

'Plan? I'm not sure there is a plan.' Lucy frowned. 'As I read somewhere, *You don't always need a plan. Sometimes you just need to breathe, trust, let go and see what happens.*'

'Mandy Hale,' Garrow said.

'Sorry?'

'It was Mandy Hale who said it,' Garrow explained.

'Have I heard of her?' Lucy asked rhetorically.

'She's an author. Bit of a feminist, if I remember correcty.'

Lucy pulled a face. 'Oh, God, really?' Then she gave a little laugh. 'I've missed this. Me and you. Back and to. I forgot how clever and well read you are.'

'Had you?'

'Fancy a glass of wine?' Lucy asked. 'I've got a bottle of Shiraz open.'

'Yes, why not,' Garrow replied looking directly at her. 'As long as you don't poison me.'

Lucy gave a loud laugh as she stood up. 'Now, would I do that?'

CHAPTER 5

Ruth and Nick were now making their way across Snowdonia as they sped towards Abersoch. The night sky was black and ominous above them. Taking a cigarette from her packet, Ruth took a lighter and lit it. Then she buzzed down the window, took a deep drag and then blew a plume of smoke out so that the wind outside could drag it away.

Ah, that's better, she thought.

'What did you think of Adam?' she asked.

'Seemed like a nice bloke,' Nick replied and then grinned. 'For a Leeds fan.'

Ruth smiled. 'Yeah, well God help him if he messes Georgie around.'

Nick nodded in a agreement. 'Yeah, he'll have the both of us to deal with.'

Hearing the faintest sound of music from the car radio, Ruth turned it up. It was 'Freedom! '90' by George Michael.

'Oh, I love this,' Ruth said enthusiastically. She loved both Wham! and George Michael.

'So do I,' Nick said.

'No you don't,' Ruth protested pulling face. 'You can't stand Wham!'

'No, but I do like some of George Michael's solo stuff. It's just that I draw the line at Wham!,' Nick explained.

'That's what baffled me. How can anyone *not* like Wham? It's just such happy, fun music.'

'Or it's unoriginal, manufactured pop,' Nick chortled.

Ruth shook her head. 'Piss off. You're so pretentious. What's wrong with bloody pop music? The Beatles were a pop group.'

'Only in the early years,' Nick countered.

Ruth gave a groan. 'Fine. I don't know why I ever get into these debates about music with you!'

Nick gave her a smug smile. 'Neither do I.'

As Ruth peered out from her windscreen, she could see that up ahead of them, the dark night sky was lit up by the rhythmic blue flashes from emergency vehicles.

Turning up a steep hill, the huge glass-fronted mansion loomed into view.

Nick gave a little whistle – the house certainly had the 'wow' factor.

'Now that wouldn't look out of place on a Malibu beach,' Ruth stated.

Nick slowed the car.

There were two marked patrol cars, lights flashing, that had been pulled across the road just down from the house.

A dozen or so uniformed officers were busy rolling out evidence tape. Ruth had called ahead to tell officers that no one was to leave until she and Nick got there but it sounded as if all the wedding guests had already left before Jack Rush's body had been discovered.

Nick pulled the car over and stopped.

Ruth unclipped her seatbelt and opened the passenger door. 'It's going to be a logistical nightmare trying to track down a hundred wedding guests and getting statements.'

Nick nodded as they headed up the road towards the police corden which was being supervised by a young male police officer, twenties, stocky, with coal–black hair and quick eyes.

Ruth got the salty smell of the nearby sea as she and Nick pulled out their warrant cards to show him.

'DI Ruth Hunter and DS Nick Evans. CID Llancastell,' she said and then nodded over at the mansion. 'What have we got, Constable?'

The officer pulled out his notebook and peered at it. 'Victim is a Jack Rush. It was his stepdaughter's wedding today. Guests were based in marquees on the lawn away from the main house. Only family had access to the house as it was locked during the wedding. The last guests left in their own vehicles or by taxi at 11:30 p.m. The victim was last seen alive by his family just before twelve after they'd made a family video message together.'

'What time was the victim discovered?' Ruth asked, impressed by the officer's manner.

'12:15 a.m., ma'am,' he replied. 'Apparently, the victim's twin sons, Ed and James, both heard a noise from the upstairs office. Edward went to investigate and found the victim on the floor. He checked on him but said he wasn't breathing which is when he dialled 999.'

'So it was Jack Rush's son Edward who discovered his father and made the emergency call?' Nick asked, to clarify.

'That's right,' the officer said.

Nick nodded. 'Were you first on the scene?'

'Yes, sir,' the officer replied.

'What did you think?' Ruth asked. It was always good to get the initial reaction and instincts of the first officers on the scene.

'There were lines of white powder on the desk,' the officer explained. 'There was also a rolled up fifty-pound note. The victim seemed to have collapsed onto the floor but there was a lot of blood around his nose and mouth. My instinct was that he died from a drug overdose or a heart attack.'

'But Forensics think it's suspicious?' Nick asked.

'Yes,' the officer said. 'I'm guessing that neither an overdose or a heart attack would have caused that much bleeding.'

He's keen. And smart, Ruth thought. She'd seen it before. Young officers in uniform itching to get into plain clothes and into CID.

'Okay.' Ruth nodded. 'Does anyone think they saw anything?'

The officer shook his head. 'No, nothing, ma'am. We spoke to his immediate family who were here at that time. No one saw a thing, ma'am.'

Ruth gave a sigh. 'We're going to need a statement from everyone at the weddding. Plus contact details. We'll interview the immediate family.'

'Yes, ma'am,' the officer replied. 'I'll talk to my sarge and make sure we speak to all the guests. I assume there would have been caterers, bar staff, a band and a DJ. I'll get statements from them too once we've tracked them down.'

'Good thinking,' Nick said encouragingly.

The officer tried to hide his pleasure at getting a compliment from a senior CID officer.

'I'd like to talk to the immediate family right now, especially the two sons,' Ruth said. 'Any idea where I can find them?'

'There's a big dining room as you go in on the left,' the officer said and gave her a knowing look. 'And I mean *big*. Family are all in there.'

'Thank you, constable,' Nick said as they turned and headed towards the mansion.

Ruth looked up at its sleek glass frontage which glowed with the soft vanilla-coloured lights that were inside.

Over to their right, the white Scene of Crime forensic van was parked up. The back doors were wide open and a SOCO, in full white nitrile forensic suit, mask, rubber boots and sky-blue forensic gloves, was crouched down putting a clear evidence bag into a steel tray.

As Ruth and Nick approached, there were three more SOCOs in forensic suits close to the front door who were talking in low, respectful voices.

Flashing their warrant cards, Ruth and Nick were handed white nitrile suits and shoe covers by a SOCO. Ruth got the familiar chemically smell of the material which made a strange crunching noise as she pushed her arms through the top half. She had small feet and so the forensic foot covers she was given at crime scenes always seemed a little too big and flapped as she walked.

'Shall we?' Ruth said to Nick and gestured to the front door of the house, which was wide open.

However, Ruth was distracted by the sound of booming voices arguing nearby. Turning, she saw that a man in his late twenties was quarrelling with two uniformed police officers.

'I don't want Sofia to be here,' the man snapped in his very middle-class accent.

'Is there a problem?' Ruth asked the two officers.

'This gentleman is...' the young female officer said.

'Charlie. My name is Charlie Huntington. I'm the groom,' he said in a loud, overconfident voice. 'And my poor wife Sofia is in a terrible state as her stepfather's died. As I was trying to explain, I'd like to take my wife to a hotel where at least there's a bed if she wants to lie down. Or have a shower. Or a drink.'

Nick gave an understanding nod. 'I know that this is a very difficult time for you and your wife. And as soon as we've spoken to you and taken a statement, then we can look at allowing you to leave the premises.'

'Allowing us?' Charlie bristled. 'You can't just keep us here.'

'I'm afraid we can,' Ruth said firmly. She'd met Charlie's type before. Very entitled and often thought that they were above the law. 'This is a possible crime scene. And both you and your wife were present.'

'This is ridiculous,' Charlie growled. 'Who the hell are you, anyway?'

Ruth took out her warrant card and fixed him with a stare. 'Detective Inspector Ruth Hunter, Llancastell CID. I'm the Senior Investigating Officer here. I'd really like it if you and your wife could stay here. But I will make it a priority to take your statements as quickly as possible.'

Charlie gave an audible sigh. 'Fine. Whatever,' he said, then turned briskly and marched down the side of the house towards the back, muttering under his breath.

Ruth gave the two uniformed officers a forced smile. They were all thinking the same thing.

She and Nick headed back towards the house. As they reached the front door, Ruth spotted a familiar face approaching dressed in a forensic suit.

'Ah. I knew you two would be here before too long,' Professor Tony Amis chortled. 'I assume there's some sort of signal they shine up into the North Wales sky. And then like Batman and Robin, Llancastell's dynamic duo come to the rescue.'

Ruth had known Amis ever since she'd transferred to the North Wales Police from the London Met. He was very eccentric and a little annoying, but very good at his job. So, for the most part, she tolerated him.

'Hello, Tony,' Ruth said with a wry expression as Amis pulled his forensic mask down and looped it under his chin. His once ginger beard was flecked with silver. 'What have we got?'

'Strange one,' Amis said and then gestured for them to follow. 'I'll show you.'

There were a series of aluminium stepping plates laid out across the blocked wooden flooring and rugs.

The hallway was large, airy and ultra-modern. There were beautiful chrome lights, wooden sculptures, paintings and light blue rugs. It had an almost Scandinavian feel to it.

Ruth and Nick followed.

The open-plan living area had floor to ceiling windows that looked out over the beach and sea. The dark sky was lit up by a large moon which cast light on the inky sea below.

Wow, that must be a hell of a view in the daytime, Ruth thought to herself.

Walking down the corridor that led from the living room, she saw a smaller television room, study and laundry room.

Then the space opened up again into a vast bespoke kitchen and dining area.

In the far corner, there was a steel, spiral staircase that led to floor above.

There were two SOCOs who were dusting the banisters for prints and taking photos.

Ruth frowned. 'Have we checked if anyone was in this kitchen at the time of death?'

Amis shrugged. 'The caterers had gone apparently. And they were based down in the garden anyway. But I guess that will come out when you get the witness statements.' Amis then gestured to the staircase. 'Right, let's go up here.'

Ruth and Nick made their way up the steel staircase, moving caerfully past the SOCOs at work. The top of the staircase came out onto an incredibly long landing. Like the rest of the house, everything was tastefully decorated with paintings, small sculptures and muted colours. It looked like something you'd see inside *Vogue Interiors*. Well, it was what Ruth imagined the houses in *Vogue Interiors* to look like if she picked up a copy and actually opened it.

'Your victim's office is just here,' Amis said pointing to a set of double doors that were wide open about five yards to their right. There was blue police evidence tape across the hallway nearby.

Moving along the landing, they peered in through the doors.

The office was huge with more floor to ceiling windows. Shelves were packed with books and scripts. The walls were adorned with film posters. Ruth assumed that they were films that Jack Rush had produced over the years.

Rush was lying twisted on the floor, his white shirt soaked in dark, congealed blood. His eyes were closed and his head was tilted to one side. There was also a lot of blood around his mouth, nose and neck.

Two SOCOs were standing close to the body, using a small ruler to take measurements and scale as they took photographs.

Nick looked around and then narrowed his eyes. 'What can you tell us, Tony?'

Ruth moved around the office to get a better look at everything. She noticed the gleaming Oscar sitting on the far end of the desk. It had a tiny speck of blood on its base.

Out of the corner of her eye, Ruth saw something shiny on the desk. It was close to the far edge, away from the body.

'What's that?' Ruth said almost to herself as she went to have a closer look. It was a pretty, delicate silver ring. As far as she could see, it didn't have a precious stone in it, nor did it look particularly expensive.

Nick came over. 'Definitely not his ring.'

'No,' Ruth agreed as she looked around the room. 'It just looks very out of place there, doesn't it?'

Nick nodded. 'Yes.' He then took a step back. 'Given how wide that desk is, I'd say that it was placed there by someone standing this side.'

Ruth frowned and then looked at a SOCO. 'Can we make sure that gets photographed and bagged, please?'

'Yes, ma'am,' the SOCO replied.

'Have we checked if anything of value has been taken?' Nick asked.

'As far as I'm aware, the family told officers that nothing of any significance is missing,' Amis said and then pointed to the various film awards. 'Those are worth a fortune for starters.'

'Walk us through what you think happened,' Ruth said as she spotted the lines of white powder and the rolled fifty-pound note on the desk.

Amis walked around the desk to where the chair was. 'The victim was sitting here. He poured himself a large brandy,' Amis explained as he pointed to the crystal tumbler. 'He lit a cigar. Then we assume that he opened this drawer here.'

Ruth and Nick moved around and saw that the bottom drawer of the desk was open.

'Which is where he kept his cocaine,' Nick said.

'Exactly,' Amis nodded and then pointed to the desk. 'He chops out these lines of what he believes is cocaine. He rolls this fifty-pound note and then snorts the cocaine into his left nostril.'

Ruth looked at Amis. 'Except it wasn't cocaine?'

'No.' Amis shook his head. 'When I first got here I thought he'd either OD'd on the cocaine or had a massive heart attack.'

Ruth frowned. 'But that's not what happened?'

'No,' Amis replied and then came over to Jack Rush's body and crouched down. 'I've had a preliminary look at his nose and notrils.' Amis pointed with his gloved finger to Jack's face and his shirt. 'There's massive haemorrhaging stemming from his left nostril, hence all this blood. Neither an OD or a heart attack would have caused all this. A lot of it seems to have come from the membranes in the nose and possibly the throat.'

'Any idea what caused it?' Nick said.

'I'm not exactly sure. I've seen something similar a couple of times over the years,' Amis said as he then pointed over to the lines of white powder again. 'Whatever that white powder is, it's very, very toxic and deadly. It looks like it killed your victim in a matter of seconds.'

CHAPTER 6

Now back on the ground floor, Ruth and Nick had removed their forensic suits as they'd left the crime scene. Ruth spotted the imposing oak door to their left, went over, turned the metal handle and she and Nick went inside.

She could see what the constable meant. The dining room was cavernous with a long light wooden table that looked like it seated twenty or so diners. There were several large modern paintings on the walls. Above them, the ceiling was mainly glass so that the dark night sky and stars were visible.

Okay, well this is very nice, Ruth thought to herself.

At the far end of the table, there were about half a dozen people talking in hushed voices. A young woman in a chic cream wedding dress was sniffing and wiping her face. She was being consoled by Charlie, the pompous young man whom they'd met earlier.

Ruth and Nick took out their warrant cards and showed them as they approached.

'Hi there,' Ruth said in a low, gentle voice. 'My name is Detective Inspector Ruth Hunter. And this is my colleague Detective Sergeant Nick Evans. We're very sorry for your loss. I'm now the Senior Investigating Officer in this investigation.'

Nick nodded with a suitably sombre expression. 'I know this is a very difficult time for you all,' he said gently. 'But we are going to need to talk to all of you and get a statement.'

A rather haughty woman – forties, stick thin, pointy features, auburn hair – gave them a confused, almost patronising frown. 'I thought Jack had a heart attack?'

Ruth shot a cursory look at Nick. She assumed this was the victim's wife but she didn't look very upset. Maybe it was just shock.

'Sorry,' Ruth said looking at her. 'I didn't catch your name?'

'Charlotte Rush. Lottie,' she said almost as if she expected Ruth to have known this. 'Jack's wife.'

'I'm afraid that we're treating Mr Rush's death as suspicious. That's why we have forensic officers in the house,' Nick explained.

The bride took a deep breath but looked confused. 'Suspicious? What does that mean?'

Lottie frowned. 'Does that mean Jack's death wasn't… an accident of some kind, for want of a better word?'

'I'm afraid not, no,' Nick said.

There were several concerned looks between the family members.

A young man – twenties, slicked back hair, tanned, veneers – narrowed his eyes. 'You think someone else was involved?'

Ruth nodded. 'Yes, we think that is a possibility.'

'Oh, God,' Lottie gasped a little too theatrically. 'You mean someone killed him?'

There were a few seconds of silence as Lottie's question seemed to hang in the air.

'Yes. That is a line of inquiry that we are going to be looking at,' Ruth explained.

There were more alarmed looks and murmurings between the family.

'How?' asked Sofia, the bride, looking very distraught.

'At this stage, it's not appropriate for us to discuss the details with you, I'm afraid,' Ruth said calmly. 'We will be able to at some point.'

Everyone in that room was a suspect and Ruth didn't want to reveal her hand about any details quite yet.

The other young man who was Ed's identical twin, except that he had longer, messy hair and a patchy beard, put his head in his hands. 'Jesus,' he whispered, sounding upset.

There was an awkward silence.

'Okay. Can I ask who it was that discovered Mr Rush?' Ruth asked, looking at them.

Ed raised his hand slightly. 'It was me.'

'Are you are Edward Rush, is that correct?' Nick said.

'Ed… But yes,' he said with a nod.

Ruth then looked at Lottie. 'Is there somewhere private where we could go and talk to Edward.'

'It's Ed,' he said, sounding a little short. 'Sorry. It's just that I don't like Edward.'

'Of course,' Ruth said with a forced smile. He sounded incredibly entitled too.

'I need to come with him,' Lottie said anxiously.

Nick shook his head. 'I'm afraid we are going to have to speak to Ed on his own.'

Lottie had a panicked expression on her face. 'Does he need a lawyer?'

'No, Lottie. Don't be so bloody silly.' Ed snorted and then stood up. 'I'll be fine,' he reassured her. Then he pointed. 'We can go into the library if you like.'

As Ruth followed Ed towards the door, she saw him shoot his stepmother Lottie a look of contempt.

CHAPTER 7

Ruth and Nick sat on a rather firm, uncomfortable, dark leather Chesterfield sofa. The library looked like it had been transported from an old London Gentleman's club and felt out of keeping with the rest of the modern decor of the house. The furniture was made from dark oak and there were floor to ceiling shelves that were packed tightly with books. It had that slightly musty smell of an old library.

Ed sat forward on the leather armchair that had a brass reading light positioned over it and ran his hands nervously through his hair. 'Sorry. Would you guys like a coffee or something. I think the caterers have gone but I'm sure I can arrange something.'

Ruth put up her hand. 'Thank you, but we're fine.'

Nick took out his pen and notepad. 'Ed, in your own words, could you tell us exactly what happened?'

'Erm…' Ed blinked as he tried to compose himself. 'The wedding had finished and everyone had gone home. James and I had come upstairs.'

'So, James was with you?' Ruth asked, to clarify.

'He didn't come into Dad's office,' Ed explained. 'But we were both upstairs.'

Nick frowned. 'Why did you come upstairs?'

Ed looked a little nervous as he tapped his fingers on the arm of the chair. 'We just wanted a bit of time out from the family. You know. Chill. It'd been a long day.'

'Where were you going?' Ruth said.

'We were going to hang out in James's room. He's moved back here for a bit,' Ed replied. 'Listen to some music. Maybe play a video game.'

'Okay,' Nick said.

Ruth leant forward and looked directly at Ed. 'Can you tell us why you went into your father's office?'

'We heard a bang,' Ed said. 'I thought someone had fallen over on the landing or something. I thought it might have been Lottie having another drunken fall.'

Ruth noted this and wondered if Lottie had a drink problem of some kind.

'Can you remember what time that was?' Nick asked.

Ed pulled a face. 'Not really. Just gone twelve. Maybe a bit after that.'

Ruth narrowed her eyes. 'Definitely after midnight though?'

'Yes. I saw the time on my phone at some point. Sofia and Charlie were due to leave at 12:30 a.m. to go to a hotel before flying to the Maldives. James and I said we'd go for a chill then head back down just before they left.'

Ruth nodded slowly. 'So, you heard a bang. And you went to see what it was? Is that right?'

'Yes,' Ed said and then he thought of something. 'I saw that at the other end of the landing, the door to my father's office was wide open.'

Nick stopped writing and looked up. 'Was it open when you and James first arrived upstairs?'

Ed shook his head. 'No.'

Ruth picked up on Ed's explanation. 'Was it unusual for the doors to your father's office to be wide open?'

'Yes, they're never open. My dad keeps thems locked. And if he's in there, the doors are always closed. And no one ever really goes in there. Not if you know what's good for you,' he said in a sardonic tone.

Ruth sat forward. 'It sounds like you didn't get on with your father?' she asked.

Ed let out a sigh. 'Not really. He was a very difficult man to be around. Very demanding on me and my brother. Very controlling. And a bit of a bully.'

Ruth studied Ed for a few seconds. For a son who had found his own father dead only an hour earlier, he wasn't exhibiting the normal emotions of loss or shock. He looked as if he was numb. Was that suspicous? Possibly. It was definitely unsual. But maybe that's because Jack Rush hadn't been a very kind or loving father.

Ruth exchanged a look with Nick and then said, 'So, the doors to the office were closed. You heard a bang. And then you went out onto the landing and the doors were now open?'

'Yes,' he said.

'How long were you and James in his room before you heard the bang?' Nick said.

He thought for a few seconds. 'Ten, fifteen minutes.'

Ruth looked at him. 'And you went straight out as soon as you heard the noise?'

'Almost. Maybe a minute later.'

'Did you see anyone?' Nick said.

'No,' Ed replied a little too quickly.

'Sure?' Ruth asked, picking up on his anxiety. He was hiding something.

Ed didn't say anything and he looked away.

'Ed, whatever it is, you do need to tell us,' Ruth said gently.

'Except for my stepmother,' Ed said. 'I saw her.'

Ruth gave him an enquiring look. 'Where was she?'

'She came out of her bedroom,' Ed explained. 'It's down the opposite end of the landing to the office.'

'Did she say anything to you?' Nick said.

'Yes.' Ed nodded. 'She asked me what I was doing. Then she got angry that James and I had left the family to come upstairs and said that we needed to get back down as soon as possible as Sofia and Charlie were about to leave.'

'Did you tell her about what you'd heard?' Ruth asked.

'Yes. She told me I was being silly,' Ed stated. 'But I ignored her. The doors to the office were open so I knew something was wrong. So I just went over to look and...' Ed took a breath and blinked. 'And that's when I saw him there.'

'Did you see anyone else?' Nick said.

'No.' Ed shook his head sadly. 'No one.' Then he frowned as he recalled what he'd seen. 'There was so much blood.'

'And then what happened?' Nick asked.

'I started to shout. Then I ran down to the stairs. I saw Charlie coming up...' Ed said.

'Charlie was coming up the main stairs of the house?' Ruth asked, to clarify.

'Yes. Before I could say anything, he said he was going to see my father to sort a few things out,' Ed said. 'That's when I told him that Dad was... dead.'

Ruth thought for a couple of seconds. 'How did Charlie seem when he told you he was "going to sort a few things out"?'

Ed frowned. 'How do you mean?'

'Did Charlie seem like he was angry?' Nick said.

Ed hesitated.

'Ed?' Ruth prompted him.

'Yes. I suppose he did seem a bit angry,' Ed admitted. 'But it wasn't surprising. They didn't get on. Dad was so bloody suspicious of Charlie.'

Ruth sat forward. 'Why was that?'

'Charlie comes from old money. Big house and estate in the country but they actually haven't got a pot to piss in. Dad's words, not mine. He didn't like Charlie. Silver spoon and all that. Dad had a rather heavy working class chip on his shoulder.'

'What did Charlie think of your father?' Nick asked.

'I'm not sure. I don't think he was a fan,' Ed admitted. 'But it wasn't surprising. Dad wasn't good at hiding his feelings. And he just didn't trust anyone who had inherited wealth and hadn't had to work for it. Plus he was paranoid that someone was going to take all his money away one day.'

Ruth nodded. It was a very candid and honest appraisal of Jack Rush's character.

Nick tapped his pen against his notebook and then said, 'Can you think of anyone who might want to harm your father?'

Ed gave an ironic snort. 'You are joking, aren't you?'

Ruth gave him a questioning look. 'You think that your father had a lot of enemies?'

'God, yes. You don't get to be a successful film producer unless you fuck over a lot of people on the way up. I remember some big Sunday paper magazine did a profile on him. They described him as the sort of man who would not only elbow out those in his way as he climbed up the film business ladder but that he'd also stamp on the hands of anyone below him. I think that sums him up pretty well.'

'Could you be more specific?' Nick asked. 'Do you know the names of anyone who you genuinely believed might want to harm him?'

'Not really,' Ed admitted. 'He didn't really talk to me and James about his work. He didn't really talk to me and James about anything. We were a deep disappointment to him, I'm afraid.'

'And why was that?' Ruth asked.

'He paid for us go to Rugby School,' Ed explained. 'We boarded of course. He wanted James and I to have the kind of education that he never got in Birkenhead. And he was very clear that his ambition for both of us was Oxbridge, a blue in rugby or rowing, job as a doctor, surgeon, barrister. He didn't factor in that we both resented the overpriced education he'd forced upon us. So we rebelled. No sport for starters. Flunked our GCSEs and A Levels. James spent five years messing around at Art College in London before heading back here. I got a lowly 2.2 in Business Studies from Loughborough. Both our choices drove him insane. He was furious that he'd spent thousands on our education only for his sons to want to be utter failures.'

Ruth was fascinated by what Ed had told them. He still hadn't exhibited any kind of sorrow or grief which seemed strange. Did Ed and his brother have something to do with their father's murder. She doubted it. Ed had been incredibly open and honest about his feeling towards him. It just wouldn't make any sense to be like that if he and his brother had plotted to murder him. Unless they were playing a game of bluff?

'And everything was all right at home?' Ruth said. 'Within the family?'

Ed's face broke into an ironic smirk. 'Was everything all right?'

Ruth shrugged. She had no idea why that was such an amusing question, but she could guess why.

'Dad was having yet another affair for starters,' Ed said.

Ruth gave Nick a meaningful look. Was that significant?

'And you're sure about that?' Nick said.

'Yes. Positive,' Ed nodded. 'I heard him and Lottie rowing about it this morning.'

'Any idea who he was having an affair with?'

'No. But Lottie was yelling. And I think that whoever it was, she was a guest at the wedding today,' Ed said.

Ruth looked at Nick. Ed had certainly given them a lot of food for thought.

CHAPTER 8

Georgie and Detective Constable Jade Kennedy were sitting out in the conservatory. As with everything else in the house, it was fashionably designed with huge glass windows from the floor up. The roof was also glass, allowing a perfect view of the night sky above.

Sitting opposite Georgie and Kennedy was Rupert Bray, the wedding photographer. According to Lottie Rush, Bray had been the last person to leave the grounds of the house – with the exception of the close family who were staying there.

Bray was in his early forties, handsome with sandy blond hair and a neat beard. He was wearing a dark navy suit, waistcoat, pink shirt, and tie. They'd been talking to him for no more than five minutes. Georgie thought he was a little standoffish and pompous. But that's how she'd found everyone since she'd arrived at the mansion in Abersoch.

Ruth had decided that Bray needed to be questioned by CID as he had observed the wedding for the whole day as an outsider so might have a better angle on the events. He might have also been the last person outside of the family to see Jack Rush alive.

Kennedy had taken out her notebook and pen. 'You said that you work locally?'

Bray nodded as he reached up and loosened his tie a little. 'That's right. Weddings are a bit of sideline for me in the summer. I'm mainly a freelance portrait photographer, although I do some corporate work too.'

Georgie wondered why he'd needed to overexplain himself. Kennedy had asked merely if he worked locally.

'How did you end up as the wedding photographer today?' Georgie asked.

'Actually I photographed the mother of the groom's fiftieth birthday over in Chester a few months ago,' Bray explained. 'They hired a big house on the river there. I did some photographs for the party. Sofia and Charlie liked my work and asked if I could photograph their wedding.'

Georgie nodded and shifted in her chair as she tried to get comfortable. Being eight months pregnant, it was pretty much impossible to get comfortable anywhere.

'Did you notice anything out of the ordinary during the day?' Georgie asked.

'Out of the ordinary?' Bray asked cautiously.

Georgie sat back and moved a cushion so that it was behind her back. 'Was anyone acting strangely? Were there any arguments?'

'I don't think so,' Bray replied. 'Mrs Rush seemed to have everything under control. Very organised.'

'Lottie Rush?' Kennedy asked, to clarify.

'Yes, that's right,' Bray nodded.

'And Jack Rush? How was he acting?' Kennedy said.

'He seemed to be having a great time. Very proud as he walked Sofia down the aisle in the garden. Great speech after the dinner,' Bray explained. 'Right balance of humour and sentiment.'

'And the bride and groom were having a great time too?' Georgie asked.

49

Something about the question seemed to bother Bray for a moment.

Georgie latched on to his hesitation. 'Whatever it is, however small, you do need to tell us. It could be very important.'

Bray pulled a face. 'I have my reputation to think of and…'

Kennedy interrupted him. 'Whatever you tell us, we will try to let it stay between us. But it might be important.'

Bray narrowed his eyes. 'I don't see how it could be. I was led to believe that Mr Rush died from a drugs overdose. I assumed you wanted to know what his state of mind was during the day.'

Georgie looked directly at Bray. 'I'm afraid that we are now treating Jack Rush's death as suspicious.'

Bray's face fell. 'What? You mean… You think that someone killed him?' he asked in a whisper.

'I'm afraid that this is now a murder investigation,' Kennedy said. 'So anything you can tell us, however insignificant it might seem, might help us to catch whoever did this to Jack.'

'Okay.' Bray then considered his words for a few seconds. 'If this is staying between us, the groom, Charlie, was definitely worried about something. I don't think I saw him smile naturally more than once. I could see it in his face every time I took a photograph. He just drifted away into his own thoughts. It was definitely very strange given that it was his wedding day.'

CHAPTER 9

'Is this going to take long?' Lottie asked in a withering tone. 'I need to be with my family. My daughter is just devastated. Well, we all are, of course.' Then she started to blink as her eyes filled with tears. 'Sorry I…'

Ruth wasn't sure that she completely bought the whole distraught wife act. There had been something distinctly fake and mannered about Lottie the whole time Ruth had been in her presence.

'It's fine,' Ruth reassured her gently. 'No need to apologise. It's been such a traumatic day for all of you.'

Ruth and Nick had been interviewing Lottie Rush in the library for less than a minute before she had begun to lose her patience. But Lottie struck Ruth as a woman who continually lost her patience, especially with those she deemed to be of a lower social status or wealth to her and her family.

Lottie nodded. But Ruth noticed that suddenly the prickly, hard-edged veneer had gone. She looked brittle and vulnerable. 'Poor, poor Sofia. Her wedding day. I just can't believe it. And dear Charlie.'

Ruth reached into her coat pocket where she always kept fresh tissues. She handed them to Lottie. 'Here you go.' It looked like the shock had cracked Lottie's hard, cold veneer. At least for now.

'Thank you,' Lottie said taking a long, deep breath and then blowing out her cheeks. 'I just can't believe that he's gone.' She shook her head. 'It doesn't seem real. Like it's not really happening.'

Ruth gave her an empathetic nod. 'It's a very difficult time,' she agreed.

Nick looked over from where he was sitting with his notepad. 'We'd like to ask you a few questions, if that's okay?' he said in a low voice.

'Yes, of course' Lottie sniffed as she dabbed at her eyes and nose. Then she pulled out a small compact mirror to check her eye make-up.

As Ruth peered closely, she could see that Lottie had had fillers, botox and some collagen in her lips. It was all very subtle but Ruth was close enough to spot it. It wasn't surprising. A very wealthy woman, probably in her late forties and married to a famous film producer. Ruth was actually surprised that Lottie hadn't had more work done than was immediately obvious.

'I'm afraid that I need to tell you that we are now treating your husband's death as very suspicious,' Ruth said gently.

Lottie narrowed her eyes and looked at her. 'Sorry? I don't understand. Jack collapsed in his office. He had a heart attack or something didn't he?'

'I'm afraid not,' Ruth said. 'Our Chief Pathologist believes that Jack was poisoned.'

'What? That doesn't make any sense.' Lottie looked horrified. 'What do you mean poisoned?'

'We believe that the white powder that Jack took, which he thought was cocaine, was in fact a deadly poison,' Ruth said.

'Oh, my God!' Lottie put her hand to her face. 'No. How could that happen?'

'That's what we're going to try and find out,' Nick reassured her.

Lottie shook her head in shock. 'No. That doesn't make any sense.'

'I'm afraid that *is* what happened,' Ruth said quietly. 'I understand that it's very difficult for you to hear that.'

Lottie closed her eyes and took a deep breath.

'We understand from Ed that you were upstairs close to the time when your husband collapsed and died?' Ruth said.

Lottie narrowed her eyes again. She clearly didn't like the tone of Ruth's question and suddenly the haughty prickliness was back. 'I don't know when my husband collapsed and died,' she snorted as if this was a ridiculous question. 'So how am I meant to know that?'

Nick frowned and then consulted his notebook. 'Ed told us that he and James heard a noise just after midnight. Ed went out to investigate. He saw you coming out of a bedroom. You told him that he and James needed to be downstairs. He told you about the noise but said that you weren't interested and left.'

'I wouldn't have put it quite like that,' Lottie said with an irritable shrug.

'Ed went to his father's office,' Nick continued. 'Where he found your husband. We assume that the noise that Ed and James heard was the sound of Jack falling to the floor. Which was only about a minute before your conversation with Ed.'

Lottie frowned as she took all of this in. 'I'm not sure where you're going with all this.'

Ruth leant forward, trying to keep her patience. 'Can you tell us what time you came upstairs?'

'Five minutes before I saw Ed,' Lottie replied defensively. 'I've no idea what time it was.'

'And can you tell us why you came upstairs and went into the bedroom?' Ruth said.

'Really?' Lottie gave a frustrated sigh. All her vulnerability that she'd demonstrated a few minutes ago had simply vanished. Then she tapped the earrings she was wearing. 'The clasp on one of my earrings broke. I came upstairs to change into another pair. I was upstairs for about five minutes.'

'Did you hear anything?' Nick said.

'No. Of course not,' she snapped. 'Don't you think that if I'd heard something, I would have gone to find out what was going on?'

It was a fair point *if* she had nothing to do with her husband's death.

'And apart from Ed, did you see anyone else?'

'No. I just went back downstairs,' she explained.

Ruth moved a strand of hair from her face and said, 'Could you walk us through what happened next?'

'I went outside to check that all the guests had left so we could start to lock up,' Lottie explained. 'Then I heard some shouting. I hurried back inside. Ed was shouting and yelling. He said that Jack had collapsed and wasn't breathing. I raced upstairs with him and that's when I saw Jack in his office. And then I called 999.'

Ruth waited for a few seconds as she played through what Lottie had told them.

'Can you think of anyone who would wish to harm your husband?' Ruth said.

'No,' Lottie replied immediately. 'Jack was a well-respected film producer at the top of his game. He'd won awards. There were rumours of a lifetime achievement award from BAFTA in the next year or two. Possibly an MBE for services to the film industry. And Jack had come from such humble beginnings.' Lottie looked at them and shook her head. 'I don't understand who would do something like this.'

Nick leant forward. 'Had Jack been involved in any disputes recently?'

'Oh, God,' Lottie snorted. 'Jack was a film producer. All he did was argue and dispute. That's the job. But I just don't see that this would have anything to do with his work. Maybe it was some kind of accident?'

'I don't think it could have been an accident,' Ruth explaiend. 'Your husband was deliberately targeted.'

'But why?' Lottie asked and then she closed her eyes. 'Oh, God, this is going to be all over the papers and television. There are going to be bloody TV crews all down the road.'

Ruth shot a look at Nick. It seemed a strange thing to be concerned with when your husband had just been murdered.

Ruth knew that she had to somehow touch upon Ed's comment that Jack was having an affair, that they had rowed about it earlier in the day and that the woman Jack was sleeping with was a guest at the wedding.

'How would you describe yours and Jack's marriage?' Ruth asked.

Lottie's face dropped in disgust at the question. 'What?'

'I'm afraid we have to explore every avenue of Jack's life,' Ruth explained calmly. She could see that Lottie was about to explode. 'And our experience is that most homicides are committed by people close to or well known to the victim.'

Lottie's face contorted as if she'd sucked a lemon. 'You think I killed my husband?'

'No. I'm simply asking what your marriage was like,' Ruth said pushing back a little.

'Fine. Our marriage was fine,' Lottie snapped.

Nick thumbed back through his notebook. 'When we spoke to your stepson earlier, he told us that he'd heard you and Jack arguing this morning. That you accused him of having an affair and that the person he was having an affair with was a guest at your daughter's wedding.'

Lottie let out a booming laugh of derision. 'What utter nonsense! I'm afraid you can't take anything that dear Edward tells you as true. He might be my son, but he's a complete fantasist and an inveterate liar. He loves to stir things up to cause a drama.'

Ruth gave Lottie a suspicious look. 'You think that your son is capable of completely fabricating something like this when answering questions about his father's murder?'

Lottie fixed Ruth with an icy stare. 'Are you calling me a liar?'

'No. But I've been doing this job for a very long time,' Ruth explained assertively. 'I find it difficult to believe that Edward would invent this. After all, his assertion that Jack was having an affair and that you knew makes you a suspect in his murder.'

'Oh, for God's sake,' Lottie sighed scornfully. 'Jack has been having affairs throughout our whole marriage. And I've tolerated them all. It's just how our marriage works… Or worked.' Lottie got up from where she was sitting.

'Now is there anything else? I'd like to get back to my family if that's okay?'

Lottie didn't wait for Ruth to answer and she waltzed towards the door and left.

CHAPTER 10

Georgie and Kennedy were still sitting in the conservatory. The forensic team outside had brought up huge halogen arc lights along with a generator to light up the grounds around the house as they searched for vital clues. There might have been some who would have argued that it would be better to wait for daylight. But Georgie knew the statistics. The first twenty-four hours of a murder investigation were key to finding the killer. And that meant finding and analysing as much evidence as they could as quickly as they could. So it was vital that a fingertip search of the area around the house took place before dawn.

As they waited for the bride, Sofia, Georgie scrolled through her social media.

'I've got a weird feeling that I know the bride,' Georgie said under her breath.

Kennedy looked at her notebook. 'I only saw her at a distance, but she looks the same age as you.'

'Here we go,' Georgie said with growing interest. 'Yes, of course. We used to hang out in the same social circle in our early twenties. It must have been before she met Charlie.' Georgie looked over at Kennedy. 'We were both single. I'd split up with Jake. We went out in Chester and Liverpool a few times. Clubs. And then we went over to Ibiza.'

'Ibiza?' Kennedy gave her a knowing look. 'I didn't have you down as an Ibiza kind of gal,' she teased her.

'Oh, it was the other side of Ibiza, darling,' Georgie said, putting on a posh, middle-class accent. 'It definitely wasn't San Antonio, drinking shots and foam parties.'

'No?' Kennedy asked.

'In fact, I think it was Jack Rush's villa that we all stayed in. I didn't know Sofia that well. She was a friend of a friend.'

'What's she like?' Kennedy asked.

'Nice. Really nice actually,' Georgie admitted. 'Some of the people we went away with were right snobs. Especially the boys. All public school types. But Sofia was down to earth. We got on really well.'

Then Georgie remembered something else. She and Sofia had had a drunken snog sitting by the pool at dawn after a mad night out. It hadn't led to anything else. But it hadn't felt weird either. Just one of those things. Georgie felt herself blush as she got a momentary flash of the kiss.

'You okay?' Kennedy asked, clearly noticing that Georgie was lost in thought.

'Fine, fine,' Georgie reassured her. She wasn't about to tell her about what she'd just remembered. Well, not at that moment anyway.

'Hi there,' said a soft voice.

Georgie looked up and saw that Sofia was standing by the doorway to the conservatory with a uniformed police officer beside her.

'I understand you'd like to talk to me?' she said, but her face was lost in her grief.

Kennedy glanced at the uniformed officer. 'Thank you, constable. We'll take it from here.'

As Sofia came in, Georgie got up and approached her very slowly.

'Hi, Sofia,' she said, wondering if the penny would drop. If it didn't, Georgie wasn't going to remind her. Not given the terrible circumstances.

'Georgie, isn't it?' Sofia said, recognising her instantly.

'Hi,' Georgie said gently. 'I'm so sorry.'

Sofia came over and they hugged.

'I'd heard that you were a police officer,' Sofia sighed. 'I didn't know you were a detective.'

Georgie gestured to a large, cream-coloured sofa. 'Why don't you come and sit down?'

Sofia frowned, looking a little lost as she came and sat down.

'This is my colleague, Detective Constable Jade Kennedy,' Georgie explained and they nodded a hello to each other. 'Are you up to answering a few questions?'

'Yes,' Sofia said as her voice dropped to a whisper. 'It just doesn't feel real.'

'Of course,' Kennedy said empathetically as she clicked her pen ready to write notes.

Georgie peered at Sofia. She had long black hair that had been curled into tresses with a small, discreet white flower headpiece. Her skin was olive and her eyes a deep chestnut colour. She looked beautiful.

'We were meant to be flying to the Maldives in the morning,' Sofia said in a confused voice and then looked at Georgie. 'I'd completely forgotten that.'

Georgie nodded slowly and then waited for an appropriate amount of time before asking, 'Sofia, could you just walk us through the day for a minute?'

Sofia took a deep breath to settle herself and curled her feet under her on the sofa. 'It was just how Charlie,

Mum and I had planned it.' She then pointed out of the window to the gardens. 'Weather was perfect. The service was down at the old gazebo that's just before the walled garden. Then we had champagne and photographs. Jack had got these two beautiful marquees in the garden...' At the mention of her stepfather, Sofia got visibly upset and her eyes filled with tears. 'Oh, God, sorry. It just keeps hitting me that he's gone. And that...'

'It's okay,' Georgie said quietly. 'Just take your time, okay?'

Sofia nodded. 'The catering was incredible. Jack used some film caterers that he said were the best in the business. Speeches. The best man Miles's speech was hilarious. And Jack...' She blew out her cheeks and took another deep breath. 'Sorry I...'

'Please don't apologise,' Kennedy reassured her. 'There's no hurry. Just whenever you're up to it?'

'Jack's speech was amazing. Charlie said a few words and so did I,' Sofia explained. 'We had our first dance to Stevie Wonder. Then drinks and dancing. Everyone left... And then poor Ed came running from the house, telling us what had happened.'

'Thank you.' Georgie gave Sofia an encouraging nod.

'Did you go upstairs?' Kennedy asked quietly.

Sofia shook her head. 'No. I didn't want to see him like that.' Then she wiped more tears from her eyes. 'The funny thing is, people keep saying that it's so much worse because it was my wedding day.' Sofia looked at Georgie. 'But it's not. I don't care about my wedding day. It's not important. He's... gone. And he's never coming back.' Then Sofia dissolved into sobs. 'I'm never going to see him again. How can that be? It just doesn't make any sense to me.'

Georgie left a few seconds and then asked, 'I know this is a difficult subject to broach but...'

Sofia nodded. 'It's fine. I know you've got to ask me stuff that might make me uncomfortable,' she reassured them.

Georgie frowned. 'Did you know that your father used cocaine?'

Sofia nodded. 'Yes, of course,' she said in a tone that suggested that her father was a regular user. 'But I don't understand how he could have overdosed.' Then she gave Georgie a quizzical look. 'Or was it a heart attack? No one seems to be able to tell me what actually happened.'

Georgie leant forward. 'Actually, we're not convinced that your father's death was an overdose or a heart attack.'

Sofia furrowed her brow. 'I don't understand. That's what we were all told. That's what Ed said had happened.'

'Yes. And initially that's what our officers thought had happened. But The Chief Pathologist has been up to your father's office,' Georgie explained gently. 'On initial tests, the lines of white powder that are on your father's desk aren't cocaine.'

'What is it then?'

'We think it's some kind of poison,' Kennedy said.

'Poison? Oh, my God,' Sofia protested. 'How could that happen? Jack wouldn't have done that on purpose.'

'No,' Georgie agreed. 'Our theory is that someone switched his cocaine for the poison.'

Sofia looked horrified. 'You mean you think that someone killed him?'

Georgie nodded slowly. 'I'm sorry, but that's what it looks like to us.'

Sofia wiped more tears from her face and sniffed. 'But who?' she whispered.

'We were hoping that you might be able to provide some kind of answer to that?' Kennedy said.

Sofia took a few seconds to compose herself.

'Sofia,' Georgie said softly. 'Is there anyone that you can think of that might want to harm your father?'

Sofia gave a little sigh. 'Jack's fallen out with countless people over the years. He's a film producer. And he's utterly ruthless. But nothing that would make someone come and do this to him.'

'Had there been any arguments in the past few weeks?' Kennedy enquired.

Sofia shook her head. 'Mum and him were always arguing. But they've been doing that for years.' Then Sofia paused as if something had suddenly occurred to her.

'Whatever it is, however small, it might be significant,' Georgie said supportively.

'James and Jack had a huge row about two weeks ago,' she admitted. 'You could hear it all over the house.'

'Do you know what they were arguing about?' Kennedy asked.

Sofia nodded. 'James wanted Jack to pay for him to go to Les Beaux-Arts de Paris for a year.'

Georgie pulled a face. 'Sorry, but I don't know what that is,' she confessed.

'It's the most prestigious art school in Paris. *And* the most expensive,' Sofia explained. 'But given that James has already spent five years at the Royal Academy of Arts in London, Jack told him no.'

'And how did James react to that?' Georgie asked.

'He was furious,' Sofia explained. 'He said that Jack had ruined his life. But James is incredibly spoilt and entitled. Both he and Ed are.'

'It sounds like you don't get on with your brothers,' Kennedy observed.

'I don't,' Sofia admitted. 'They're just like their mother.'

'And what was their relationship like with your step-father?' Georgie said.

Sofia gave them a dark look. 'Very troubled. He's made no secret of how disappointed he is with them both. And they only tolerated him for the money. I actually think they hated him.'

Georgie shot a look over at Kennedy. Ed and James were now clear suspects in their father's murder.

CHAPTER 11

'And what time did you hear this bang?' Nick asked as he scribbled in his notebook.

They were sitting opposite James Rush and had been talking to him for about five minutes. Although James and Ed were identical twins, they couldn't have been more different in appearance.

James had scruffy long black hair that fell over his face a little. He kept running his hands through it to push it off his face. His hands were tattooed – which led Ruth to assume that most of his body was also. He had silver rings of various designs on nearly every finger and bracelets on his wrists. His appearance seemed to clash with the smart navy suits that he and his brother Ed were wearing.

'It was just after twelve, I suppose,' James mumbled as he looked at the floor.

'All the guests had left at 11:30 p.m., is that right?' Nick asked, to clarify.

'Yes. It was just the immediate family after that,' James replied.

Ruth looked at him. 'And you were with your brother Ed in your bedroom, is that right?'

James nodded but he was lost in his own thoughts.

'And what were you and Ed doing when you heard this noise?' she said.

James shrugged. 'Just hanging out. You know. Listening to some music, doing stuff on our phones,' he explained nonchalantly.

'Can you tell us what happened next?' Nick said.

James pushed the hair off his face as he fidgeted nervously, turning one of the rings on his finger with the other hand. 'Ed went to see what the noise was. Then he came back.' James visibly took a deep breath. 'He said that Dad had collapsed.' James then blew out his cheeks as he got upset and wiped away a tear. 'So we went to see if we could help him but…'

'It's okay, take your time,' Ruth reassured him.

'We went into Dad's office,' James explained as his voice dropped to a virtual whisper. 'And he was just lying there. On the carpet. He had… He had blood…' Then James motioned to his own face to show that Jack Rush had blood all around his nose and face.

'Did you go to help him?' Nick asked quietly.

James nodded. 'Sort of. Ed pushed his fingers against his neck and then put his ear close to his mouth.' There were more tears and James wiped them away. 'Ed said that Dad was dead so he called for an ambulance and then went to tell everyone what had happened.'

Ruth looked at him. 'And what did you do?'

James took a few seconds as he looked upset again. 'I stayed with him.' He looked at Ruth with a distraught expression. 'I couldn't leave him there. Like that. I just wanted to stay with him.'

'Of course,' Ruth said in an understanding tone. 'And then what happened next?'

James's expression then changed as he narrowed his eyes. 'And then *she* came upstairs to see what had happened.'

Ruth gave a questioning frown. 'She?'

'My wonderful stepmother,' he snorted ironically. 'She screamed and then did this whole fainting act. It was an Oscar-winning performance. But it was also pathetic.'

Ruth frowned. 'Why do you say that?'

'That woman didn't love my father,' James growled. 'She never did. It was all about the money and prestige of being married to *Jack Rush, the film producer.*'

There was clearly no love lost between James and Lottie which seemed different to Ed's relationship with her.

'What was your father and Lottie's marriage like?' Nick asked.

James gave a withering sigh. 'Jesus. Volatile at best. My father is a serial philanderer. He seems to think that it's his right to sleep with anyone he likes.'

'And Lottie knew about this?' Ruth asked.

'Of course!' James laughed. 'That was the deal when she married him. But it drove her mad. She hated him for cheating on her.' He shook his head. 'What the hell did she expect? But she was also so incredibly desperate to keep all the perks of my father's wealth. The holidays, cars, clothes... you name it.'

Ruth nodded and then said, 'So your father and Lottie would argue a lot?'

'Argue?' James frowned. 'They would fight.'

Ruth leant forward. 'You mean physically?' she asked seeking clarification.

'Yes, physically,' James replied with a dark smile. 'I've seen Lottie attack my father with a knife when she's drunk. Throw wine glasses at him.'

Nick looked over. 'And he was physical towards her?'

James shrugged. 'Only to restrain her when she lost it. He'd grab her arm or push her when she was having one of her little fits. I did see him slap her face once when she tipped a cup of boiling coffee over his lap.'

Jesus, Ruth thought. *That all sounds very volatile.*

Lottie had painted a very different picture of her marriage to Jack and her tolerance of his many affairs.

Ruth shot a look over at Nick. James's description of Lottie's behaviour towards Jack certainly put her in the frame as a suspect in his murder.

'Is there anyone who you think might want to harm your father?' Ruth asked.

'My bloody stepmother,' James said without hesitation. 'I've just told you what she's like.'

Ruth narrowed her eyes. 'Do you really think that Lottie could have murdered your father?'

James shrugged. 'Why not? She didn't love him any more. He was cheating on her left, right and centre. If she killed him, she would stand to inherit millions of pounds.'

Nick stopped writing and glanced over at him. 'Do you know the details of your father's will?'

'No,' James said defensively. 'But my assumption is that Dad would have left everything to her. She's a cold-hearted, gold-digging bitch.'

CHAPTER 12

Georgie and Kennedy were outside on the rear patio of the house, sifting through the pile of statements that the uniformed officers had taken from wedding guests who were staying in nearby hotels. The night air was warm and the smell of white daisies and lavender moved in from the gardens. Beyond that, the large round moon was a mottled gold and shone on the satin surface of the sea. In the distance, the tiny lights of two boats were moving slowly across the water.

'Are you detectives?' said the voice of a girl.

Georgie looked to her right and saw a girl of about twelve approaching. She had dark plaited hair and was wearing a cream-coloured dress and slip-on shoes.

She had a black bag with a shoulder-length strap. If Georgie was to guess, she'd have said that it was a camera bag.

'Erm, yes we are,' Georgie replied with a slightly bemused smile.

'I'm Jasmine,' the girl said by way of an introduction. 'But my friends call me Jas.'

'Right. Good to know,' Kennedy nodded.

Jasmine pointed into the house. 'I was inside with my family but it was getting boring. Everyone's terribly upset about what's happened to my father.'

Georgie had been told that Jack Rush had four children – two sons and two daughters. And so Jasmine was the youngest by quite a few years. She had no idea why or if it was relevant to the investigation. Probably not.

'So it's your job to go around, ask lots of questions and find out what happened. Is that it?' Jasmine asked.

'Yes, I suppose it is,' Georgie replied.

It struck her that Jasmine didn't seem at all concerned that her father had died only a few hours ago. Maybe she was just too young to process what had happened.

'Yes, that's right,' Kennedy said and then gave a curious look. 'What's in your bag?'

'My camera,' Jasmine said suspiciously. 'I'm in charge of making the video of the wedding.'

Georgie frowned. 'What about the official photographer?'

'Oh, yes. Rupert,' Jasmine snorted. 'But he's an idiot. Dad put me in charge of making the video. I'm going to be a film director when I'm older. This is all part of my learning process. Dad said that I had a real eye for it and…' Then Jasmine trailed off and suddenly looked very upset.

'Are you okay?' Georgie asked her gently. It was as if the enormity of what had actually happened had just hit her.

Jasmine shook her head as she rubbed her face with the back of her hand. 'No,' she whispered.

'Do you want to come and sit down next to me?' Georgie asked.

Jasmine nodded and sat down.

Reaching into her pocket, Georgie took a packet of tissues and handed one to Jasmine. 'Here you go.'

'Thank you,' Jasmine said as she dabbed at her face and then blew her nose.

Kennedy leant forward. 'This must be so difficult for you. Do you want one of us to take you back to your mum?'

'God, no,' Jasmine said pulling a face. Whatever that was about, Jasmine clearly didn't relish spending time with her mother, despite the trauma of what had happened.

Georgie gave Jasmine an empathetic look. 'Well you can sit here with us for as long as you like.'

Jasmine nodded and sighed. 'I'll go and find Sofia in a minute. She's the only one that I want to talk to. She's my sister so she understands me. She's the only one.'

'You're very close to your sister Sofia, then?' Georgie asked, trying to probe a little for the true dynamics of the Rush family.

'Yes. She protects me, you see?' Jasmine said.

Georgie didn't like the sound of the word 'protects' and the dark connotations that went with it.

Kennedy narrowed her eyes. 'Why does Sofia need to protect you?'

Jasmine blinked as if she was trying to make sense of what she wanted to say in her own mind. 'I'm not in danger.' Then she turned to look directly at Georgie. 'My family are very, very strange. Mum says that we're completely... dysfuntional. Is that the right word?'

Georgie shrugged. 'It might be. It depends what your mum means I suppose.'

'Except my mum always adds a very bad swear word when she says we're dysfunctional,' Jasmine explained.

'What about your brothers? Do you get on with them?' Kennedy asked.

'*Stepbrothers*,' Jasmine corrected her rather curtly. 'No. I don't have anything to do with them. They're both...'

Jasmine searched for the word and then said in a conspiratorial tone, 'Sofia says that they're creepy.'

'What about your dad?' Georgie asked as softly as she could.

Jasmine shrugged a little defensively. 'What about him?'

'Were you close?' Georgie asked.

Jasmine thought for a second and then shook her head.

'No?' Georgie asked, trying to encourage her to say a little more.

'He was never here,' Jasmine said with hint of resentment. 'Always away filming. Or his offices in London or LA.' Jasmine frowned. 'My father was a bad man. You do know that?'

'A bad man?' Georgie repeated quietly. 'Why do you say that?'

Jasmine gave them a knowing look. 'God, don't you know? That's what everyone said. Just go online and you can read about it.'

Georgie then pointed to the camera bag. 'Did you video the whole day, Jasmine?'

Jasmine gave her a slightly supercilious look. 'Of course I did. That was my job.'

'Then I think we're going to have to have a look at what you filmed,' Georgie explained.

'But I haven't edited it all together yet,' Jasmine protested.

'Oh, we won't keep it,' Georgie reassured her.

Jasmine opened the bag and then took out the camera. 'Why don't I just download all the files onto a memory stick for you to take away. I can go and do that now?'

Georgie looked at Kennedy who nodded.

'Okay,' Georgie said with an uncertain expression. 'Are you sure that you're up to it? I can take the camera and get our technical experts to do it?'

'It'll take me ten minutes in my bedroom,' Jasmine explained and then frowned. 'Don't you trust me?'

'No, that's fine,' Georgie reassured her.

'Okay,' Jasmine said in a light voice. 'Won't be long.'

Georgie and Kennedy watched Jasmine as she walked away.

'I'm not sure what to make of her,' Georgie admitted.

'No, me neither,' Kennedy agreed. 'Definitely not your average twelve-year-old.'

'My mother would have described her as precocious,' Georgie said.

CHAPTER 13

Ruth and Nick entered the dining room where most of the family were sitting quietly. Charlie was leaning close to Sofia, holding her hand and comforting her.

'Charlie,' Ruth said softly. 'If it's okay, we'd like to ask you a couple of questions.'

He gave Sofia a concerned look.

Charlie was in his early thirties, smart suit and handsome.

'It's okay,' Sofia reassured him. 'I'll be fine here. You go.'

Ruth gave Charlie an empathetic look. 'Just routine. Nothing to worry about.'

Charlie followed Ruth and Nick out of the dining room and down the long hallway towards the library. The walls were painted a subtle shade of pale duck-egg green. There were impressionistic, modern paintings at intervals dotted along the walls. Ruth assumed they were originals and worth a lot of money.

'Let's go in here,' Ruth said gesturing to the open door of the library and then closing it behind them.

Charlie walked over to a Chesterfield leather armchair and sat down slowly. As with most of the others, he looked as if he was dazed by the events of the evening. However, Ruth had compared notes with Georgie and Kennedy. It seemed that the official photographer thought that there was something distinctly 'off' about the way Charlie had behaved during the day.

Ruth and Nick sat down on the sofa opposite and Nick got out his notebook and pen.

'I'm so sorry that this has happened, especially on your wedding day,' Ruth said gently.

Charlie nodded. 'Thank you.' He reached down and fiddled nervously with his cufflinks.

Nick sat forward a little on the sofa. 'Could you tell us the last time you actually saw Jack?'

Charlie thought for a second. 'All the guests had gone. So Jas asked the whole family to say a few words to Sofia on camera. Jas is making our wedding video.'

'Oh, right,' Ruth said sounding a little surprised. Even though she hadn't spoken to Jasmine, she knew that she wasn't more than twelve years old.

Charlie looked at Ruth. 'Jas is a real talent when it comes to making films. I know she's young, but she's really gifted.' Then a sad expression came over his face. 'It's horrible because I always assumed that Jas would end up being a film director and that Jack would produce those films. But now...' His voice trailed off.

'And you were in that video?' Nick asked.

'No. It was just the family,' he said. 'Jack, Lottie and the children. But I watched them. And I'm pretty sure that was the last time I saw Jack.' Charlie peered over at them. 'I just can't believe he's gone. It's so awful. He and Sofia were so close.'

Ruth gave him a sympathetic nod. 'Of course.'

'And what was your relationship like with Jack?' Nick asked.

Charlie reacted for a second as if he didn't like Nick's question. Then he composed himself. 'Well, I was marrying his daughter,' he said with an ironic laugh. 'And he was very protective of Sofia.'

'Did you get on with him?' Ruth asked.

Charlie gave them a quizzical look. 'Sorry. I'm not trying to be difficult but I've been told that you think that Jack was deliberately killed or something. I don't see how the questions that you're asking me are relevant to that.'

'How did Jack seem today?' Ruth asked, trying a different tack.

'Fine. He was having a great time,' Charlie shrugged. 'He was father of the bride so he was lapping up all the attention.'

'It didn't seem that anything was bothering him?' Ruth said.

'No. God, no. Far from it.' Charlie shook his head. 'He was having a really good time.' Then Charlie shook his head. 'Who would want to kill him?'

Ruth looked at him. 'I know you're not directly related, but can you think of anyone that might want to harm Jack?'

'Well, he wasn't the easiest of people to be around. He loved an argument. And he was never wrong about anything which could be tedious,' Charlie admitted. 'But I can't think of anyone who would want to do this to him. It's so terrible.'

'As an outsider, what did you think about Jack and Lottie's marriage?' Ruth asked.

Charlie laughed. 'They fought like cat and dog. And then they made up again. Sofia said it was the Italian passion. Her grandmother is half Italian. Latin temperament or something.'

'But you thought they got along?' Nick asked, to clarify.

'I don't suppose it's something that you can ever really know,' Charlie admitted. 'But form the outside, they seemed to make it work. And Jack was away a lot, so Lottie was the boss in the house.'

Ruth moved a strand of hair from her face and looped it over her ear. 'What about his children? How did Jack get on with them?'

'Well, naturally he doted on Jas,' Charlie said. 'She's the baby of the family. And maybe I'm biased, but Jack and Sofia had a very special bond.'

'A special bond? How do you mean?' Ruth said.

'The whole father and daughter thing,' Charlie replied. 'And they were very similar in many ways. They were very close. I don't know how Sofia is ever going to get over this.'

'And what about the twins?' Nick said. 'Ed and James?'

Charlie paused for a few seconds as he considered how best to answer. 'If I'm brutally honest, Sofia told me that they were a great disappointment to Jack. And I think he let them know that. I didn't agree with some of the things he did when it came to them though.'

Ruth wasn't quite sure what Charlie was referring to. 'Could you explain what you mean by that?'

'Sofia told me that Jack had threatened to disinherit Ed and James from his will if they didn't sort themselves out.'

'And do you know how they reacted to that?' Nick said.

Charlie pulled a face. 'I think they were very angry.'

CHAPTER 14

Ruth lit a ciggie as she leant back against her car which was now parked directly outside the Rush mansion. The SOCOs forensic search of the house and surrounding areas was ongoing and wouldn't finish for several more hours. Nick leant back against the car.

Ruth took a deep drag of her cigarette and blew out a plume of smoke.

That's better, she thought to herself.

'Problem is,' Nick said, thinking out loud, '...anyone who had access to the house in the past day or two, would have had access to Jack Rush's office. They could have swapped the cocaine for whatever killed him.'

'True,' Ruth agreed as she tapped the ash off the end of her cigarette. 'But firstly you'd need to know that Jack used cocaine on a regular basis. And secondly, you'd need to know where he kept it.'

Nick shrugged and then pointed to the vast glass-fronted mansion to their right. 'He's a multimillionaire film producer who lived in a house like that. Not a big surprise that he takes coke.'

'No,' Ruth said, but before she could continue, two men came out of the main front door carrying a black body bag on a steel stretcher. They headed for the black windowless van that belonged to the coroner's office. Jack Rush's body would be taken to the nearest mortuary for a post-mortem to establish cause of death. There would also be more forensic tests on his body there.

Georgie and Kennedy came out a few seconds later and approached.

'That's everyone in the family interviewed now, boss,' Kennedy said with a sigh.

'Good work, guys,' Ruth said as she finished off her cigarette. Then she gave them a questioning look. 'Anything interesting?'

'It was pretty clear that Jack Rush was a ruthless film producer, so he'd probably made many enemies over the years,' Kennedy replied.

Nick nodded. 'Yeah, that's the picture we got too.'

Ruth narrowed her eyes. 'But given the access needed to Jack's office and the knowledge where he kept his cocaine, my instinct is that we start our investigation looking a lot closer to home.'

'I actually know Sofia Rush from way back,' Georgie admitted. 'We used to socialise together for a few years. She always struck me as being pretty down to earth. And she's cleary devastated by what's happened.'

'She told us that James Rush had fallen out with his father recently because he'd refused to pay for him to go to art school in Paris,' Kennedy explained.

'Right,' Ruth said. 'That's interesting. James Rush seemed convinced that his stepmother was involved. He clearly has no time for her.'

'And Ed Rush told us that he'd heard Lottie and Jack arguing early this morning,' Nick said. 'He claims that she'd accused Jack of having another affair. But when we asked Lottie about this, she admitted it but was very dismissive. She told us that she'd tolerated Jack's affairs over the years and it wasn't anything new. She claimed that she wasn't remotely angry about it.'

Ruth took a few seconds and then glanced at her watch. It was 3:30 a.m. 'Right, guys. Let's get home and get some sleep. Back in CID at seven a.m., please, and we can get the rest of the CID team up to speed.'

CHAPTER 15

Ruth opened the fridge in her kitchen quietly and took out a cold bottle of wine. She knew that the sensible thing to do was to have a cup of tea or even milk. But a large glass of white wine would take the edge off nicely after a very busy night.

Pouring the wine, she then took the glass and wandered down the hall and into the living room where she slumped onto the sofa and gave an audible sigh. She was exhausted. And she'd only get three or four hours' sleep before she had to be back into Llancastell CID.

For a few seconds, she wondered what it would feel like to be retired. Leisurely morning with Sarah. Pub lunch. Pick up Daniel from school. Didn't sound too shabby. Ruth had come pretty close to retiring when she'd been shot and almost died earlier in the year. But she'd maintained that she'd be bored not having the cut and thrust of being a Senior Investigating Officer in CID. It was at times like this when she wondered if she'd made the right choice.

The soft sound of footsteps on the stairs broke her train of thought.

Leaning forward, Ruth peered out the door and saw Daniel walking down the stairs and then along the hallway towards the kitchen.

Ruth leant forward. 'Daniel!' she whispered loudly.

Daniel turned, looked at her and rubbed his eyes.

'Are you okay?' she asked in a low voice.

He nodded. 'Just wanted a drink of water.' Then he pointed to the sofa. 'Can I come and sit with you for a little bit?'

'Of course you can,' Ruth said with a smile. She could feel herself relax just at the thought of Daniel wanting to come and sit with her.

For a second, Ruth was transported back to when her daughter Ella had done something similar when she was younger than Daniel. That must have been fifteen years ago. Maybe more. They'd been living in a flat at the top of Balham Hill in South London. It wasn't that long after Ella's dad had walked out on them for another woman. She and Ella had snuggled under a thick blanket and watched TV together until she fell asleep.

Daniel appeared and plonked himself right next to her. He sipped at his water and then peered at her.

'Have you been out at work?' he asked.

Ruth nodded. 'I just got back.'

He looked confused. 'But you were here when I went to bed.'

'I got a call very late. I had to go over to Abersoch,' she explained.

'What's Abersoch?' he said.

'It's over on the coast. It's very nice. Lots of wealthy English people live there or go on holiday there, including Wayne Rooney and his family,' she said.

Daniel's face lit up. 'Wayne Rooney? Wow.'

There were a few seconds of comfortable silence as Ruth drank her wine.

Daniel was deep in thought and then he asked, 'Does that mean that someone got hurt badly?'

Ruth nodded.

'Did they get killed?'

'I'm afraid so,' Ruth said. She didn't want to lie to him.

'Why did they get killed?' he asked.

Ruth looked at him. 'We don't know yet. It's our job to find out why.'

'Like with what happened to my dad?' Daniel asked. His father had been shot dead the previous year and Ruth and her team had brought his murderer to justice.

'Yes, that's right,' she replied. Daniel had a photograph of his father beside his bed. Ruth thought that it was important that Daniel remember him and be able to talk about him whenever he wanted. 'Do you miss your dad?'

'Sometimes.' Daniel nodded. 'Especially when the other kids at school talk about doing stuff with their dads. Callum Moorscroft's dad is going to be manager of the Bangor-on-Dee football team for our age. They're having trials for next season on Saturday.'

'Do you want to go?' Ruth said.

Daniel shrugged. 'Maybe.'

Ruth wondered why he wasn't being more enthusiastic. Daniel loved football and he was often in the garden with the ball. 'I thought you'd be itching for the chance to play.'

Daniel pulled a face. 'I haven't got any boots.'

Ruth rolled her eyes. 'I'll buy you a pair of boots, silly.'

His face lit up. 'Really?'

'Of course.'

'Adidas Preditor Leagues with fold-over tongues?' he asked excitedly.

Ruth laughed. 'You just said a load of words that I didn't understand. But yes. I'll buy whatever football boots you want.'

Daniel immediately gave her a hug. 'Thank you, Ruth.'

She put her hand on his head and ruffled his hair. 'If you need anything, you just need to ask me or Sarah, okay?'

He nodded and smiled at her. Then he sipped his water and got up.

'Maybe I should go back to bed,' he suggested.

'Probably a good idea,' she agreed.

'What about you?' he asked.

'I will do in a minute.'

Then Daniel had a thought and furrowed his brow.

'You know the man that you said that got murdered in Abersoch,' he said.

'Yes,' Ruth said hesitantly, wondering why Daniel was back to that.

'Was he a bad man?'

'To be honest, we're not sure yet,' Ruth admitted. 'But we're going to find out.'

CHAPTER 16

Nick walked down to the kitchen to get a glass of milk before going to bed. Megan and Amanda were upstairs, presumably fast asleep. As he opened the fridge, he noticed a small bag of rubbish sitting on the floor by the back door. Amanda must have forgotten to put it in the bin. And it was bin day tomorrow.

Unlocking the back door, Nick went outside. He took the bag with him and opened the lid of the blue wheelie bin. As he dropped the bag inside, he spotted something out of the corner of his eye. The top inch of a wine bottle that had been shoved down the side of the rubbish bags.

Oh, my God. His heart sank.

Both he and his wife Amanda were in recovery and attended regular AA meetings. Although, he had noticed that Amanda's attendance had tailed off in recent months. She had put it down to returning to work as a Team Leader in Social Services.

Trying not to panic, Nick pulled the empty bottle of red wine from the bin. Had Amanda really had a drink and relapsed? He prayed that she hadn't but what other explanation was there? As far as he knew, there hadn't been any visitors in recent days that might have drunk red wine. He put it back while he decided what the best thing to do was.

He then crept up the stairs, along the landing and then stopped at the door to his daughter Megan's bedroom. Pushing the door open very gently, he saw that she was fast asleep in her pink princess bed. She looked so peaceful and innocent. He couldn't believe that he'd been lying on that bed only nine hours ago reading Caitlin a bedtime story.

Pulling the door so that it was open by about an inch, Nick went quietly into the bedroom he shared with his wife Amanda. His head was still whirring with what he'd seen in the bin. Did he confront her right now or see how she was and if it seemed as if she'd been drinking?

As soon as he walked in, he saw that her face was lit up in the darkness by the light of her mobile phone. She was wearing her reading glasses.

'What are you doing up?' he whispered as he closed the bedroom door behind him.

'I couldn't sleep,' she admitted. Then she pointed to her phone. 'Did you say that you'd been over to Abersoch?'

Her voice sounded normal. No hint of a slur. And her eyes were clear.

'Yeah,' Nick said as he started to undress.

'Jack Rush?' she asked.

'That's right,' Nick said with a slight nod.

'It's all over the news,' Amanda explained. 'What were you doing there so long? Everything online is saying that he died from a drug overdose.'

Nick shook his head. 'We were there because he didn't die from an overdose. Someone switched his cocaine for some kind of poison and it killed him.'

'Jesus!' she said as her eyes widened and she sat up in bed. 'Someone murdered him?'

'Looks like it,' Nick said as he folded up his clothes.

'There must be people lining up to do that,' she said.

Nick frowned. He didn't know what she was talking about. 'How do you mean?'

'When all that Harvey Weinstein stuff and the #MeToo campaign was going on, there were various stories about Jack Rush. Just rumours of bad behaviour, sexual harassment, NDAs. I don't think anything ever came of it though.'

Nick was pretty sure now that Amanda hadn't been drinking. She just seemed very coherent and lucid, rather than trying to hide anything from him. He was so relieved. He'd wait until tomorrow to bring up the empty wine bottle.

Nick gave a knowing nod. 'Where there's smoke...' It was definitely something that they needed to look at in their investigation into Jack Rush's murder.

'Don't you remember that actress? What's her name,' Amanda said clicking her fingers. 'Elizabeth Davies.'

Nick shook his head. He didn't know what she was talking about.

'Yes, you remember. She accused Jack Rush of sexually assaulting her on a film that she was working on. A period drama. She was very young. Early twenties. Then she went public and said that Rush had blackballed her from the film industry and she couldn't even get an audition. And then she took her own life. Drug overdose, I think. It was a big scandal around the time of the millenium.'

Nick nodded as he folded up his clothes. 'Yes, I do remember that. I think her sister wrote an article about it in the Sunday papers.'

Amanda frowned as she looked at Nick. 'Why are you putting your pyjamas on?'

Nick looked puzzled and then the penny dropped.

Amanda grinned at him as she pulled the duvet back.

CHAPTER 17

The following morning, Ruth pushed through the double doors into the Llancastell University Hospital mortuary, followed by Nick. The air was thick with the smell of preserving chemicals and detergents, and the temperature dropped to a ghostly chill.

Ruth looked around at the mortuary examination tables, gurneys, aluminium trays, workbenches and an assortment of luminous chemicals. Then she spotted Jack Rush's body on the far side of the room. Chief Pathologist, Professor Tony Amis, was taking photographs, using a small white plastic ruler to give an indication of scale. Attached to his pastel blue scrubs was a small microphone, as post-mortems were all now digitally recorded.

'Here they are again,' Amis said with a cheery wave.

Ruth shot Nick a bemused look. Amis seemed to be so happy in his work that it was sometimes quite unnerving.

He wandered over, grabbing a mug of tea as he went.

'Morning, Tony,' Ruth said as brightly as she could after only three hours' sleep. 'What have you got for us?'

'Potassium iminomethanide,' Amis said.

'Sorry?' Ruth said with a frown.

'That's what killed your victim. Although you'd know it as potassium cyanide. Luckily for the killer, it comes in a handy white powder.' Amis pointed over to the body. 'Once he'd snorted a line of that, he would have been dead in seconds. And even though its use is restricted, it's relatively easy to get these days online.'

'Cyanide?' Ruth asked, to clarify.

'Yes,' Amis said. 'Nasty stuff. And quite old-fashioned.'

'Would there be any signs if you had handled it?' Nick asked.

'Yes.' Amis nodded. 'It causes redness and a rash if it's exposed to the skin. It could also cause headaches or dizziness for a while.'

'But it's not fatal?' Ruth said.

'No. It needs to be ingested to be fatal,' Amis explained and then he gave Ruth a knowing look. 'I did find something else which surprised me.'

'Go on,' Ruth said, her interest now piqued.

'I'll show you,' Amis said as he gestured and walked over to the body.

As they got closer, Ruth saw that the chest cavity had been opened and the ribs, lungs and heart were all visible inside. It had been a while since Ruth had seen the insides of a human body.

'You can see the black discolouration of the lungs,' Amis said as he went closer and pointed with his gloved forefinger.

Nick frowned. 'What is it?'

'Lung cancer,' Amis said. 'Stage four. Although I'm not an expert, I'd say that it's progressed to the point of being inoperable.'

'Meaning?' Ruth asked.

'I'd say that your victim had less than a year to live,' Amis replied.

Ruth thought about this for a second and then said, 'You don't think that snorting cyanide was Jack Rush's way of taking his own life? If he thought he was going to have a painful death from cancer, maybe he just decided to control when and how he died?'

Amis looked doubtful. 'Snorting cyanide is an incredibly painful way to die. It's agony. From what I know of your victim, he was a shrewd, intelligent man. If he was going to end his life, he would have found a far more dignified, painless way to go.' Amis looked at them. 'If you want my opinion, I'm sticking with my original thesis. Someone replaced his cocaine with cyanide and he was murdered.'

CHAPTER 18

Ruth sat at her desk in her DI's office in Llancastell CID. Reaching over, she grabbed her coffee and took a sip. It was still piping hot which is how she preferred it. Since returning from the mortuary at Llancastell University Hospital, she'd been mulling over the implications of what Professor Amis had told them about Jack Rush's cancer. Was it at all relevant to his murder? Did any of Jack's family know that he was dying?

Nick knocked on the open door and looked in. 'I've spoken to Jack's private GP. He tried to fob me off with doctor–patient confidentiality until I told him it was a murder case.'

'What did he say?' Ruth asked.

'He confirmed what Amis suspected,' Nick explained. 'Jack had scans two months ago that revealed that his treatment for lung cancer was no longer working and that it had spread to other parts of his body. The consultant had given Jack eight to nine months to live.'

Ruth sat back in her chair and looked at Nick. 'I don't know about you, but I didn't get the feeling from anyone that we spoke to in the family that Jack was dying.'

'No.' Nick agreed. 'In fact, it would have been very strange for Lottie not to have mentioned it when we spoke to her.'

Ruth shrugged. 'Which suggests that Jack had kept it a secret from his family.'

'Possibly,' Nick said and then he pointed to the CID office where the team of detectives were now assembled. 'Shall we?'

Glancing at her watch, she saw that it was eight a.m. and it was time for her to take the briefing. 'Oh, right. I'd better get out there,' she said grabbing her coffee. 'Morning everyone,' Ruth said as she came out of the DI's office and then moved across the CID office towards the front of the room. A scene board had already been created. At the centre was a picture of Jack Rush dressed in a bow tie and dinner suit at an awards ceremony. To one side there were photographs of the members of his family – Lottie, Ed, James, Sofia, Jasmine and Charlie. Underneath his photo there was writing with his date of birth – *23.05.65.*

'Okay, let's get everyone up to speed,' Ruth said and then she sipped her coffee before putting it down on the desk next to her. 'This is our victim. Jack Rush. Oscar-winning film producer and multimillionaire. Aged fifty-nine. We believe that Jack went up to his office at around midnight last night after the guests had left from his daughter's wedding. He took a bag of what he believed was cocaine and snorted some of it. However, the forensic toxicology report has identified that the white powder was in fact potassium cyanide which is a deadly poison. It's our theory that at some point before midnight last night, someone went into Jack's office and switched his cocaine for the cyanide deliberately, which makes this a murder investigation.'

Garrow looked over with a quizzical expression. 'Is there any way of narrowing down who had access to the house in the past few days?'

It was good to see Garrow back at his desk and asking pertinent questions. He'd been though the mill in recent weeks so she hoped he was back on track as she thought he was an excellent detective.

'We're not sure yet,' Ruth admitted and then went over to the other photos. 'It's something we need to check but clearly Jack lives with his second wife, Lottie, his twin sons from his first marriage, Ed and James. And then his two daughters, Sofia and Jasmine. Plus, Charlie, Sofia's new husband, was staying over in the days leading up to the wedding. We believe that all these family members had some access to Jack's office, although we can't be sure.'

Georgie looked over. 'Does that mean we're concentrating our investigation primarily on members of Jack's family?'

'Until we have evidence that points us elsewhere,' Ruth said. 'Then yes, I think that the focus of our investigation needs to start with the family members.'

'We checked with Lottie, Ed and James,' Nick said as he consulted his notebook. 'The main house was locked and alarmed while the wedding was taking place. Jack was incredibly paranoid about people snooping around the house generally.'

'Who had keys?' Garrow asked.

Nick flicked over a page. 'Every member of the family had keys, except for Charlie and Jasmine, as she was too young and didn't need them.'

Kennedy sat forward. 'So, while the wedding was taking place, there were only five people who could have entered the house?'

'That's right,' Ruth said. 'But Jack kept his office locked when he was out of the house, so no one could have got into his office to make the switch during the day.'

Garrow frowned. 'And for all we know, the cocaine was switched a week ago,' he pointed out.

'Ah,' Ruth said knowingly. 'Lottie is certain that Jack took some cocaine on Thursday night. She said he was wired. So, we have a window of when Jack went to bed which was around midnight on Thursday and when Jack returned to the house at midnight last night. That's a forty-eight-hour window.'

'Was Jack's office locked overnight?' Georgie said.

'Lottie wasn't sure,' Nick explained. 'If Jack had been in his office during the evening, he would leave it open. It was only when he left the house that he was a stickler for locking it up.'

Kennedy looked down at the notes that she was making. 'And there was only one bag of what Jack thought was cocaine?'

'Yes,' Nick replied.

'And who exactly was in the house on Friday night?' Garrow enquired.

Ruth went to the photos in turn. 'Lottie, Ed, James, Sofia, Charlie and Jasmine.'

Georgie looked surprise. 'Charlie stayed overnight? But he's the groom?'

Nick shrugged. 'Apparently Sofia and Charlie had been living together over in Chester for the past three years. Sofia thought it terribly old-fashioned to spend the night apart.'

'What about Charlie's parents?' Kennedy asked.

'It's just his mother,' Ruth said as she looked over to Nick for confirmation. 'Jenny?'

'That's right,' Nick nodded. 'Charlie's father died about ten years ago.'

'I would think that Lottie has a very strong motive,' Georgie snorted. 'Jack was a serial adulterer with accusations of sexual harassment in his past. They were heard arguing about his latest affair the morning of the wedding by Ed. Jack was also a very, very rich man, which means that she stood to inherit millions.' Georgie gave a dark smile. 'I'd be tempted to kill him.'

Ruth shook her head at Georgie's little joke. Sometimes dark humour was the only way to survive as a police officer.

'Unless she signed a prenup?' Garrow pointed out.

'Good point, Jim. Let's get onto Jack's lawyer,' Ruth said. 'Find out if Jack made Lottie sign a prenup before they got married.'

Nick held up his pen to make a point. 'We also know that Jack had turned down James's request to attend the Paris School of Art. They had a blazing argument about it and James was furious.'

Kennedy narrowed her eyes dubiously. 'And maybe he thought he'd pay his father back by killing him? Doesn't that seem like a stretch?'

'Maybe not,' Ruth said thinking aloud. 'We also know that Jack had threatened to disinherit both his sons as he claimed that they were a bitter disappointment to him.'

'If that's true, the brothers could have plotted together to buy the cyanide and then swap it,' Georgie suggested.

'Like the Menendez brothers in America,' Nick said.

The Menendez brothers had gunned down and killed both parents at their luxury Beverly Hills mansion in 1989. They tried to pass the killings off as a mafia hit but it was claimed that they killed their parents so that they could inherit.

A phone rang and Garrow picked it up.

Ruth perched herself on a table. 'We're going to need to see Jack Rush's will as soon as possible. We need to know if he really did remove his sons from the will. And what Lottie stood to gain on his death.'

Kennedy looked over. 'Are we ruling out the others?'

'I'm not sure yet,' she admitted.

'Boss, I've got some of the photographs sent over from Forensics.' Kennedy then pointed at the screen. 'One of them is Jack Rush's diary. There's an entry for Friday morning. There's a scribble – *Meeting with M.*'

'M?' Nick asked.

'Just the letter M?' Ruth said, to clarify.

'Yes.' Kennedy said. 'We know that Jack had been at the house for several days before the wedding. If he had a meeting with "M", would that have taken place in his office at home? If it did, that would mean whoever he met also might have had access to his office and the cocaine.'

'That's a very good point, Jade,' Ruth agreed. 'Can we see if we can find out who M might be. It might have been a business meeting or it could have been something to do with the wedding. Either way, let's find out who that is and where they met, please.'

CHAPTER 19

Ruth came out and saw the CID office was a hive of activity. Detectives were mainly at computers or making phone calls. Others were out on interviews or chasing leads. For a moment, Ruth was swept up with a lovely feeling of pride for the team. It was at moments like this that she was reminded how little she missed working at the London Met.

27 March 2017.

It was a date etched in her memory. It was the evening that she'd made the decision to leave the Met once and for all. She was working with officers from Operation Trident, a special unit that had originally been set up in 1998 to crack down on 'Black on Black' gun crime. As the unit developed, it focused particularly on organised criminal gangs that were battling each other over London's drug trade.

It was the events of that night that convinced Ruth that enough was enough. It wasn't the worst incident that she'd ever been to. That had been a triple fatal shooting in a crack house in Camberwell in 2012. But she could remember that night in March as if it was yesterday.

Even though it had been March, it was freezing cold. Ruth and her team had been called to a rough estate, Crane House, in Peckham SE15. She'd led the Armed Response officers to the front door of a flat belonging to Kossi Asumana, aka Taz, a low-level drug dealer and member of the infamous Peckham Boys gang. They had been linked to murders and crime as far back as the 1970s. Neighbours had reported hearing screaming and a gunshot.

Smashing down the door, Ruth found Zaria Asumana, Taz's wife, sitting in the living room holding a handgun and sobbing. Taz's blood-soaked body was lying on the sofa. They'd had a row and she'd shot him. After a frantic search of the flat for their two young daughters, Ruth eventually found them hiding in a cupboard in terrified shock. It was the expression on their faces and the blood on their little white trainers that convinced Ruth that it was time to move to a different force and start again.

'Boss,' said a voice that broke her train of thought.

It was Georgie. She was at her desk and holding a document with blue latex forensic gloves.

'What is it?' Ruth asked.

'These are some of the documents that were retrieved by the Scene of Crime officers from Jack Rush's lawyers in Chester,' Georgie explained. Then she put the document down on her desk and closed it so that the front was showing. From what Ruth could see, it was some kind of legal document.

'Is that his will?' she asked hopefully. Although they would be able to have access to Jack's last will and testament from his lawyers as this was a murder investigation, it would be useful to have a look at it right now. She had no idea how long the lawyers would drag their feet.

'No.' Georgie shook her head. 'It's a prenuptial legal agreement.'

Ruth asked. 'Between him and Lottie?' From what she remembered, Lottie came from a wealthy family in Shropshire.

Georgie looked at Ruth. 'Between Sofia and Charlie Huntington.'

'Really?' Ruth said, now interested. Then she gestured. 'What does it say?'

'It stipulates that Charlie has no rights to Sofia's family money or anything that she inherits from her parents,' Georgie explained.

'Right,' Ruth said thoughtfully as she processed this. 'I suppose Jack Rush was a very wealthy man and wanted to protect his money.'

'The strange thing is,' Georgie said as she then turned the document over to the final page. 'Jack hasn't signed it.'

Ruth narrowed her eyes. 'What?' Then she looked.

There was a signature and date by Charlie's name but nothing beside Jack's.

'Isn't that really weird?' Georgie asked.

'Yeah, it is,' Ruth agreed. 'Because without Jack's signature, that prenup is invalid. Come on.'

'Where are we going?' Georgie asked.

'If the lawyers are in Chester, then we're going to Chester,' Ruth replied.

'Can I drive?' Georgie said.

'You're eight months pregnant,' Ruth said. 'So, no.'

'How do you think I get to work?' Georgie asked with an amused smile.

'It's still no,' Ruth laughed.

CHAPTER 20

As Ruth and Georgie sped towards the border and Chester, the clear azure-blue sky stretched out before them. Hovering over a field to their right were two peregrine falcons who bobbed and soared elegantly on the thermals.

'So… Adam,' Ruth said after a while.

Georgie rolled her eyes. 'I knew you were going to ask me about him once we got into the car.'

Ruth gave a defensive shrug. 'I was just going to say that I really liked him when I met him on Sunday. He seems like a nice bloke. And Sarah and Ella gave him a five-star approval. In fact, they both thought he was really "fit".'

'Oh, right,' Georgie chortled. 'Well, he is really "fit".'

Looking up, Ruth saw the sign that read ENGLAND as they crossed the border into Cheshire.

'Have you run him through the PNC yet?' Ruth asked with an amused expression.

The PNC – Police National Computer – was the UK National database that stored convictions, cautions and arrests from all forces.

'No,' Georgie exclaimed defensively. 'Of course not. I'd lose my job for starters.'

'Depends on who found out,' Ruth pointed out. 'Want me to check him out?'

Georgie narrowed her eyes. 'I think you might be taking this whole protective thing a bit too far.'

Ruth nodded. 'Okay, I'll back off. I just want you and your baby to be safe. And this Adam seems to have come out of nowhere.'

'Not nowhere,' Georgie said. 'He just moved in next door, that's all.'

'Good. That's good,' Ruth said as if she was actually convincing herself.

They drove around a large roundabout and into the middle of Chester.

'God, are you like this with Ella?' Georgie joked.

'Sometimes,' Ruth admitted. 'I think that we see such terrible things as police officers, that we can be a bit overprotective.'

'I'm fine. I can handle myself,' Georgie said and then looked over at Ruth. 'But it is sweet that you care so much.'

'Yeah, well we can stop all this mushy stuff,' Ruth said as they pulled into a small private car park beside a building close to Chester Station. 'We're here.'

Ruth parked up in a visitors bay and they got out. They walked around to the main entrance and headed for the main reception desk.

'Have we got a name?' Ruth asked Georgie quietly as they approached.

'Karan Patel. He owns the firm,' Georgie replied.

As they arrived at the reception desk, a rather snooty woman in her early fifties looked at them enquiringly. 'Can I help?' she asked in a very middle-class accent.

Ruth and Georgie flashed their warrant cards. 'DI Ruth Hunter and DC Georgie Wild. Llancastell CID. We'd like to speak to Karan Patel?'

'Llancastell? You've come a long way,' the woman said as if this was somehow amusing to her.

God, she's getting right up my nose, Ruth thought to herself.

'Is he in?' Georgie asked.

The woman tapped at the computer. 'Do you have an appointment? *Mr* Patel is incredibly busy.'

Ruth took a breath and forced a smile. 'I'm running a murder investigation so it would be useful if we could see *Karan* right now,' she said through gritted teeth.

The woman gave Ruth a supercilious look. 'Now? Oh, I'm afraid Mr Patel is in a partners meeting. But if you can wait…'

Don't lose it, Ruth, she said to herself.

Ruth leant closer to the desk and then spotted a name plate by the woman's computer – *Maggie Goodwin*.

'Okay, Maggie,' Ruth said in a very quiet but threatening voice as she fixed her with an icy stare. 'This is what you're going to do. You're going to find Karan Patel and tell him that we're here to talk to him right now about a client of his that was murdered less than ten hours ago. Otherwise, I'm going to come back with half a dozen uniformed officers and seize every computer, file and piece of paperwork that I want in connection with this investigation and haul it all the way over to Wales.'

'You can't do that,' Maggie said looking shocked.

Georgie gave Maggie a little smug smile. 'She can. And she will. I've seen her do it and it's not pretty. Absolute chaos. And we'll probably keep all the stuff we seize for months.'

Maggie grabbed the phone and quietly explained what was going on.

Within a few seconds, a very smartly dressed man in his early sixties came marching out and approached.

'Detective Inspector Hunter?' he said as he came over and shook Ruth's hand. 'Karan Patel. Please come through to my office.'

'Thanks for all your help, Maggie,' Ruth said giving her a smug smile.

Ruth and Georgie followed Karan through some glass double doors and along a corridor. Everything about the place said, 'Corporate Law Firm.'

'Here we go,' Karan said ushering them into a huge corner office with windows that overlooked the canal.

The office was stylishly decorated with an area on one side with two sofas facing each other. A large desk, computer and chair were on the other side. The walls were adorned with various photos of Karan with the great and good – Boris Johnson, Richard Branson, Sir Alex Ferguson, etc…

Ruth and Georgie sat down on the large sofa.

'Can I get you something?' Karan said politely. 'Coffee, tea, water?'

'We're fine, thank you,' Ruth said.

'You've come to talk to me about poor Jack,' Karan said with a sombre expression. 'Such a terrible tragedy. Was it accidental?'

'Actually, we think that Jack's death is suspicious,' Ruth replied. 'And we're treating it as a murder case.'

'Oh, my God,' Karan said with a shocked expression. 'Murder? I… Do you have any suspects or know why Jack was targeted?'

Georgie leant forward. 'We can't really discuss the details of an ongoing investigation at the moment.'

'Of course.' Karan gave an understanding nod. 'I understand that my office has sent over most of the paperwork and documents that pertain to our work for Jack?'

'That's right,' Ruth said and then reached into a small bag that she was carrying. She pulled out a photocopy of the prenuptial legal agreement and showed it to Karan. 'This is your signature as witness to Charlie Huntington's signature. It's dated last Thursday. Is that correct?'

'Yes. We drew up this prenuptial agreement for Jack for his daughter Sofia,' Karan explained. 'Charlie came in and signed it in this very office. And I witnessed it.'

Georgie took out her notebook and pen. 'Do you draw up many of these prenuptial agreements?'

'We're seeing more and more of them actually,' Karan admitted. 'It's a trend we got from the States.'

'How did Charlie seem when he signed the agreement?' Ruth asked.

Karan looked confused. 'Seem? I don't understand.'

'Was he happy to be signing the document?' Georgie said, to clarify.

'Not really,' Karan replied. 'But he loved Sofia and wanted to marry her.'

Ruth turned the photocopy to show Karan. 'Can you tell us why Jack hadn't signed the agreement.'

'Typical Jack.' Karan sighed and shook his head. 'Once I'd called him to tell him that Charlie had signed it, Jack said his mind was at rest. I told him that it wasn't legally binding.'

'What did he say to that?' Ruth asked.

'He joked that it wasn't as if he was going to drop dead between Saturday and today,' Karan said quietly.

Georgie raised an eyebrow. 'Today?'

Karan looked at them. 'The sad irony is that Jack was going to pop in today to sign it and get a copy.'

Ruth looked directly at him. 'Am I right in thinking that this prenup agreement isn't valid because it's not signed?'

'Yes, that's right. And of course, the agreement will never be valid,' Karan replied.

'And that means that whatever Sofia inherits from her father's estate,' Ruth said, 'Charlie will be entitled to half of it because no agreement was signed?'

Karan nodded. 'Yes, that's exactly right.'

Ruth narrowed her eyes. 'Did Charlie know that Jack wasn't going to be signing the agreement until today?'

Karan frowned for a few seconds. 'Actually, yes. He did ask but I didn't think anything of it.'

Ruth gave Georgie a dark look. Charlie Huntington knew that if Jack died before the prenup was signed, it would be invalid. That now made him their prime suspect.

CHAPTER 21

Nick was trawling through the video footage of Sofia and Charlie's wedding at his desk. Each video file was numbered with a small time stamp, plus there was a running time code at the bottom of the screen. Nick was just working his way through it chronologically. The ceremony had taken place in a large wooden gazebo that had been decorated with an array of colourful flowers. Even though it did look romantic and picturesque, it also reminded Nick of a slightly cheesy scene you'd see in an American film. All the seats lined out neatly on the lawn, the perfect setting, the sun shining. It wasn't that surprising that it looked like this given Jack's job.

Nick had a pad of A4 paper in front of him and was making the odd note. Most of his attention was focused on Jack as the footage played. It was vital to look closely at how Jack interacted with the members of the family. Were there any signs of tension or resentment? If they stuck with their hypothesis that someone in the immediate family had switched Jack's cocaine for cyanide, then was anyone behaving strangely. The knowledge that Jack was going to die the next time he took cocaine in his office might weigh heavily on the guilty person's mind. Were there any signs of that?

The video now showed the official wedding photographer lining up various shots of the happy couple along with parents, relatives and friends. Meanwhile, guests were being handed flutes of champagne and canapés on the lawn by smartly dressed waiters and waitresses who effortlessly drifted between them.

Out of the corner of his eye, Nick spotted something that didn't look right. The photographer was gesturing for Sofia and Charlie to have their photograph taken with Jack and Lottie.

However, for a few seconds Jack and Charlie seemed to move to one side for a talk. They were very close to each other. They were clearly talking very quietly as the microphone on the video camera didn't pick up any sound from them until Jack gave a loud laugh and then turned and walked away.

Nick wound the video back to watch it again. Jack and Charlie are talking intently. Jack laughed and as he turns to walk to where the photograph is to be taken, Charlie reaches out and grabs at his forearm angrily.

What the hell is that about? Nick wondered.

Using the zooming in tool, Nick watched it again. He could now see that Charlie's face was twisted in anger by whatever Jack was saying to him. When Jack laughed, Charlie's facial expression was one of fury as he grabbed at Jack angrily.

'Anything interesting?' asked a voice.

Nick turned and saw Kennedy walking over towards his desk. Ever since Ruth had 'poached' her from Cheshire Police Force, she had proved herself to be a very resourceful, hard-working and instinctive detective. However, he had to admit that he didn't know her any better than the day she'd arrived. She was a very private person and kept her cards close to her chest. He didn't mind that. Some officers kept their work and personal life very separate. He could see that was sensible for lots of reasons.

'I'm not sure,' Nick admitted. 'Watch this and tell me what you think.'

Kennedy came closer and peered at the screen as Nick played the video again.

'Wow,' Kennedy said. 'Whatever Jack says to Charlie, it's definitely rattled him. He looks like he's about to explode and hit Jack.'

'Yeah. Something is very wrong,' Nick said, glad that Kennedy had confirmed his suspicions.

He noticed that Kennedy had a thoughtful expression on her face as if something had just occurred to her.

'You okay?' Nick prompted her.

She nodded. 'Yes.' Then she gestured to a computer printout that she was holding. 'That might fit in this forensic report that I've just been given.'

'What does it say?' Nick asked.

'It's the initial sweep of the crime scene,' Kennedy explained. 'They've cross-matched the fingerprints and DNA that they found in Jack's study with the family elimination sample.'

An elimination sample was when forensic officers take the fingerprints and DNA of anyone who lives or works in a crime scene. They can therefore, by process of elim- ination, discover any DNA or fingerprints that can't be accounted for.

Nick looked at her with interest. 'Why? What does it say?'

Kennedy pointed to the report. 'Naturally Jack Rush's prints and DNA are all over the office. But they also found Charlie Huntington's fingerprints all over the office too. On the desk, the drawers, the chair. Everywhere.'

Nick's eyes widened. It was a significant discovery. 'Right. Looks like Charlie has got some explaining to do for various reasons. I'll call the boss. Thanks, Jade.'

'No problem,' she said as she turned and walked back to her desk.

Grabbing his phone, Nick quickly dialled Ruth.

'Nick?' Ruth said as she answered the phone. It sounded like she was in the car.

'Boss. We've got a couple of significant developments here,' he explained.

'Go on,' she said.

'Forensic report came back on Jack Rush's office. Charlie Huntington's fingerprints are all over the place. Desk, chair, drawers.'

'Okay,' Ruth said slowly.

'I've been watching the wedding video,' Nick continued. 'Jack and Charlie get into some kind of argument when the photographs are being taken. Jack laughs in Charlie's face and he goes to grab Jack's jacket.'

'That might tally with some of the details that were disclosed to us about the prenup agreement,' Ruth said. 'I think it's worth bringing him in, don't you?'

'Definitely,' Nick agreed.

CHAPTER 22

Ruth and Georgie pulled up outside the Rush's Abersoch mansion. There was still blue and white cordon tape across the road which fluttered noisily in the sea breeze. Two uniformed officers wearing high-vis jackets that read *HEDDLU POLICE* stood at the gates chatting.

On the road outside there were several television camera crews and various other journalists. Jack Rush's death was major news. North Wales Police had made the decision overnight to go public that this was now a murder investigation. Ruth had fielded several calls from the police media liaison team from St Asaph asking if she planned to hold a press conference. Her superintendent had suggested that she should. She knew that it wasn't a 'suggestion'.

The positive news was that they had enough to arrest Charlie Huntington and take him back to Llancastell nick for questioning. And that would allow Ruth to hold a press conference and announce that they had made an arrest which would appease everyone, at least for a few days. She knew that there would be increasing pressure from the chief constable and her superiors to get a quick result as North Wales Police were now not only in the UK media's spotlight, but across the globe, which made the pressure intense.

Ruth got out of the car and slammed the door. The sky above them was a soft baby blue, and even though they were close to the sea, the clouds were static. The small white clouds that were dotted symmetrically across the horizon looked like they had been painted delicately onto the skyline.

Ruth and Nick began to walk purposefully towards the house, flashing their warrant cards to the two uniformed officers as they went. Ruth recognised one of them and gave her a half smile of recognition. She could never understand those CID officers who treated uniform with disdain or condescension. That type of behaviour had been far worse when she'd first joined the Met in the Nineties. Uniformed, female police officers were treated like secretaries or dogsbodies by male CID officers. Definitely not the 'good old days'.

'Sofia is going to be devastated,' Georgie said quietly as they got to the front door where another uniformed officer – twenties, male, thick black beard – was standing.

Ruth nodded but she hoped that Georgie wasn't getting personally involved given that she knew Sofia socially a few years ago. She needed to keep an eye on that.

'Ma'am,' the bearded officer said as they showed him their warrant cards.

'We're looking for Charlie Huntington,' Ruth explained and then gestured. 'Any idea if he's inside?'

'Yes, ma'am,' the officer nodded as he opened the huge white front door. 'Everyone is in at the moment.'

'Thank you, constable,' Georgie said as they went inside and looked around the hallway. The aluminium stepping plates were now gone and most signs of the Scene of Crime Officers' work were no longer apparent.

Ruth's eye was drawn to a huge modern canvas on the wall in front of them. A heady swirl of oranges, greens and blues. Not something she would have chosen. It was a little too chaotic for her taste.

Her train of thought was broken as a figure appeared at the top of the stylish oak and glass staircase.

It was Jasmine. She was holding a large ginger cat in her arms.

'Hello,' Jasmine said with a curious expression as she came down the stairs confidently.

'Hi, Jasmine,' Georgie said with a friendly tone.

'Are you looking for clues?' Jasmine asked them.

'Sort of,' Ruth replied.

'And who is this?' Georgie asked gesturing to the cat.

'This is Marmalade,' she said as she stroked his white and ginger fur. 'It was my dad's idea. It was his favourite thing to have on his toast. But I didn't like it. I think marmalade is disgusting.'

Well, she's a curious little thing, Ruth thought to herself with a bemused smile.

'Yes, I'm not a big fan. Very bitter. Strawberry jam for me every time,' Georgie said.

Ruth looked at Jasmine. 'I'm really sorry about what happened to your father. You must be very sad.'

'I am.' Jasmine nodded and then gestured around the house. 'No one is really talking at the moment. I don't think anyone knows what the right thing is to say. If that makes sense?'

That's very perceptive.

Georgie nodded. 'Yes, it does,' she said reassuringly.

'It must be very difficult for all of you?' Ruth said gently.

Jasmine shrugged. 'I don't think Mummy is that upset really.'

Ruth gave her a quizzical look. 'What makes you say that?'

Jasmine shrugged again. 'I just know things. Just because I'm twelve, everyone thinks that I'm irrelevant and don't understand anything.' Then she tapped at her ear. 'But I hear everything.'

'Why do you think your mum isn't upset?' Ruth asked in a soft tone.

'I think she'd had enough of him. He wasn't very nice to her,' Jasmine sighed. 'And they were always fighting. He had lots of lady friends.'

Ruth nodded slowly. 'Did he?'

'Oh, yes. There was a new one,' Jasmine said in a very matter-of-fact tone. 'Amelia something.'

Ruth and Georgie exchanged a meaningful look.

'Are you sure?' Georgie asked.

'Oh, yes,' Jasmine nodded. 'I heard them arguing about it a few times.'

'And you're sure that Amelia was the name?' Ruth asked.

Jasmine nodded her head. 'Yes. Certain.' Then she gestured to a corridor off the hallway. 'I've got to feed Marmalade now, if that's okay?'

'Of course it is,' Ruth said gently 'Do you know where Charlie is?'

Jasmine pointed. 'He's sitting out on the terrace with Sofia.'

'Thank you,' Georgie said.

They watched as she walked away.

CHAPTER 23

Ruth and Georgie pushed open the large glass door that led out to a sweeping terrace. As they walked out into the sunshine, the air was instantly warm and fresh with the salty smell of the sea. The view across Abersoch beach was spectacular with the sea a silvery, metallic blue strip in the distance. It was speckled with various boats in all shapes and sizes. Over to the right, someone was water skiing behind a speedboat.

Glancing around, Ruth spotted Sofia sitting on a reclining chair reading a book. She was wearing big black Gucci sunglasses and a burgundy baseball cap.

'Sofia?' Georgie said as they approached.

Sofia sat up, lowered the sunglasses down the bridge of her nose and peered at them. 'Hi, Georgie,' she said quietly. Her eyes were a little puffy from where she'd been crying.

'How are you doing?' Georgie asked with an empathetic expression.

Sofia shrugged and looked a little lost. 'Up and down.'

Georgie nodded and gestured to Ruth. 'This is DI Ruth Hunter who is our Senior Investigating Officer.'

'I'm so sorry for your loss,' Ruth said gently.

'Thank you.'

'We're actually looking for Charlie,' Georgie explained.

Sofia pointed to the garden. 'He's gone to the garden. We…'

Georgie gave her a searching look.

'It doesn't matter. We just had a little bit of a tiff that's all,' she said looking a little embarrassed. 'I think that everyone's emotions are running high at the moment.'

Ruth gestured to two chairs that were close by. 'Mind if we sit down with you for a minute?' she asked. If they were bringing in Charlie for questioning, Ruth wanted to get a clear idea of Sofia. How much did she know about what Charlie had been doing? If Charlie was guilty of Jack Rush's murder, was Sofia complicit in any way?

'Erm, no. Of course not,' Sofia replied but she now looked concerned.

Ruth and Georgie moved the chairs over and sat down. Then Ruth had to readjust where she was sitting as the sun was bright and in her eyes.

'Why do you need to talk to Charlie?' Sofia asked. 'Should I be worried?'

Ruth leant forward and looked at her. 'We've been made aware of the prenuptial agreement that Charlie signed.'

Ruth watched Sofia to see what her reaction was.

Sofia took a moment to respond and pulled a face. 'Oh, that. Yes, that was a bit of a bone of contention.'

Ruth loved the way that the moneyed upper middle classes always underplayed anything emotional.

'I assume that was your stepfather's idea?' Georgie asked delicately.

'Of course.' Sofia nodded. 'Jack was a very protective and suspicious man. Don't get me wrong, I loved him but when it came to money…'

'How did Charlie react when you told him that your father wanted him to sign the agreement?' Ruth enquired.

Sofia winced. 'Well, he wasn't pleased. I did try to explain what Jack was like to him and not to take it personally. But it did make everything a bit awkward. Charlie said that he understood but I could see he was hurt that Dad didn't trust him.'

Georgie narrowed her eyes. 'Did you know that Jack hadn't got round to signing the agreement?'

There was an awkward silence.

'No. I had no idea.' Sofia furrowed her brow. 'I don't understand. Why didn't he sign it?'

Ruth couldn't tell if Sofia was lying to them. Her reaction seemed genuine but Ruth wasn't sure.

'According to your father's lawyer, Karan Patel, he'd planned to drive to Chester to sign it today,' Ruth said. 'He was satisfied that Charlie had signed it so he thought it didn't matter if it wasn't done until today.'

'But that means...' Then Sofia looked perplexed. 'So, it's invalid?'

'Yes.' Georgie nodded and then gave Sofia a meaningful look. 'And Charlie knew that your father had left it unsigned.'

'No. That can't be true.' Sofia shook her head adamantly. 'He would have mentioned it to me.'

Ruth looked at her. 'According to Karan Patel, Charlie definitely knew that your father had planned to sign the agreement today.'

'Why wouldn't he tell me that?' Sofia asked under her breath as she looked away. The seriousness of what they were suggesting wasn't lost on her.

'We don't know,' Georgie replied and then leant forward. 'Maybe he forgot in all the excitement of the wedding. But we are going to have to take Charlie back to the station for questioning. There are a few things that don't add up that we need to talk to him about.'

The colour visibly drained from Sofia's face. 'Are you arresting him?'

'Charlie is helping us with our inquiries,' Ruth said diplomatically.

Sofia looked distraught. 'You can't possibly think that Charlie had anything to do with what happened to Jack. That's ridiculous.'

'We've seen the wedding video,' Georgie said. 'There is a moment when the photographs were being taken when your father and Charlie have cross words. Charlie actually grabs at Jack and appears very angry. Do you know why he's so angry?'

'No,' Sofia muttered as her eyes filled with tears. It was all getting too much for her. 'I would have noticed if something like that had happened. I was there.'

'Everything all right?' asked a voice.

It was Charlie.

He looked concerned as he came out onto the terrace towards them.

'Charlie Huntington?' Ruth said as she stood up. 'I'm afraid that we're going to need to take you back to Llan-castell Police Station for questioning.'

Charlie looked shocked. 'What?' he snorted arrogantly. 'Am I under arrest or something?'

'We just need to ask you a few questions,' Georgie explained.

Charlie narrowed his eyes. 'I can answer your questions here,' he said in a tone that suggested he thought it was very inconvenient.

Ruth fixed him with a stare that was intended to show him that this was serious. 'We'd prefer to do it at the station.'

'Do I need a lawyer?' Charlie asked starting to look worried.

Ruth nodded. 'You are entitled to legal representation if you feel you need it, yes.'

CHAPTER 24

Ruth pressed the button on the recording equipment and said, 'Interview conducted with Charlie Huntington, 1:30 p.m., Interview Room 1, Llancastell Police Station. Present are Charlie Huntington, Detective Constable Georgie Wild, duty solicitor Simon Kestler and myself, Detective Inspector Ruth Hunter.'

Ruth sat down and looked over at Charlie who seemed scared.

'This is ridiculous,' Charlie said very quietly. He looked lost and broken. 'I didn't kill Jack. How could you think that?'

Ruth ignored him, reached over and took a document from a folder. She turned it for Charlie to look at. 'For the purposes of the recording, I am showing the suspect Item Reference 945M. This is a forensic report from a search that was made of Jack Rush's office on the night of his murder.' Ruth looked directly at Charlie. 'As you can see, your fingerprints were found in multiple places in Jack's office.' Ruth pulled out a photograph of the drawers on Jack's desk where they were convinced his 'cocaine' had been kept. 'This photograph shows your fingerprints on all of the drawers of Jack's desk. Is there anything you can tell us about that?'

Charlie took a deep breath to steady himself and then shook his head. 'I'd been into Jack's office. So what?'

Georgie frowned. 'Why did you go into his office?'

Charlie looked down at the floor and then ran his hands nervously through his hair. 'I don't know,' he replied quietly under his breath.

Ruth gave him a puzzled look. 'You don't know why you went into Jack's office and searched through his shelves, drawers and desk? I'm assuming he wasn't in there when you did that?'

Silence.

Georgie leant forward. 'What were you looking for, Charlie?' she asked in a low voice.

Charlie leant in to talk to the duty solicitor. They spoke very quietly for about a minute.

Ruth shot Georgie a suspicious look. She was concerned about what the duty solicitor was advising Charlie to do.

The duty solicitor then looked at them. 'I'm advising my client to answer "no comment" to any further questions that you have for him today. My concern is that my client will inadvertently incriminate himself for a crime that he did not commit.'

Ruth gave a frustrated sigh and looked at Charlie. 'This is a voluntary interview, Charlie. If you choose to answer "no comment" to our questions, then you are suggesting that you have something to hide. And that's very suspicious.'

Charlie just looked over at Ruth and shrugged. 'No comment.'

'You're not helping yourself, Charlie,' Georgie said in a quiet voice. 'You just need to answer our questions.'

Ruth was losing her patience now. 'You knew that Jack Rush hadn't signed the prenuptial agreement that you *had* signed in Karan Patel's office. You also knew that if Jack

Rush died before he got to sign that agreement, it would be invalid. And if you were ever to divorce Sofia, that would make you a very wealthy man.' Then Ruth stared at him but he avoided eye contact and looked away. 'Is that why you swapped his cocaine for potassium cyanide? Is that why you were rummaging around Jack's office?'

'No comment,' Charlie mumbled as he looked uncomfortably at the floor.

The duty solicitor leaned in to talk to him again. Charlie nodded at what he was saying.

The duty solicitor then leaned forward. 'I'm not comfortable with the tone of your questioning, Detective Inspector. And as this is a voluntary interview, and my client isn't under caution or arrest, then we are now going to leave this police station. Unless you have plans to arrest or charge my client?'

Ruth closed the folder in front of her in frustration. 'No, not at this time.'

CHAPTER 25

An hour later, Ruth was perched on the edge of a desk in the CID office, looking at the scene boards. Her eyes roamed across the various photos of the family members. Something about the forensic evidence against Charlie didn't quite add up.

Nick joined her. 'We don't have enough evidence to arrest him, do we?'

'No,' Ruth replied quietly.

Georgie approached. 'Boss, PNC check on Charlie Huntington. Nothing there. Clean as a whistle. As they say, "Not even a parking ticket."'

Ruth frowned at them. 'We have Charlie's fingerprints all over Jack's office. His desk and the drawers where we think he kept his cocaine. *But* we don't have any finger-prints on the actual plastic bag that contained the cyanide. Why is that? Why would he leave his fingerprints all over the place and then somehow carefully avoid leaving them on that bag?'

Nick nodded in agreement. 'No, that doesn't make sense, does it?'

'And Charlie is an intelligent man,' Georgie pointed out. 'And he would know that if Jack died, the whole of his office would be swept for prints and DNA.'

Garrow looked over from where he was sitting. 'It's a very big mistake to make.'

Nick frowned. 'But we still have the prenup and the quarrel with Jack at the wedding.'

'I don't think we're ruling him out,' Ruth admitted. 'I'm just not as convinced as I was. Has anyone found out who Jack Rush met on Friday morning yet? The mysterious letter M?'

'We've drawn a blank so far, boss,' Garrow admitted.

'And when is Jack Rush's last will and testament going to be read?' Ruth asked looking around the room.

'It's going to take at least three days for the paperwork to be processed,' Georgie explained. 'They have to get a death certificate from the coroner's office.'

Garrow wandered over. 'Boss, just had a call from the guys in Digital Forensics. They think they've found something significant on one of the laptops that was taken from the Rush house.'

CHAPTER 26

Ten minutes later, Ruth and Nick were sitting with a Digital Forensics officer, on the ground floor of the building opposite Llancastell nick, where the Digital Forensics team were housed. The room comprised two rows of state-of-the-art computers facing each other. Above this were black shelves that contained audio and digital tracking machinery, which glowed and made low humming noises.

The officer – thirties, neat beard, designer glasses – pointed to the screen in front of them.

Ruth frowned. 'What exactly are we looking at?'

'Okay, so this is the data and internet history from James Rush's computer,' the officer explained. He then pointed to something on the screen. 'He's used an encryption code to try and hide what he's looking at.'

Nick narrowed his eyes. 'Which is suspicious in itself.'

'What has he been looking at?' Ruth asked, wondering why they'd been called down to have a look.

'He's been on "the Dark Web",' the officer explained.

The Dark Web was a part of the World Wide Web that was difficult to access and very secretive. A plethora of illicit sites selling drugs, guns, child pornography, even people.

'Do we know why?' Nick asked.

'I can see some of the sites that he's browsed,' the officer replied. 'But it's impossible to see if he's interacted with any sellers or made any purchases.'

Ruth peered at the screen. The Dark Web was a mystery to her but she knew how dangerous it was to those that could access it.

'Anything that helps us?' she asked.

The officer pointed. 'This is a site based in Houston, Texas. The seller offers every drug known to man. But there is also a section on his drop-down menu that lists poisons.'

'Cyanide?' Ruth asked.

The officer nodded. 'Yes.' He pointed to the screen. 'Here we go. *Cyanide – the classic killer used by eveyone from the Roman Emporer Nero to the villains of Agatha Christie novels.*'

'Nice sales pitch,' Nick said dryly.

Ruth peered at the screen in disbelief. It was laid out like any other internet shopping page with prices, photos and even a basket to pop your purchases in.

'So we do know that James Rush went onto this site?' Ruth asked, to clarify.

'Yes.' The officer nodded. 'But we just can't prove that he purchased anything.'

'Have you got a date for his search?' Ruth asked.

'Yes, ma'am,' the officer replied. 'Ten days ago.'

Ruth looked at Nick. 'Then we can cross-reference that with any bank account or credit card that James Rush has. And I think we should confront James with this and see what he has to say for himself.'

CHAPTER 27

Ruth and Nick were heading away from Llancastell towards Abersoch. Taking a cigarette from a packet, Ruth buzzed down the window. Then she lit it, took a drag and blew a plume of smoke out of the window.

The sun was blazing down and reflecting brightly off the windscreen. Taking out her black Ray Ban Wayfarer sunglasses, Ruth popped them on.

That's better, she thought as she took another drag on her cigarette.

'Hello, Maverick,' Nick joked as he looked over at her, referring to the Tom Cruise character in the *Top Gun* film.

'Yeah, well that makes you Goose,' Ruth joked, referring to Tom Cruise's sidekick in the film. 'Anyway, I was going for Molly Ringwald.'

'Molly who?'

'Oh, God. Molly Ringwald. *Pretty In Pink, Sixteen Candles, The Breakfast Club*?'

'You've just mentioned three films that I've never seen,' Nick laughed.

'What?' Ruth said looking aghast. 'Classic Eighties Brat Pack movies directed by John Hughes.'

'Sorry, lost on me,' Nick shrugged as he stared intently in the rear-view mirror.

'Oh, dear,' Ruth chortled. 'You need to see *The Breakfast Club*. It's a classic. One of the great lines of dialogue is when Judd Nelson says to his teacher, "Does Barry Manilow know that you raid his wardrobe in the morning?"'

But Nick wasn't listening. Instead he was peering into the rear-view intently.

'Everything okay?' Ruth asked as she turned and glanced back.

There was a black Range Rover with tinted windows behind them.

'I'm not sure yet,' Nick admitted.

'Are we being followed?' she asked.

'I think so,' Nick nodded. 'Number plate looks foreign to me.'

Ruth reached for the car's Tetra radio. 'Control from three-six, are you receiving me, over?'

The radio crackled. 'Three-six, this is Control. We are receiving you. Go ahead, over.'

'I need a licence plate check on a vehicle,' Ruth said as she looked at the wing mirror to see the reflection of the Range Rover's registration. 'Gamma-two-four-seven, yankee-zebra, over.'

'Okay, three-six, stand by,' the Computer Aided Dispatch (CAD) replied.

As Ruth watched, the Range Rover sped up so that it was very close behind them.

'That plate doesn't have any flag on it, does it?' Ruth asked under her breath.

Nick shook his head. 'No.'

Looking forward, Ruth could see the winding country road ahead of them.

'Three-six from Control, are you receiving, over?' crackled the radio.

Ruth clicked the grey button. 'Control, this is three-six, we are receiving, over.'

'The car is registered to a Russian national, Aleksandr Pitrov,' the CAD said.

'Do we have an address?' Ruth asked, wondering why on earth a car driven by a Russian national would be following them.

'Yes, ma'am. The address is in central Moscow. I can text it to you, over?' the CAD operator suggested.

'Thank you, over and out,' Ruth said.

'Moscow? Do you want me to stop to see what they want…?'

Suddenly, there was a little jolt.

Ruth and Nick were knocked forward.

The Range Rover had rammed into the back of them.

'Are you bloody joking?' Ruth growled as she reached over and hit the lights and sirens. She hoped that would signal that they were police officers and the car would back off. Unless they knew they were police officers and that was why they were being followed.

Ruth started to feel very uneasy as the lights and sirens burst into life.

Nick glanced at the rear-view mirror again. 'It doesn't look like they're going anywhere.'

Ruth peered again in the wing mirror.

Nick floored the accelerator and the Astra's 2.0L fuel-injection engine roared. 'Let's see how serious they are about fucking with us.'

'Be careful,' Ruth said as they came hammering around a bend and she had to grip the seat to keep her balance. She felt the back tyres slip a little.

'Problem is that if we stop, we're in the middle of nowhere,' Ruth pointed out as her pulse quickened.

The Range Rover's engine revved as it came speeding up behind them again.

Ruth looked at Nick. 'This is not good. I'm calling for backup.' She took the radio again. 'Three-six to Control, are you receiving us, over?'

'Three-six from Control, are you receiving, over?' crackled the radio.

Ruth clicked the grey button. 'Control, this is three-six, we are receiving, over. I need backup asap.' Ruth glanced over at the digital GPS map on the dashboard. 'We're heading west on the A497, approaching Petrefelin, over.'

'Three-six, received, stand by, over.'

Nick's eyes were glued to the rear-view mirror.

Ruth lowered her head so she could look in the wing mirror. The Range Rover was now about twenty yards behind. Her pulse was now racing.

'Are they trying to force us off the road?' Ruth asked. Her mouth was dry. The mention of Moscow and Russia had thrown her.

'I don't think so,' Nick said uncertainly. 'If I was to make a guess, they're trying to scare us.'

'Well, they've succeeded,' Ruth groaned. 'We're in the middle of nowhere.'

'What the hell is a car registered to someone in Moscow doing in the middle of Snowdonia?'

'No idea,' Ruth admitted. 'Bloody long way from home though.'

The Tetra radio crackled. 'Control to three-six, over.'

Ruth glanced in the wing mirror again. The Range Rover was just sitting on their tail.

What the hell do they want?

'Three-six receiving. Go ahead, Control,' Ruth said.

'I have patrol unit gamma–delta–one heading your way,' the CAD explained. 'ETA seven minutes, over.'

'Thank you. Over and out,' Ruth said ending comms.

There was a deep roar of an engine from behind.

'Oh, here we go,' Nick said darkly with his eyes fixed to the mirror.

'What is it?' Ruth asked as she spun around to look.

The Range Rover was now on the opposite side of the road and speeding down the side of them as if to overtake.

Or ram them off the road.

'Shit,' Ruth hissed under her breath as she watched the enormous Range Rover pull alongside.

There was a man in his forties – shaved head, tough-looking, designer sunglasses – sitting in the passenger seat. He looked over directly at Ruth and smirked as if it was some kind of joke.

'Hold on,' Nick said.

'Why?' Ruth asked.

'Just hold on.'

Nick slammed on the brakes.

Ruth was flung forward and felt the seatbelt cutting into her right shoulder.

The car skidded from side to side.

The Range Rover, which was now about thirty yards ahead and still on the wrong side of the road, applied its brakes, slowed a little and then pulled over to the left-hand side of the country road.

The Range Rover stopped in the road ahead of them.

Then its white reverse lights came on.

'Shit,' Ruth said.

Then with a squeal of its tyres, the Range Rover sped away at high speed.

Ruth blew out her cheeks. 'What the bloody hell was all that about?'

Nick took a deep breath and glanced over at her. 'No idea, boss.'

CHAPTER 28

Kennedy sat at her desk tapping away at her computer. Reading through her emails, she noticed one from an old work colleague at Chester Town Hall nick. She'd worked there before transferring to North Wales Police. The email was from DC Johnny Bellamy. He informed her that her old boss and head of Chester CID, DI Simon Weaver, had transferred over to Merseyside. DC Bellamy had written *Good bloody riddance!*

The thought of DC Weaver sent a little shudder down her spine. As an SIO, Weaver couldn't have been more different to Ruth. He was arrogant, petty and childish. His management style was woeful and most of the CID team couldn't stand him. He was also fiercely ambitious and continually looking to climb up the ladder to the upper echelons of the forces' hierarchy. It struck her that it was officers like Weaver – often men – who ended up in positions of power because their sole focus was promotion and reputation. Often this came at the detriment of the job in hand – criminal investigations. Kennedy thought that the force would be far better if officers such as Ruth ran it. But officers like Ruth weren't interested in those positions. They were in the job for the right reasons, getting their hands dirty and solving cases.

Sitting back, Kennedy gave a little sigh and thought how glad she was that Ruth had 'tapped her up' and offered her the transfer across the border.

It felt a long way from the Park Estate in Streatham, South London, where she'd grown up. She'd worked so hard at school because she knew that the only way was to move away and make a life for herself. Having secured a place at Chester University to do a degree in Criminology, she decided to stay north and put roots down there.

Garrow wandered past and then stopped. 'I'm going to the canteen. Fancy a coffee?'

Kennedy smiled. 'Yeah. That would be lovely. Flat white, no sugar.'

'Same as the boss,' Garrow observed and nodded.

Kennedy went to get her bag. 'Here, I'll get you some money.'

Garrow shook his head. 'Don't be silly. On me,' he reassured her with a wave of his hand.

She watched him walk away. Although she didn't know all the details, she knew that Garrow had had a rough few weeks. She hoped he was okay. Not only was he a good copper, he was also a decent bloke.

Out of the corner of her eye, Kennedy spotted that another email had landed in her inbox, although it had been forwarded to the whole of Llancastell CID by the station's inquiry team.

The thing that then really caught her attention was the email address – whistleblowerrushproperties@gmail.com.

Rush properties? That must be connected to Jack Rush? she thought.

With a quick search, Kennedy soon established that *Rush Properties & Construction* was a Chester-based limited company. The Managing Director was Edward Rush, although Jack Rush was Chairman and the majority share-holder.

The email read:

> To whom it may concern,
>
> I have worked in the Chester office of Rush Properties for the past three years. After I saw that Jack's death was now being treated as murder, I felt compelled to contact the police. Ed and Jack had a terrible argument behind closed doors last week. Jack threw several cups across Ed's office because he was so angry. There have been rumours that the company has been mismanaged by Ed over the years and is about to go bankrupt.
>
> My name is Annabelle Blackman. I am willing to talk to the police off the record about what I know but I don't want it to be known that I have spoken to the police.

Getting up from her desk, Kennedy scoured the office for Georgie.

'Looking for someone?' said a voice which startled her.

It was Georgie who was standing behind her.

'Oh, bloody hell, Georgie,' Kennedy laughed. 'I'm looking for you actually.'

Georgie gave her a puzzled look.

'Email has arrived from a whistle-blower at a property and construction company that was owned by Jack Rush, but run by Ed Rush. Apparently, it's about to go bankrupt and Ed and Jack had an almighty row last week.'

Georgie raised an eyebrow. 'Interesting?'

Garrow approached and handed Kennedy her coffee. 'Here you go, Jade.'

Georgie looked at Garrow with mock indignation. 'Hey, where's mine, Jim?'

Garrow pulled a face. 'Sorry. I did look for you,' he said apologetically.

Georgie touched his arm. 'I'm just kidding,' she laughed.

Kennedy gestured towards the doors. 'Shall we go?'

CHAPTER 29

Ruth and Nick were sitting at the long oak table in the vast open-plan kitchen at the Rush's home in Absersoch. They had told James that they needed to ask him a few questions. A female housekeeper, Gwyneth – fifties, with a thick North Wales accent – came over with a tray of coffees and a plate of biscuits.

'Here we go,' she said with a friendly smile. 'James, I've put goat's milk in yours.' She looked at Ruth and Nick. 'He's lactose intolerant, aren't you?'

James nodded but he had looked incredibly nervous since their arrival. 'Thank you, Hettie,' he mumbled as he pushed his hair from his face.

'I'll leave you to it then,' Gwyneth said as she wandered away out of the kitchen.

Nick pulled out his notepad and pen.

Ruth was still a little preoccupied by their encounter with the Range Rover. What was a Russian national doing in Snowdonia and why had they decided to try and intimidate two police officers? It had definitely left her feeling uneasy.

Trying to take her mind off of it, she reached for her coffee and took a sip.

Okay, that's very good coffee, she thought to herself. Although it should be given the state-of-the-art La

Marzocco coffee maker in the corner of the kitchen. *You wouldn't get much change out of £3,000 for that.*

'Okay, James,' Ruth said looking over at him. 'We've got a few things we'd like to clarify with you. How would you describe your relationship with your father?'

James shrugged defensively. 'I don't understand what you mean.'

'Did you and your father get on?' Ruth clarified.

'I suppose so.'

'We understand that you were angry at your father for not funding you to go to art college in Paris?' Nick asked as he clicked his pen open.

'Art college?' James snorted arrogantly. 'Les Beaux-Arts de Paris isn't an art *college*. It's arguably the best art *school* in the world.'

Well at least he's not entitled, Ruth thought sardonically to herself.

Nick didn't react to this. 'Well, semantics aside,' he said calmly, '…were you angry that your father had refused to pay for you to go to Paris?'

'I think "angry" is a very strong word,' he sighed. 'I was disappointed. Of course. But I could see my father's point of view too. I've studied art in London for five years already.'

Ruth frowned and leaned forward. 'We understand that you had a blazing argument with him? An argument that could be heard throughout the house?'

'Good God, no!' James laughed. 'Who told you that? My stepmother no doubt.'

'I can't reveal the details of our investigation, I'm afraid,' Ruth explained. 'Are you saying that you didn't have any kind of argument with your father?'

'No.' James shook his head adamantly. 'I loved my father but as you're probably becoming aware, he was a terrifying, controlling bully when he wanted to be. I wouldn't have dared argue with him. The only person who dared to do that was Lottie.' He virtually spat her name in disdain from his mouth. 'Anyway, my father made me a counter offer.'

'Which was?'

'He said that he'd buy me a flat and an artist's studio over in Chester,' James explained. 'You see it wasn't only the fees for Les Beaux-Arts de Paris that he was so against. It was that I would be living in Paris. He likes...' Then James corrected himself as he realised he'd used the present tense. 'He liked...' James swallowed as if recalling that his father was no longer alive had got to him. 'Sorry. He liked to have everyone in his family nearby and under his control. Of course, he was a very rich man so he could use money to control us. It was okay when I lived in London because he bought me a flat close to his offices in Notting Hill. But Paris. He just didn't want me to move away.'

Ruth was surprised at the level of control that Jack Rush held over his grown-up children and the extent to which he would go to exert it.

Nick turned a page of his notebook and looked over. 'What can you tell us about the Dark Web, James?'

The question seemed to throw him for a few seconds.

'The Dark Web?' James asked but he was clearly rattled. 'What do you mean?'

'Have you ever been on it?' Ruth asked.

'Yes,' he replied cautiously. 'Why? Am I in trouble or something?'

Ruth ignored this. 'What did you do when you were on the Dark Web?'

'I just looked around,' James shrugged. 'It fascinates me. The dark side of humanity has always fascinated me. It's what my work is about. How we are all essentially primeval deep down. It's in our DNA.'

'Can you tell us what you bought on it?' Ruth asked. Even though they had no evidence that James had purchased anything, it was worth throwing in the question to see what he'd tell them.

James frowned and paused for a second. Then he gave a little shake of his head. 'I didn't buy anything. I don't know what you're talking about.'

Ruth pulled a computer printout from her case. It was a screenshot of the site that the Digital Forensic team had discovered that James had been trawling.

'Have you ever been on this website, James?' Ruth asked calmly.

James peered at the screenshot for several seconds with a furrowed brow as if he was trying to remember.

Ruth wasn't buying it. *Cut the bullshit.*

'Let me help you. Our Digital Forensic team have discovered that you *have* been on this site,' Ruth said.

James shrugged defensively. 'So what? It's not illegal, is it?' Underneath the sullen bravado, he looked agitated.

'Did you buy anything from this site?' Nick said.

'No. I told you that already,' he snapped.

'Would it surprise you that this site sells various poisons that are lethal to human beings?' Ruth asked.

'It wouldn't surprise me, no,' James replied. 'There's all sorts of weird shit on there.'

Ruth narrowed her eyes. 'But you're sure that you didn't purchase any kind of poison from that site?'

Then the penny dropped. 'My father was poisoned?' James said almost to himself in a low tone.

Ruth nodded. 'Yes.' The exact details of how Jack Rush had died still hadn't been made known, just that he had snorted something instead of cocaine that had killed him.

Then James looked at them both. 'And you think I had something to do with that?'

'Did you?'

'No. I loved my father. How many times do I have to say it?' James sneered nervously. Then he shook his head. 'I keep telling you. It's her.'

'You mean Lottie?' Nick asked, to clarify.

'Yes. Lottie,' James sighed angrily and then his expression changed as he thought of something. He looked up at them. 'Someone switched his cocaine for poison? Is that what happened?'

Although Ruth wouldn't usually divulge the details of a murder investigation to a possible suspect, she could see that James might have something important to tell them. 'Yes, that's right. Your father ingested a poison thinking that it was cocaine.'

'Well, there you are then,' James said with a gesture. 'Lottie sources Dad's cocaine most of the time.'

Nick stopped writing for a second. 'Lottie buys your father's cocaine for him?'

'Yes. Of course. She used to be a right coke head back in the day,' James explained. 'Not as much these days but she gets it for him. I've heard them arguing before when Dad had taken all the coke and Lottie was pissed off because she had to try and get more.'

Ruth looked over at Nick. It could be significant.

CHAPTER 30

Kennedy and Georgie sat in a very chic cafe in Chester called The Jaunty Goat. Opposite them was Annabell Blackman, the employee from Rush Properties, who had sent them the whistle-blowing email. They had arranged to meet her there rather than at the office.

A waitress arrived with a black circular tray and placed down three coffees.

'Thank you,' Georgie said with a kind smile. She then took her decaf flat white and slid it over so that it was in front of her. She'd been drinking decaf ever since she'd discovered that she was pregnant. Her baby was proving to be very lively, kicking her at various points of the day and night. Caffeine wasn't going to make that any better.

Annabelle was in her late twenties, fashionable glasses, blonde, pretty, with lots of make-up, nice clothes and immaculate nails. She looked incredibly nervous as she lifted her coffee.

Kennedy took out her notebook and pen. 'Annabelle, thank you for agreeing to meet us. I know it must have been difficult to send that email.'

'I didn't know what to do.' She gave a slight nod. 'But I knew that I had to tell someone what was going on after what had happened to Jack.'

Georgie noticed her casual use of 'Jack'. 'Did you know Jack Rush?'

'Not really.' Annabelle's eyes widened when she spoke.

'But he did come into the offices in Chester?' Kennedy asked.

'Yes, once in a while,' Annabelle replied. 'You could tell when he was coming in because everyone was on edge.'

'And why was that?' Georgie asked, although she had a pretty good idea.

'He was just scary. He had a way of looking at you...' Annabelle looked frightened even just thinking about it. 'And if he lost his temper, then all hell broke loose.'

Kennedy frowned. 'Did he often lose his temper?'

'Sometimes.' Annabelle said. 'And sometimes he could be very sweet. He'd come in and tell us to close the office and he'd take us to an expensive restaurant for lunch. There'd be champagne. And of course he'd pay for everything.'

'How would you describe Jack and Ed's relationship?' Georgie asked.

Annabelle pulled a face. 'Difficult. Jack was a...' Then she stopped herself.

'Go on,' Georgie prompted her.

'I feel so bad talking about him after what's happened,' Annabelle admitted in a soft voice.

'Please. We want to find out who did this to Jack. And to do that, we need to get as full a picture of Jack and his life as we can,' Kennedy explained encouragingly.

Annabelle gave an understanding nod. 'Jack was a bully. Especially when it came to Ed. Nothing Ed did seemed to be good enough. Sometimes he'd give Ed a dressing-down in front of the whole office. It was embarrassing for him. Even though I wasn't Ed's biggest fan, I felt so sorry for him when Jack did that. It was horrible to see Ed so humiliated. Like a little boy.'

'And when was the last time this happened?' Georgie asked.

Annabelle thought for a few seconds. 'Last week. It was Monday afternoon. Jack came in. I think he'd been drinking because his eyes were glazed. And he just went crazy.'

'Why was he so angry?' Kennedy said.

'There had been rumours for a few months that the company was losing money. We'd even heard that we were going to go out of business,' Annabelle sighed. 'Ed had got involved in this big development down on the canal. But it had all gone wrong in the past year.'

Georgie frowned. 'Gone wrong? How do you mean?'

'A structural survey had missed a major fault in the foundations of the warehouses we'd purchased. It set us back months and cost a fortune to rectify,' she explained.

'So that wasn't Ed's fault?' Kennedy asked, to clarify.

'No,' Annabelle replied adamantly. 'It was the structural engineer's fault. But Jack laid the blame with Ed. Last Monday, Jack marched Ed into his office. The door was closed but Jack was shouting so loudly that we could hear what he was saying. We heard something being thrown in there.'

Georgie frowned. 'What were they arguing about?'

'Jack was going to pull the plug on the company. Everyone was going to lose their jobs. And that was all Ed's fault because he was useless and pathetic. Then he told Ed he'd have to give up his flat in Chester and move back to the family home in Abersoch. And then...' Annabelle stopped talking and looked away.

'And then what, Annabelle?' Georgie asked gently.

Annabelle pulled a pained expression.

'It's okay,' Georgie reassured her.

'Ed said that the world would be a far better place for so many people if Jack was dead.'

CHAPTER 31

Ruth and Nick were searching the house looking for Lottie. Coming into the vast living room, they spotted Lottie sitting over in the corner nursing a large glass of wine. She was smoking a cigarette and blew the smoke out of the door to the terrace.

Hearing them approach, Lottie looked up and frowned. 'What is it? Have you found a suspect yet?'

'I'm afraid not,' Ruth said as they reached her. Then Ruth pointed to the cream sofa and asked, 'Mind if we sit down? We've got a few things we'd like to ask you.'

'Of course you have,' Lottie said with withering sarcasm. 'Do I have a choice?'

Nick narrowed his eyes. 'You don't want to help us find the person who killed your husband?'

Lottie gave a wry snort. 'Very good. I like the way you turned that back on me.' Then she took a long drag on her cigarette and blew the smoke up into the room. A shard of light caught the smoke as it swirled up to the high ceiling and pendant lights above.

'Mind if I smoke?' Ruth asked, wondering if that might get Lottie a little more onside.

Lottie smiled. 'Not at all. In fact, you've just gone up a hundred per cent in my estimation. No one smokes these days.'

'I know,' Ruth agreed as she took the packet from her jacket. 'Very boring, isn't it?'

'Very, very boring. You're right,' Lottie laughed. 'Glass of wine?'

Ruth shook her head. 'Tempting, but not while I'm on duty.'

Nick took his notebook and looked at his notes. 'Does the name Amelia mean anything to you?' It was the name that Jasmine had told them she'd heard Jack and Lottie arguing about.

'Amelia?' Lottie frowned, not giving anything away.

Ruth took a drag of her cigarette and then blew the smoke away from where they were sitting. 'It was Jasmine that mentioned it actually.'

Lottie gave them a wry smile. 'God bless Jasmine. She creeps around this house like a mouse, listening to what's going on. Making her little films. Unfortunately, she knows everyone's business, which in a house like this, isn't particularly appropriate for a twelve-year-old girl.'

There were a few seconds of silence as Lottie reached over and stubbed out her cigarette in a large blue glass ashtray.

Ruth gave her a half smile. 'You didn't actually answer the question, Lottie.'

'I know.' She gave a little laugh. 'The only person that I can think of is Amelia Wharton.'

'And who is Amelia Wharton?' Nick asked looking over.

'She's Jack's Head of Development,' Lottie explained. 'He calls her Milly actually. She finds writers, scripts, books and then develops film projects. She's been with Jack for only a year or two. I really like her. And she's bloody good at her job.'

'And were you and Jack having an argument about Amelia?' Ruth asked.

'No. I don't see why we would have been,' Lottie shrugged. 'Jasmine is prone to exaggeration, I'm afraid. Fantastic imagination but she does get carried away.'

Ruth leaned across and also stubbed out her cigarette into the ashtray. 'Jack wasn't having an affair with Amelia?'

'An affair?' Lottie gave a booming laugh. 'No. No way.'

Ruth frowned. 'You seem very certain?'

'That's because Amelia is gay,' Lottie said in a condescending tone.

Ruth looked at Nick. 'We should probably talk to her.'

Nick nodded in agreement.

'Where does Amelia live?' Ruth asked Lottie.

Lottie hesitated. 'Her mother lives locally to here. Over in Bala. She's staying with her for a few days. I'm sure I can get the address if you need it.'

'Thank you,' Ruth nodded. Then she left a few seconds before challenging her over James's assertion that it was Lottie who supplied Jack with his cocaine. 'There is something else that I need to ask you about which might be a little sensitive. As you're aware, Jack was taking what he believed to be cocaine when he died. We've had that powder tested in our forensic labs and it turns out that it was actually cyanide, which is a deadly poison.'

'Oh, my God,' Lottie said pulling a horrified face. 'That's terrible.'

'Yes,' Ruth agreed sensitively.

'How the hell did that happen?' Lottie asked as if talking to herself. Her breathing had become shallow and then she took a large gulp of wine.

'We thought you might be able to help us with that?' Nick said quietly.

Lottie took a few seconds to process what Nick had said. Then she furrowed her brow. 'Sorry? I don't understand what you mean by that.'

'You used to supply Jack with his cocaine, didn't you?' Ruth said.

'Who told you that?' Lottie asked indignantly.

Ruth looked at her and waited for several seconds. 'Lottie, we're not interested in the illegality of you buying cocaine for yourself, Jack and anyone else in the house. But we are interested in how that cocaine was switched with cyanide.'

Lottie looked at them both as she weighed up her options. 'Well, I certainly didn't switch it.'

'But you did supply it to him?' Nick said.

'I don't like the word "supply",' Lottie said witheringly. 'I bought some cocaine for Jack and I to use recreationally. He kept it in his office away from prying eyes.'

'When did you buy it?' Ruth said.

'Two or three weeks ago,' Lottie replied.

Nick scratched at his beard and asked, 'Had you or Jack taken any of it before Saturday night?'

'No. Well I certainly hadn't,' Lottie admitted. 'I don't know if Jack had. He took if more often than I did.'

'On his own?' Ruth said.

'Oh, God, yes,' Lottie snorted.

'But he didn't mention that he had taken cocaine from the last bag that you'd bought?' Nick said.

'No. But I don't think he would have, to be perfectly honest,' Lottie said. 'He could be a bit secretive about it. Sometimes he'd claim that he'd taken it all so he could keep some for himself like a little child.'

Then something occurred to Ruth that no one had yet thought of.

'And when you handed the cocaine to Jack, it was in a small, clear plastic bag?' Ruth asked.

Lottie looked puzzled. 'Yes.'

Ruth went onto her phone where she had photos of the crime scene logged away. She scrolled through and eventually found a SOCO's photo of Jack's desk with the white powder cut into lines and the clear plastic bag beside them.

'Could you confirm that this is the bag that you gave your husband?' Ruth asked as she turned the phone so that Lottie could see the photo.

'Yes,' she said peering at it intently.

'You weren't wearing gloves?' Ruth said.

Nick looked at Ruth. The penny had dropped. The forensic lab had only found Jack's fingerprints on the plastic bag. If Lottie had handed it to him, then why weren't her fingerprints on there too? It didn't make sense. In fact, the only conclusion she could draw was that whoever switched the cocaine for cyanide had found an identical bag – which was unlikely – or they had wiped the bag to remove any prints.

'Gloves?' Lottie snorted. 'I'm sorry, but I really don't understand why you're asking me all this.'

From her reaction it was clear that Lottie had no idea what she was getting at. And her confusion would suggest that Lottie had nothing to do with Jack's death. Unless she was an incredible actor and had thought all this through. Ruth's gut instinct was that she was telling them the truth and that her bewilderment at the questions was genuine.

Ruth looked at her. 'Our forensic team only found Jack's fingerprints on that bag,' she explained as she put her phone away.

Lottie shook her head. 'No. That's impossible.'

Nick gave Ruth a meaningful look. Something wasn't right about what they'd discovered.

CHAPTER 32

Garrow was at his desk, trawling through the wedding video that Jasmine Rush had shot. He was looking for anything suspicious but had found nothing so far. His phone buzzed with a message.

Taking the phone from his jacket pocket, he saw that it was a message from Lucy:

> Meet me in the car park. I've brought lunch
> Xx

Garrow was pretty sure that meeting Lucy in the car park for lunch wasn't a sensible thing to do. He messaged her back:

> Not a good idea. And I'm busy xx

He added then took away the kisses – but then added them again. If they were going to play this little game then he had to be all in.

> Shame. I brought cous cous. And I can tell you stuff about Jack Rush xx

Garrow allowed himself a bemused smile. The mention of 'Jack Rush' intrigued him.

> 5 mins xx

She messaged back.

> New car. Black Audi A3. And I'm wearing a blonde wig. All part of the fun xx

Garrow shook his head, got up from his desk and pushed his chair under it. Then he strode out of CID, headed down the corridor towards the back staircase. Two minutes later he came out of the back entrance of Llancastell nick and scoured the car park excitedly.

There was a black Audi A3 parked over to the right, facing away from him.

Jesus, what are you doing, Jim? he asked himself. But something was compelling him to keep the charade going.

Getting to the car, he leaned down and looked in through the passenger window. Lucy was actually wearing a blonde wig. It really suited her.

She clicked the central locking open and beckoned for him to get in.

Opening the door, Garrow slid into the passenger seat and closed the door.

Before he could even settle or look at her, Lucy passed him a small bowl of cous cous salad.

'Okay, so this is my famous summer cous cous salad,' she said as she then passed him a plastic fork and paper napkin.

Garrow looked dubious. 'It's famous, is it?'

'Very. And once you've tried it, you'll want the recipe,' she explained. 'So, we have the cous cous. Then cucumber, vine tomatoes, finely sliced radishes, beetroot and shallots. Bit of mint, parsley and dill. Then the dressing which has plenty of zingy lemon.'

'Zingy lemon, eh?' Garrow asked with a wry smile. 'Good to know.'

Garrow took his fork but then hesitated. He looked over and met Lucy's eyes which were watching him intently.

'Oh, my God, Jim,' Lucy sighed in frustration as she rolled her eyes. 'I'm not going to poison you. That's not my MO.' Then she reached over with her fork, took some and ate it. 'See?' Then she grabbed at her throat, making a terrible gurgling sound before roaring with laughter.

'Very funny,' Garrow said as he started to eat.

'It's good, isn't it?' Lucy asked excitedly.

'Yes, it's very good,' Garrow agreed. 'What are you going to tell me about Jack Rush?'

'Oh, we're getting straight down to business, are we?' she said pulling a mock sad face. 'That's very tedious.'

Garrow ignored her. 'Jack Rush?'

'Powerful man. I'm guessing lots of enemies. You don't get to be a big film producer without fucking over a lot of people,' Lucy said. 'By all accounts a bully and control freak. And a misogynist given that he's Generation X and made his name in the Nineties. *Power corrupts and leads men towards arrogance. It narrows a man's vision and is the worst form of addiction. Men will fight to the death to maintain the power they have worked so viciously to attain.'*

Garrow gave her an amused frown and then remembered. 'John F. Kennedy?'

'Very good,' Lucy said with a patronising tone.

'Condescending. Great,' Garrow sighed. 'You haven't told me anything about Jack Rush that we don't already know.'

'The first news reports said that Jack Rush had died from a drug overdose,' Lucy said narrowing her eyes. 'Has to be cocaine. He's a film producer. He's not going to be taking smack, Ket, crack or meth. So, first reports were that Jack Rush had died from a cocaine overdose. That was what the first officers on the scene thought when they found his body. Is that right?'

Garrow shrugged. 'Keep going.'

'That means that whatever Jack Rush snorted, thinking it was cocaine, killed him,' Lucy said peering at him.

'Maybe.'

'Maybe means yes,' Lucy said triumphantly.

'No, it doesn't,' Garrow protested but he could see how by a process of deduction, Lucy had worked out the circumstances of Jack's murder. In a different life, Lucy should have been a detective with analytical skills like that.

'That means that someone substituted a substance that was lethal for his cocaine,' Lucy said. 'How am I doing?'

'Pretty warm,' Garrow admitted.

CHAPTER 33

Kennedy and Georgie pulled up outside the Rush's Abersoch mansion and spotted that Ruth and Nick's car was parked outside. The sun was dropping lazily in the sky, casting a powdery golden light across the building and its grounds. The immaculately clipped lawns either side that descended out of sight were so green that they didn't look real. Box hedges of raspberry-coloured spiraea rattled in the gentle breeze. Over to their right, the sea was a silvery-blue. The tide was out and there was the distinctive black and white oyster catchers who waded in the shallows pecking and eating at muscles and cockles.

Kennedy looked up at the mansion that seemed to glow vanilla in the low afternoon sun. 'It's funny. You'd assume that living in a place like this, with this view and more money than you need would make you happy. But it just doesn't work like that, does it?'

'No,' Georgie agreed as she looked up at a window. 'Some of the most miserable and screwed up people I've ever met were filthy rich.' She spotted Sofia looking out of a first-floor window across the sea. She looked deep in thought and hadn't noticed their arrival.

But then Sofia looked down at them and quickly moved out of sight.

That's a bit weird, Georgie thought as they came to the front door and rang the doorbell.

A few seconds later, the Family Liaison Officer – fifties, female, short dyed-black hair – opened the door.

Georgie and Kennedy flashed their warrant cards as they didn't recognise her. 'Afternoon, constable. We're looking for Ed Rush? I'm assuming he's in?'

'Yes,' the FLO replied. 'All the family are here at the moment.'

'Thanks,' Kennedy said as they went in. 'Any idea where he might be?'

'Sorry.' The FLO pulled a face. 'I'm basing myself in the kitchen so they know where I am if they need me. But I haven't seen Ed for a couple of hours. Maybe try the library?'

'Right you are,' Georgie said with a kind smile as they turned, walked across the hallway and past the bottom of the stairs.

Out of the corner of her eye, Georgie spotted someone moving at the top of the stairs. As she looked up, she could have sworn that she saw Sofia disappear out of sight. That was twice now that Sofia had avoided her.

Georgie gestured to the stairs. 'I'm just going to pop up here for a second. Why don't you scour the ground floor and outside? I've got my phone, so call me if you find Ed?'

Kennedy gave Georgie a quizzical look but shrugged. 'Okay. It'll certainly be quicker.'

Georgie turned and made her way up the glass and wood designer staircase. There were small circular lights embedded at knee height in the wall.

As Georgie reached the top of the stairs, she saw Sofia hurrying away along the landing.

'Sofia?' Georgie called after her.

She kept walking.

157

'Sofia?'

Then Sofia stopped, turned and gave Georgie a little wave of recognition. She began to walk slowly back towards her.

'Oh, hi,' Sofia said with a half smile. 'I didn't know you were here.'

Yes, you did. Why are you lying to me? Georgie wondered.

'How are you doing?' Georgie asked with an empathetic expression.

'Not great,' Sofia admitted. 'I keep thinking that I'm going to see him walking down the stairs or sitting drinking coffee in the kitchen. And then it just hits me that I won't see him ever again.' She visibly took a breath as she spoke.

'Of course. Such a difficult time for all of you,' Georgie said quietly but there seemed to be something distinctly 'off' about her. Something other than grief.

Sofia avoided eye contact and pointed down the landing. 'Anyway, I've got a few things to do.'

For a few seconds, Georgie watched her. Then Georgie decided to go after her and delicately challenge Sofia about her distinctly strange behaviour.

'Sofia?' Georgie called after her.

Sofia stopped and then slowly turned. Her breathing was shallow as if she was panicking.

'Everything okay?' Georgie asked as she approached.

Sofia nodded but it clearly wasn't.

'I couldn't help notice that you avoided me twice after I'd arrived,' Georgie said calmly. 'And I can see that you're very jittery just standing here.'

'No,' Sofia snapped. 'My stepfather's been murdered. How do you expect me to act?'

Georgie wasn't buying it. 'Are you worried about Charlie? Is that why you're angry at me?'

'Charlie?'

'Are you avoiding me because we questioned Charlie?' Georgie asked, but the mention of Charlie's name seemed to have made her even more anxious.

Having spotted this, Georgie was now suspicious. 'Where is Charlie?'

The blood drained from Sofia's face. She shrugged unconvincingly. 'I don't know. He's around here some-where.'

Bullshit!

'Sofia?' Georgie said sternly, sensing that Sofia was now hiding something about Charlie from her.

'What?'

'Please don't lie to me,' Georgie said making direct eye contact for a few seconds. 'Where is Charlie?'

'He's gone,' Sofia said. Her voice was shaky.

'Gone where?' Georgie asked as her pulse quickened. Had Charlie done a runner? 'Do you mean he's gone out?' She knew that's not what Sofia meant.

Sofia shook her head as her eyes filled with tears. 'No,' she whispered.

'You mean he's gone on the run?' Georgie asked, to clarify exactly what she meant.

Sofia nodded again.

'Where? Is he trying to leave the country?' Georgie asked now with a sense of urgency.

Sofia didn't answer as she wiped tears from her face.

'Sofia, please. Tell me where he is before he disappears and makes everything a hundred times worse,' Georgie urged her.

Sofia still didn't say anything.

'Do you think Charlie killed your stepfather?' Georgie asked

'No, of course not. He'd never do something like that,' Sofia sobbed.

'Then tell me where he is or where he's going right now.'

'He's got a friend with a speedboat down in Abersoch,' Sofia whispered. 'I overheard him saying that he was going up to Holyhead to get a ferry to Ireland.'

'How long ago did he leave?'

'Half an hour.'

Georgie reached out and touched Sofia's arm reassuringly. 'Thank you.'

Then Georgie turned and jogged as best she could towards the top of the stairs.

This is not what I need to be doing two weeks before my due date!

Grabbing her phone, Georgie came down the stairs carefully. She needed to ring Kennedy and they needed to get to Abersoch to stop Charlie.

'Georgie?' said a voice.

As she got to the bottom of the stairs, she saw Ruth and Nick heading her way.

'Boss,' Georgie said, now a little out of breath. 'Charlie Huntington has done a runner. He's meeting a friend down in Abersoch who has a speedboat. He left about half an hour ago.'

'Right,' Ruth said as she looked at Nick.

They turned and ran out towards the front door.

CHAPTER 34

Ruth and Nick sped towards Abersoch with the blues and twos flashing. They hurtled towards a car pulling a caravan so Nick had to pull onto the opposite side of the road.

As they looked to their left, the long estuary that led into Abersoch was littered with dozens of boats. They were mainly small sailing boats along with a few larger cruisers.

'Jesus,' Nick groaned. 'There are bloody boats everywhere.'

Ruth grabbed the Tetra radio. 'Three-six to Control, are you receiving, over?'

After a few seconds, the radio crackled. 'Three-six from Control,' the CAD operator said. 'Go ahead, over.'

'We have a suspect, Charlie Huntington, male, late twenties, dark hair, who is attempting to leave Abersoch by speedboat. I need as many units as we can get to search the area and arrest him, over.'

'Received, three-six. Stand by.'

Nick slowed the car as they both scoured the area for signs of movement.

Ruth reached over and turned off the lights and sirens. She didn't want to advertise their presence.

As the road veered round to the right into the centre of Abersoch, Ruth spotted two figures standing in the distance.

Two men untying ropes from a large black speedboat that was on a trailer attached to a BMW 4x4.

Charlie Huntington.

'There!' Ruth said pointing.

'How do we get over there?' Nick asked as he glanced around and stopped the car.

There was a large stretch of wet sand and then a steep, grassy bank between them and where Huntington was standing.

Nick turned off the ignition.

The man with Charlie Huntington got into the BMW and started to reverse the trailer and speedboat towards the water.

'Yeah, I don't think we've got time to try and find out,' Ruth said as she unfastened her seatbelt.

They jumped out of the car and then quickly climbed over the low drystone wall that separated the road from the bank that then led down to the sandy flats.

Trying to find her footing, Ruth clambered down the grassy bank. She lost her balance, slipped and landed on her side.

'For fuck's sake!' Ruth groaned.

'You okay?' Nick asked stopping and holding out his hand.

'Brilliant!' Ruth snapped sarcastically. 'And I'm not your nan so I'm not holding your bloody hand.'

'Sorry,' Nick apologised.

I'm way too old to be doing this!

Getting to the wet flat of sand, they had now lost sight of Charlie, his friend and the speedboat. It was only a matter of minutes before the boat was in the water and they'd be gone. She didn't want to have to explain to her superiors why a suspect in a murder investigation had managed to leave the house in Abersoch and escape on a speedboat undetected.

It was about fifty yards across the sand flats. Their feet splashed on the surface water making splatting sounds as they went. Ruth felt the cold water go into her shoes and soak her socks. She didn't have time to give it more than a second thought.

A few moments later, they got to the bottom of the steep, grassy bank.

Ruth was gasping for breath but she knew that it was her own fault. No exercise, cigarettes and wine.

Blowing out her cheeks, she started to climb up the bank. Her foot slipped and she reached out to grab the long grass to stop herself from falling.

'You okay?' Nick called back to her.

'Will you stop asking me if I'm okay, Nick,' she said grumpily.

Nick smirked. 'It's just that you've gone a funny shade of red in your face.'

'Oh, piss off,' she said with a sarcastic smile.

The climb up the bank was really taking it out of her. She sucked in air as she felt her lungs burn with the effort. Her thighs and calves were starting to really ache.

Glancing up, she saw that the top of the bank was about ten yards away.

'Thank God,' she gasped under her laboured breath.

I'm not going to be able to read him his bloody rights at this rate, she thought to herself.

They got to the top of the bank.

Ruth wiped the sweat from her brow and top lip.

Charlie and his friend were manoeuvring the speedboat from the trailer into the water about thirty yards away.

A gull squawked noisily above them as Ruth ran, as if mocking her.

Running along the concrete of the quay, Ruth could see that Charlie was putting several bags from the car into the boat.

The sound of their running clearly alerted Charlie to the fact that they were approaching.

His face fell as he looked around for an escape route.

'Charlie!' Nick bellowed. 'Stay where you are!'

Charlie jumped out of the water, clambered onto the quayside and started to sprint.

'Are you actually joking now!' Ruth moaned. Her lungs felt like they were on fire.

Nick was now a good twenty yards ahead of her.

Where the hell is he going?

There didn't seem to be any way of getting off the quayside.

Pumping her arms, Ruth could feel herself running out of breath and energy.

'Oh, Jesus Christ,' she gasped as she stopped running. 'I feel sick.'

Charlie turned, looking frantically for a means of escape.

'Stay there, Charlie!' Nick shouted at him. 'You've got nowhere to go.'

Charlie looked terrified as he slowed.

As he turned to run again, Nick rugby-tackled him to the floor.

Ruth started to jog towards them.

Nick turned Charlie over and cuffed his hands behind his back.

CHAPTER 35

Georgie and Kennedy had tracked down Ed to the furthest reaches of the garden where he was sitting wearing sunglasses and looking out at the beach and the setting sun. However, Georgie's mind was still processing the fact that Charlie had tried to disappear. Ruth had called to say that Charlie had been arrested and was being taken back to Llancastell nick for further questioning. Although Charlie's decision to try to run wasn't an admission of guilt, it was incredibly suspicious. Why run if he had nothing to hide? And they'd had him in for questioning already.

'Mind if we interrupt?' Kennedy asked as they approached.

Ed turned, took off his sunglasses and peered witheringly at them. 'Do I have a choice?' he said rather sourly.

Georgie ignored him as Kennedy grabbed two chairs and they sat down.

Ed looked less than pleased at their appearance but Georgie really didn't care.

Kennedy fished out her notebook from her jacket pocket, opened it up and then sat forward. 'We need to ask you about Rush Properties and Construction.'

'Really?' Ed asked in a pompous tone. 'I don't think this is the appropriate time.'

'You're the managing director of that company, is that correct?' Kennedy asked, ignoring him.

'Yes,' Ed said sounding cautious.

'But your father owned the company?'

'Yes, that's right.'

Georgie looked at him. 'How would you describe the current state of the business?'

Ed frowned. 'I'm not sure I know what you mean?'

'Is the business flourishing and profitable?' Georgie clarified.

Ed took a few seconds to think. 'I'm sorry, but someone murdered my father yesterday. I found his body. I just don't see why you've come here to ask me about the family property business.' His tone was distinctly arrogant. Georgie could see why he wasn't popular with the staff in the Chester office.

Kennedy stared at him. 'You didn't answer the question, Ed.'

'That's because I'm struggling to see what relevance it has to an investigation into my father's death,' Ed said as he started to sound flustered. 'You're sitting here, wasting my time and yours when you should be focusing on who actually killed him.'

Georgie waited for a few seconds before stating, 'Let me put it like this, Ed. We know that Rush Properties was on the verge of bankruptcy. We know that the development that you had on the canal front had run into issues and had gone way over budget.'

'How the hell do you know all that?' Ed snapped angrily. 'Who have you been talking to?'

Georgie ignored him again. 'Your father came into the Chester office on Monday, is that correct?'

Ed snorted. 'You tell me, seeing as you seem to know everything,' he scoffed defensively.

Kennedy turned the pages of her notebook. 'According to a witness, you and your father had a heated argument in your office. Is there anything you'd like to tell us about that?'

Ed shrugged. 'Are you trying to suggest that because I had a disagreement with my father last week, that I'm somehow involved in his death? Jesus, if that's all you've got to go on at the moment, then God help us,' he sneered.

He's starting to get right up my nose, Georgie thought to herself.

Georgie fixed him with a stare. Underneath all the bluff and arrogance, she could see that Ed was floundering. His breathing was shallow and quick and his blinking was a giveaway.

'So, you did have an argument with your father last week?' Georgie asked in a stern tone. She was losing her patience.

Ed gave a very animated shrug and laughed a little too loudly. 'Yes. So what?'

'Can you tell us what that argument was about?' Kennedy said.

Ed shook his head. 'No. It was private matter and it's confidential.'

Georgie let out an audible sigh as she gave Kennedy a frustrated glance.

'Okay, Ed,' Georgie said, resorting to a tactic she'd used at various points in her career as a detective. She stood up and Kennedy did the same, picking up on her cue. 'We're going to take you back to Llancastell Police Station for further questioning. You can have a legal representative if you feel that you need one.'

Georgie made direct contact with Ed's eyes. She could see that he was now thrown.

He then held up his hands. 'Okay, okay. The company was on the verge of bankruptcy. My father came to tell me that he was pulling the plug on the company and it was all my fault.'

'How did that make you feel?' Georgie asked lowering her voice.

'Great. Brilliant,' Ed said sardonically. 'How do you think it made me feel?'

Kennedy leaned forward on her chair. 'I assume that it made you feel angry?'

'Angry?' Ed shook his head. 'No. Not angry. Just ashamed that I'd made such a mess of everything.'

Kennedy looked down at her notebook. 'That's strange because colleagues overheard you saying to your father that you thought the world would be a better place if he was dead.'

Silence. Ed's eyes moved around as he tried to think of how to reply.

'It's a very long way from telling your father that you wished he was dead in the heat of the moment, to actually killing him,' Ed said quietly.

'Is it?' Georgie asked. 'I'm not sure it is.'

'Well, we'll agree to differ then,' Ed sighed.

'But you were angry?' Kennedy said.

'Yes. Of course,' Ed said. 'Rather than help me save the company, he was happy to let me fail. It was almost as if he was pleased that he had been right all along, that I was useless and a failure. That this proved to him that he'd been right.'

'It sounds as if you felt very humiliated by what he did?'

'Listen, if you have any more questions then I'm happy to get myself a solicitor and you can talk to me back at the police station.'

Georgie looked over at Kennedy.

'That's all for now,' Georgie said as she got up. 'I'm sure you've already been told but we'd like you to stay in this area while the investigation is in progress.'

CHAPTER 36

Georgie and Kennedy walked up through the gardens and headed towards the rear terrace. The light of the day had faded and the air was filled with the sound of evening birdsong and the smell of lavender plants that were in enormous terracotta pots along the pathway. The wind picked up and there was a chill in the air.

'What do you think?' Kennedy said.

'To be honest, I'm just not sure,' Georgie admitted. 'Ed definitely has means, motive and opportunity to have killed his father. I get the feeling that Jack's bullying and controlling behaviour has damaged both his sons.'

'I agree. But my instinct is that he wasn't involved,' Kennedy said hesitantly.

'Mine too.' Georgie said. 'Although he has to remain a suspect.'

'Of course,' Kennedy nodded as they went across the terrace and then entered the house. 'You think Charlie did it?'

'I think that everything is pointing that way,' Georgie said. 'Why would you try and get out of the country if you didn't have something to hide?'

As they made their way down the hallway towards the front door, a figure appeared walking towards them.

It was Jasmine and she was holding her video camera as if she was filming.

'Hello, Jasmine,' Georgie said, spotting that the red recording button on the camera was on. 'Okay if you turn that off for us?'

Jasmine frowned. 'But I'm making a documentary.'

'Well, we haven't agreed to be in your documentary,' Georgie explained gently. 'So, you are going to have to stop filming us.'

Jasmine shrugged nonchalantly. 'Your loss but okay.' Then she looked at them with a quizzical expression. 'How is the investigation going?'

'It's going okay,' Georgie replied, still bemused by Jasmine's quirky behaviour.

'Have you found Charlie yet?' Jasmine asked knowingly.

Georgie frowned. 'You know about that?'

Jasmine laughed. 'I told you already. I know everything that goes on in this house. I'm like this ghost that no one sees. So, have you found him or did he get away?' she asked in a slightly excited voice.

'No, we arrested him,' Kennedy said.

'Oh, that is a shame,' Jasmine sighed.

'Why is it a shame?' Georgie asked.

'Well, I just think some police manhunt for my brother-in-law would be incredibly exciting, don't you?'

'Not really,' Georgie said thinking that this was a strange thing for her to say.

'Plus, I'd get to film the whole family here, all panicking about Charlie and if he'd managed to escape,' Jasmine said and then she frowned. 'It's funny because if someone had asked me who had the most reason to kill my father, I'd have said Ed and James.'

Georgie raised an eyebrow quizzically. 'You mean together?'

'Of course. They're identical twins,' Jasmine replied as if it was obvious. 'In fact, their mother, the late Natasha, dressed them in the same clothes until they were teenagers. You probably haven't noticed, but they think exactly the same. They finish each other's sentences. It's sometimes like they're just one person. It's very spooky.'

'Is there something about their involvement in your father's death that you're not telling us?' Kennedy asked.

'No,' Jasmine replied in a nonchalant tone. 'But Father was incredibly cruel to them. I don't know why. You could see how hurt they were by the way he treated them. I wouldn't blame them if they had decided to do it.'

And with that, Jasmine turned and walked away.

Georgie looked at Kennedy. Was Jasmine just speculating or was she trying to tell them something?

CHAPTER 37

Ruth pressed the button on the recording equipment and said, 'Interview conducted with Charlie Huntington, 6:30 p.m., Interview Room 2, Llancastell Police Station. Present are Charlie Huntington, Detective Constable Georgie Wild, solicitor Caleb Thomas, and myself, Detective Inspector Ruth Hunter.'

Charlie had protested his innocence for about ten minutes on the way back to Llancastell nick before shutting up. Since then he hadn't said a word apart from responding to questions from the custody sergeant. Charlie had also opted to be represented by his own very expensive solicitor, rather than the duty solicitor.

Ruth sat down and looked over at Charlie who seemed lost in his own thoughts. She waited for an appropriate amount of time to pass before asking, 'Charlie, can you tell us why you decided to try and leave the country today?'

Charlie looked to his solicitor Caleb Thomas who gave him a surreptitious nod.

'No comment,' Charlie said as he pushed his hair off his face nervously.

Ruth gave an audible sigh. It wasn't that surprising that Charlie was going 'no comment' for the interview but it was still frustrating.

Nick clicked his pen open and moved the A4 pad of paper so that it was in front of him. Then he frowned as he looked over at Charlie. 'Charlie, you do understand that trying to leave the country is incredibly suspicious?'

Charlie shifted nervously on his chair. 'No comment.'

'We have already questioned you regarding the murder of Jack Rush,' Nick said. 'We have evidence that you had been into his office and gone through his belongings and opened drawers. You also had motive to murder Jack Rush because he had forced you into signing a prenuptial agreement. However, you also knew that Jack hadn't signed that agreement and so his death would render that document useless.'

Ruth leaned forward and looked directly at him. 'And we clearly instructed you and everyone who was at the house in Abersoch at the time of Jack Rush's murder not to go anywhere. And certainly not to secretly leave the country. Is there anything you can tell us about why you decided to ignore that?'

Charlie sighed and looked at the floor. 'No comment.'

There was a knock at the door. It opened and Kennedy looked at Ruth. 'Can I have a second, boss? It is urgent.'

Ruth nodded, got up and headed for the door. She wondered what was so important that Kennedy needed to interrupt an interview.

'For the purposes of the recording,' Nick said, 'DI Hunter has left the room.'

Ruth went outside into the corridor. 'What is it?' she asked with a questioning expression.

'Two things,' Kennedy said. 'PNC and HOLMES search on Aleksandr Pitrov has shown that his intel is classified.'

Ruth frowned. 'Okay. And?'

Kennedy was holding two printouts. '*And* we got some more results from the forensic sweep of Jack Rush's office.'

Then Kennedy showed Ruth a close-up photograph of the clear plastic bag that had contained the lethal cyanide. 'You see here. There's the tiniest fibre of clothing that has caught on the plastic seal at the top of the bag.'

'Tell me they've matched it to Charlie,' Ruth said hopefully.

Kennedy nodded a half smile. 'The clothing fibre is an exact match to a jacket that Forensics found hanging in the wardrobe in the bedroom that Charlie and Sofia were using before their wedding. It's Charlie's jacket.'

'Brilliant. That's great,' Ruth said taking the printouts from Kennedy. 'Let's see how he explains this.'

Kennedy nodded. 'You think we can charge him?'

Ruth shook her head. 'I'm pretty sure that we haven't met the CPS threshold to charge him with murder yet. It's all very circumstantial unfortunately. But it does apply more pressure and he might just decide to confess if it all gets too much for him. It's not as though Charlie is a seasoned criminal.'

'True,' Kennedy agreed.

'Thanks, Jade,' Ruth said as she opened the door and went back inside the interview room.

'For the purposes of the tape, DI Hunter has entered the interview room,' Nick said.

Ruth took her time as she came over, pulled her chair out and then lay the images out on the table in front of her.

Then she glanced over at Charlie who was peering at the printouts with an anxious expression.

Then Ruth turned the images so that Charlie could take a proper look. 'For the purposes of the recording, I am showing the suspect Item Reference 743C. This is a forensic photograph of the clear plastic bag that contained the potassium cyanide which killed Jack Rush. Can you take a careful look at that image for me, Charlie?'

Charlie leaned forward and stared at the image.

'Have you ever seen that bag before?' Ruth asked him calmly.

Charlie looked confused and then shook his head, momentarily forgetting his solicitor's advice.

'You see the problem we have is that a fibre of clothing was found on that bag,' Ruth explained. Charlie's eyes were flitting nervously around the room as he tried to fathom what she was about to say. 'And that fibre has been matched to the jacket that we found in the bedroom that you were using in the Rush's home. Is there anything you can tell us about that?'

The blood had visibly drained from Charlie's face. 'No comment,' he whispered as he tried to get his breath.

Nick stopped writing and looked over at him. 'You see you've just told us that you've never seen that bag before. Can you tell us how a fibre from your jacket was found in the seal of that bag?'

Charlie shook his head but he was starting to visibly shake. His chest was rising and falling very quickly. He was having a panic attack and starting to hyperventilate.

Thomas looked at him. 'Charlie? Are you all right?'

Ruth got up. 'He's having a panic attack,' she said as she went around to him. She'd dealt with panic attacks in interview rooms before. 'Long, deep breaths, Charlie. Okay?'

But Charlie was struggling, his eyes wide with fear.

'Look at me, Charlie,' Ruth said. 'Breathe in for five, hold for five, breathe out for eight. Can you do that for me? Nice and slowly.'

Charlie nodded as he followed her advice. After a minute or two, his breathing started to slow down.

Thomas looked at Ruth. 'I think my client is going to need some medical attention.'

'I agree.' Ruth said.

Nick went to the door. 'I'll get the FME,' he said.

Ruth glanced at her watch. 'Interview terminated at 6:44 p.m.'

CHAPTER 38

It was pitch dark by the time Ruth drove over the old, cobbled bridge that crossed the River Dee and led into her village, Bangor-on-Dee. Although the current bridge had been built in the 1600s, there had been a crossing there since medieval times. The car juddered on the cobbled road surface as Ruth slowed her car down to 5mph.

And then, as she glanced in her rear-view mirror, she saw the headlights again. She had been concerned that a car had been following her ever since she left Llancastell nick. It hadn't come close enough for Ruth to actually see the make, model or licence plate. But now she could see it was just a few yards behind her.

A black Range Rover with the registration G247 YZ. It was the same car that had bumped them earlier and was registered to the Russian national, Aleksandr Pitrov. Why was he following her and why was access to any information classified on the PNC and HOLMES?

Looking at the river that flowed either side, Ruth felt a sudden jolt of anxiety in case the Range Rover decided to try and ram her off it into the River Dee. She got to the other side and drove slowly past St Dunawd's Church, keeping her eyes fixed on the mirror and the car behind. Then she patted her jacket to check where her phone was in case she needed to call for some kind of backup.

Suddenly the Range Rover drove down the side of her car, before swerving right down the road that ran to the side of the church and disappeared.

What the hell was that all about? Ruth wondered to herself. It had definitely spooked her. Maybe that had been the intention this afternoon and tonight. But why? Was it somehow connected to the investigation into Jack Rush's murder. She couldn't see how it could be.

Ruth pulled up onto her drive. What she needed right now was a cigarette, a large glass of wine and a cuddle from Sarah. As she walked up to the front door and took out her keys, she heard a car engine in the distance. Turning around, she checked that it wasn't the Range Rover returning. She didn't want whoever it was anywhere near her home with Daniel and Sarah inside.

The noise of the car engine drifted away.

Opening the door, Ruth went in and let out a little sigh of relief to be home.

'Hey,' whispered a voice.

Sarah appeared from the living room and smiled. Then her expression changed to one of concern. 'Are you okay?' she asked in a low voice. 'You look like you've seen a ghost.'

'I'm fine,' Ruth reassured her. Now wasn't the time to tell her that she'd been followed home by an unknown Russian national with a car registered in Moscow. 'Just a very long day that's all.'

'Wine?' Sarah asked.

'No, it's okay. I think I'll have a mug of green tea,' Ruth said with a deadpan expression.

Sarah looked baffled. 'Really?'

Ruth shook her head and laughed. 'No, silly. I need a glass of wine before I can even think about going to bed.

And I don't care that I've got to be back in in less than five hours. I need to sit and chat to you.'

'Come on then,' Sarah beckoned.

CHAPTER 39

Coming through the front door, Nick quietly took off his shoes. He assumed that Caitlin and Amanda would be asleep given how late it was. As he padded down the hallway, he saw that there was a light on in the living room. Peering in through the half-opened door, he spotted that Amanda had fallen asleep on the sofa which was very unusual for her.

As he went over to wake her, he got a waft of alcohol. *Oh, shit!*

Starting to panic, he raced over to Amanda and gently woke her up.

As she came to, she looked bewildered. 'Nick? What's going on?' Her voice wasn't slurred.

Sitting down on the edge of the sofa, he took her hand. He couldn't be cross with her. Being an alcoholic wasn't a lifestyle choice. It was a horrible, overwhelming addictive disease that both he and she had been afflicted with.

'You've had a drink?' Nick asked in a virtual whisper.

Amanda met his eyes, gave an imperceptible nod and then began to sob. 'I'm so so sorry,' she gasped.

Taking her in his arms, he hugged her. 'It's fine. Seriously,' Nick tried to reassure her. It was frustrating that Amanda had drunk but he could see how devastated she was.

'It isn't fine, is it?' she sobbed.

'How much?' he asked.

'I drank a glass and then I just poured the rest away,' she whispered with a shameful expression.

'Any more in the house?'

She shook her head. 'No, I promise.'

'Okay. Let's get you up to bed,' Nick said as he helped her to her feet.

'God, I'm so ashamed,' she sighed shaking her head.

'Don't be. We'll ring your sponsor in the morning and get you to a meeting tomorrow,' Nick said trying to be positive. 'Just a slip. And you can't do anything about it now. You do the next right thing, okay?'

'I thought you were going to go mad with me,' Amanda said as she wiped her face.

Nick shook his head. 'No. I saw this coming. What's that saying? *Lots of AA meetings, big chance. Some meetings, some chance. No meetings, no chance.*'

'I'm such an idiot,' she sighed.

'Well, you're my idiot,' he said. 'And you're going to be fine.'

He put his arm around her as they walked down the hallway and then up the stairs.

CHAPTER 40

Ruth sat back in the chair in her office and gazed out of the window. The rooftops, the church spire and the Llancastell Leisure Centre all glowed in the early morning light. Over to the east, the sky was a translucent apricot colour tinged with flamingo pink. The colours bled into the long, thin clouds that stretched over the horizon like pulled cotton wool. For those who didn't have a murder to investigate, it was going to be a glorious late summer day. But then she reminded herself that she had chosen only a few months earlier that retirement wasn't for her. At least not quite yet.

A knock at the door broke her train of thought.

She turned and saw that Nick had poked his head in through the open door. 'Boss, we're ready.'

'Okay,' she said and then gave him a look. 'I haven't had a chance to tell you yet. That Range Rover followed me back home last night.'

Nick's eyes widened. 'What? Did you check it out?'

Ruth nodded. 'Jade looked yesterday. And then I had another look when I arrived first thing.'

'And?'

'Weird one. Nothing on the PNC. But there is something on HOLMES that is very vague and classified.'

HOLMES stood for the Home Office Large Major Enquiry System. It was a computer database used by police to collate and share intel on serious criminal activity. It also provided information from other agencies within and outside of the UK Police Force.

'How classified?'

'I'm not sure but I couldn't get access so it could be Intelligence Service classified,' Ruth said.

'Which would make sense given the car and owner are both Russian,' Nick said thinking out loud.

Ruth frowned. 'But what's that got to do with us? I don't remember ever dealing with Russian gangsters at any point in my career.'

'Neither do I,' Nick agreed. 'You think it has something to do with Jack Rush?'

'I've no idea. I can't see how it can,' Ruth admitted. Then she looked out through the door into the office.

Even though Nick had engaged in the conversation with her, he seemed 'off' or distracted.

'You okay?' she asked looking at him.

He nodded but it was unconvincing.

She narrowed her eyes. 'What is it?'

'Amanda had a drink last night,' he admitted quietly.

'Oh, no,' Ruth sighed. She knew that both Nick and Amanda had several years sobriety under their belts and that their recovery was going well. At least, that's what she thought.

'Is she okay?' Ruth asked.

Nick nodded. 'She had a glass and then threw the rest away. It could have been worse. But it's really knocked her.'

'I bet it has. Poor her,' Ruth said empathetically.

'She's already rung her sponsor and she's coming over this morning,' Nick said. 'She just needs to get back on track.'

'And how are you?' Ruth asked in a genuine tone.

'A bit scared. And I'm kicking myself for not seeing all the warning signs,' Nick admitted. 'She'd stopped going to meetings. I think she took her sobriety for granted and that's dangerous.'

'But at least she's got you and you understand,' Ruth said.

'Yes. That's true,' Nick agreed. 'I'll take her to some meetings.'

'You know if you need anything, just ask,' Ruth said. 'It's about time that I babysat for my goddaughter again.'

Nick gave a half smile. 'I'll take you up on that.'

Ruth reached out and touched his arm reassuringly. 'Good.' Then she glanced down at her watch.

It was time for morning briefing. The CID team had been in since the crack of dawn as would be expected during any murder case.

'Right, we'd better get out there,' she said.

Grabbing her lukewarm coffee and a couple of folders, Ruth got up and then winced. Her calves and thighs were still very sore from all the running in Abersoch before they'd arrested Charlie.

'Bit sore?' Nick asked with a smug grin.

'No,' she lied as she took a breath. Her thighs were really painful.

Nick looked at her. 'You know the best thing for sore legs after running?'

'No,' Ruth groaned. 'But I'm pretty sure you're about to tell me,' she said sardonically.

'An ice bath,' Nick said with a nod.

Ruth gave him a sarcastic smile as they went out into the CID room where the team had assembled for morning briefing. 'Yeah, well the closest I want to come to ice is a cube in my glass of rosé,' she joked under her breath. Then she pulled a face. 'God, sorry. Not the right time to be making jokes about wine.'

'It's fine, don't worry,' he reassured her.

Ruth strode purposefully across the room towards the two scene boards that were now jam-packed with photos, maps, printouts, etc.

'Morning, everyone. And what a glorious morning it's going to be here in sunny Llancastell,' she said dryly. 'Right, as most of you know, the investigation into Jack Rush's murder is fast moving so I want everyone to be up to speed on developments. I've had my arm twisted by the North Wales Police media unit to hold a press conference mid-morning. Although we have had statements from all of the wedding guests and those who worked that day, it might still be useful to jog a few memories. But, in essence, Jack Rush was a world-renowned film producer. His murder is a huge news story across the world. And that means there is a great deal of scrutiny on North Wales Police Force and how we handle the case.'

'No pressure then,' Nick muttered with a wry smile.

'No, no pressure,' Ruth laughed. 'What's that saying these days. Pressure's for tyres.'

There was a titter of laughter from some of the detectives.

'So, there is a lot of heat coming down from the upper echelons of this fine police force for us to get a result, and fast. And a press conference is a bit of window dressing to show that we are taking this very seriously.'

Georgie shook her head. 'It's also a complete waste of time, boss.'

Ruth gave a half smile. 'I couldn't agree with you more, Georgie. But that's all above my pay grade.' She then turned to the scene board and pointed to a photo. 'Jack Rush. Someone switched his cocaine for potassium cyanide in the days leading up to the wedding and his death. Access to both the house and his office are very limited which is why we are currently concentrating on the immediate family as our prime suspects.' She pointed again. 'Okay. Let's see who we can possibly rule out. What about Jasmine and Sofia?'

Kennedy frowned. 'Jasmine. A bit strange and eccentric but she's a twelve-year-old girl.'

Ruth nodded. 'I agree. But we do have to do due diligence on everyone on this board. I'm pretty certain that Jasmine didn't murder her father. But I'd like to just check school records, stuff like that. Maybe she knows who did kill him. Maybe she's covering for them?'

Georgie pointed over to the board. 'I knew Sofia from a few years ago. She seems to trust me. As far as I can see, Sofia and Jack were very close. He doted on her. I haven't heard her say a bad word about him or anyone else in the family for that matter. I can't see that she has any motive.'

'Not one that we've found, so I tend to agree with that,' Ruth said. 'But again, bit of due diligence on Sofia, please. Get her phone records, social media, if we haven't got them already.'

Garrow looked over. 'They arrived this morning, boss.'

'Good. Just have a check through. I don't want any nasty surprises later on in this investigation, please,' Ruth said. 'Nick?'

Nick got up and went over to the board. 'Okay. We have Charlie Huntington as our prime suspect. He is currently downstairs in a holding cell. We arrested him yesterday afternoon as he tried to flee the country. Charlie has means, motive and opportunity. Jack had forced Charlie to sign a prenup to protect his wealth if Charlie and Sofia were ever to divorce. We understand that Charlie was very upset about it but Sofia had persuaded him to go through with it. However, Jack had put off signing the prenup until Monday which was being held by his lawyers in Chester. Of course, Jack never got to sign it because he was murdered so the prenup is worthless. We also have Charlie's fingerprints all over Jack's office. We know from interviews that the only person who ever really went into Jack's office was Lottie. The forensic shows Charlie's fingerprints all over Jack's desk, including the drawer where we believe he kept his cocaine. We also now have a fibre from Charlie's jacket inside the seal of the plastic bag that contained the potassium cyanide.'

'Was Charlie staying at the house?' Garrow asked.

Nick nodded. 'Charlie and Sofia arrived two days before the wedding, on the Thursday. That gives Charlie plenty of opportunity to get into Jack's office.'

Kennedy sat forward on her chair. 'And doing a runner and trying to leave the country doesn't exactly scream innocence, does it?'

'No, it doesn't,' Ruth agreed. 'Unfortunately, Charlie gave us another 'no comment' interview last night. Unless we find something really concrete, we are going to have to release him again this afternoon.' Ruth then got up from where she had been perched on the edge of a desk and went over to the scene board. 'Then we have James Rush. Jack and he had recently fallen out when Jack refused to pay for James to attend a prestigious art school in Paris.'

'Les Beaux-Arts de Paris,' Nick reminded her, using a French accent.

'Yeah, what Nick said,' Ruth nodded with a dry expression. 'Jack felt that James had already spent five years in London at art college. However, Jack had promised to buy James a flat and own artist studio over in Chester, so it doesn't feel that there was a huge amount of animosity there.'

Nick frowned. 'Although we do have James visiting a site on the Dark Web which sold poisons, including cyanide.'

'I'm not convinced,' Ruth admitted. 'I'm going to put James on the backburner for now.' Ruth pointed again. 'Then we have Lottie, Jack's wife. We know that their marriage was volatile and that Jack engaged in a number of extra-marital affairs. Lottie told us that she tolerated these and had done for many years.'

Georgie looked sceptical. 'Do we believe her?'

Ruth looked at Nick. 'My instinct was that she was telling us the truth.'

Nick nodded. 'Yeah, that was my instinct too.'

'But they were heard arguing on the morning of the wedding,' Georgie pointed out. 'Jasmine told us that they were shouting about a woman called Amelia.'

'Lottie claims that the only woman she knows by that name is Amelia Wharton,' Ruth said. 'And Lottie also maintained that Jack couldn't be having an affair with her as she was gay.'

Nick then gave Ruth a thoughtful look. 'Lottie told us that Jack called Amelia Wharton, his Head of Development, *Milly*, didn't she?'

Ruth nodded and then the penny dropped. 'Meeting with 'M'. Jack met with Amelia Wharton on Friday morning.'

'Although we have no reason to suspect her at the moment,' Ruth pointed out. 'But let's do some digging around and see what we can find out about Amelia

Wharton, please. And we should definitely go and talk to her if she did meet Jack in his office on the Friday morning. Can someone find out where she is, please? I know that Lottie Rush has her mother's address in Bala.' Ruth looked at the team. 'Okay, everyone, let's get cracking and make sure we do our best work today. Thank you.'

CHAPTER 41

Ruth walked down the corridor towards the main meeting room on the ground floor of Llancastell nick. Jane Hickson, a lawyer with the Crown Prosecution Service, had requested a meeting about Charlie Huntington. It was regarding Ruth's request to extend the amount of time they held him in custody from twenty-four to forty-eight hours.

Opening the door, Ruth saw Hickson sitting on the other side of the table. In her forties, she looked bookish and a little frumpy as she squinted at Charlie's file in front of her.

'Jane, thanks for coming over,' Ruth said with a friendly smile as they shook hands. They'd worked together in the past a few times.

'Big case,' Hickson said pointing to the case file.

'Yeah, the media are all over it,' Ruth admitted. 'Which makes our job about a hundred times more difficult.'

'Under the microscope. I bet the top brass are loving it,' she said sarcastically. Then she took off her reading glasses. Her eyes were much prettier with her glasses off. 'How sure are you about Charlie Huntington?'

Ruth took a few moments to respond. 'He's our prime suspect. Prenuptial agreement wasn't signed. He was seen arguing and grabbing the victim only hours before he was murdered. Fingerprints and clothing fibre at the scene…'

'Ruth,' Hickson interrupted her. 'I can read the file. I just want to know what your gut is telling you?'

Ruth sat back and pulled face. 'I just don't know.' She then moved a strand of hair from her face and put it behind her ear. 'I can't get a handle on this case. And my gut isn't telling me anything at all which is very unusual.'

'Any other suspects?' Hickson asked.

'Nearly everyone that was in the bloody house,' Ruth sighed with frustration. 'Jack Rush was a very difficult and often unpleasant man. His wife and sons don't really have a good word to say about him.'

'And they were all in that big house over in Abersoch at the time of Rush's murder?' Hickson asked.

Ruth nodded. 'Yes.'

'All very Agatha Christie, isn't it?' Hickson asked with a half smile.

'I suppose it is,' Ruth admitted. 'I hadn't really thought of it like that but now that you've said it…'

'If you're not convinced, why do you want to extend Charlie Huntington's time in custody?'

Ruth pulled a face. 'If Charlie did do it, more time in that cell might just apply enough pressure to break him and get him to confess.'

'Hardly secure grounds for an extension, is it?' Hickson asked knowingly.

'Not really,' Ruth sighed. 'I guess we need a result. And because the whole of the world is now focused on this case and the North Wales Police Force, I think it's skewed my thinking a bit.'

'Not like you,' Hickson said. 'If you'd told me that you had concrete evidence that you needed to verify that would secure a conviction against Huntington then I'd be happy to sign off on this. But I can't see that I can justify keeping him for an extended period in custody just to apply pressure in the hope that he'll crack.' Hickson gave Ruth a knowing look. 'But you knew that already.'

'Sorry. I've wasted your time,' Ruth apologised, feeling a little foolish by their conversation.

Hickson waved her hand. 'Glad to get out of the office. And it's always a pleasure to see you, Ruth. I wish every DI I worked with was as thorough and decent as you.'

Before Ruth could reply, there was a knock at the door.

'Come in,' Ruth said as Hickson gathered her things and stood up.

The duty sergeant opened the door and looked at Ruth. 'Sorry to interrupt, ma'am, but there are two officers from the NCA waiting to see you. They said it's very urgent.'

'Looks like you're needed elsewhere,' Hickson said as she reached over and shook Ruth's hand and gave her a smile.

CHAPTER 42

Georgie sat back at her desk and stretched out her right leg. She'd been having a twinge of cramp in her calf all day. Apparently it was another one of the numerous delights of pregnancy that was caused by too little exercise, electrolyte imbalances and vitamin deficiencies. She didn't really care what caused it. It was bloody painful.

Her phone buzzed with a text. It was Adam checking in to see how she was doing. It gave her a little thrill to see his text. She replied with a couple of emojis.

Then she looked back at the screen. She had already done a full PNC check on Amelia Wharton, Jack Rush's Head of Development. There was literally nothing on her record. Georgie was now looking at the website of Rush Pictures and the company profile of Amelia. It didn't state her age but she looked like she was in her late forties. She had curly red hair, milky skin and piercing blue eyes. In her biog, it said that she'd worked her way from being a script editor at the BBC Drama Department to various feature film development jobs at film companies that Georgie had never heard of, before landing the plum role of Head of Development for Rush.

Georgie had given Ruth and Nick the address of Amelia's mother over in Bala in Snowdonia. Georgie had spoken to Amelia's PA in London who told her that Rush Pictures had closed their London office for the week after

Jack's tragic death and Amelia was staying with her mother for a few days.

Although Georgie couldn't see how Amelia could be involved in Jack's death – there was no clear motive – she had attended a meeting with him in his office on Friday morning. And Friday morning was within the timeframe they had for the cocaine to have been swapped with the potassium cyanide.

Getting up from her desk, Georgie tried to lean down and stretch out her calves.

'You okay?' Kennedy asked as she looked over from her desk where she was typing at a computer.

'Bloody cramp,' Georgie groaned. 'And I can't seem to lean over enough to stretch properly.'

Kennedy got up, came over and gestured to Georgie's chair. 'Sit down for a second.'

'Why?' Georgie asked giving her a bemused look.

'Just do it,' Kennedy said with a smile. 'And take your shoes off.'

Georgie shrugged and did as she was told.

Kennedy moved in and pointed. 'Give me your foot.'

'Are you sexually harassing me?' Georgie quipped with a cheeky grin.

'In your dreams,' Kennedy snorted as she took Georgie's foot, slowly lifted up her leg and then gently pushed her toes back to stretch out her calf muscle. 'How's that?'

'Much better,' Georgie admitted.

'Hey, I wasn't Streatham Under-14s Girls 400 metre champion for nothing,' Kennedy chortled. 'I was always getting cramp after athletics meetings. Mainly because I didn't stretch properly or hydrate before.'

Kennedy moved the other leg before taking a step back. 'My work here is done.'

Georgie looked at her watch. 'Yeah, if you can come back on the hour, every hour, that would be much appreciated.'

Kennedy rolled her eyes. 'Don't push it.'

As Georgie turned back to her desk, she spotted Garrow's furrowed brow as he looked at his computer screen.

'Everything all right, Jim?' she asked.

'I'm not sure,' he admitted.

With a slight groan, Georgie got up and walked over. 'What are you looking at?'

'I'm still trawling through the wedding video,' Garrow said gesturing to the screen. 'But there are significant chunks missing.'

'How do you mean?' Georgie asked.

Garrow clicked onto his desktop screen and then onto the folder via his pen drive. Then he pointed. 'You see? These are all the MP4 video files here for various stages of the wedding and in the days before. Each one has a timecode to show which time period that video file covers. Except there are three files that are empty. And I can see that the file has been there but it's been deleted.'

'Any way of knowing who deleted it?' Georgie asked looking puzzled.

Garrow shook his head. 'No. But you told me that Jasmine Rush took the camera away so she could have transferred all the video files from it onto a memory stick?'

'That's right,' Georgie said.

'What if Jasmine deleted the files once they'd been loaded onto her main computer,' Garrow suggested.

'Really?' Georgie said. She wasn't convinced that Jasmine would have been that devious, although she couldn't be sure.

Garrow looked at her. 'If I'm honest, that's the only viable explanation. Jasmine had the camera, downloaded the files and then gave you the memory stick almost immediately, didn't she?'

'Yes,' Georgie replied. 'I just don't know why she would delete stuff from the wedding video.'

'Maybe there's stuff she didn't want us to see?' Garrow suggested.

'Possibly,' Georgie said as she processed what Garrow had told her. 'Maybe she's covering for someone.'

'If she knew that there was something incriminating on those files, perhaps that's why she offered to go and download the stuff for you,' Garrow said.

'Any way of retrieving those files?' Georgie asked.

'There might be. If they were first downloaded via Jasmine's main computer and she has it linked to the cloud,' Garrow said. 'Bit of a longshot but I'll run it past Digital Forensics. I've got something else to show them.'

'What's that then?' Georgie asked.

'This,' Garrow said as he used the mouse to click on a saved file. Then he clicked play and a short clip from the wedding video started to play.

Georgie moved closer to the screen. The video showed various guests dancing in one of the marquees.

'There,' Garrow said as he paused the image and pointed.

Georgie peered at the screen and frowned. 'What exactly am I looking at, Jim?' she asked.

Using his index finger, Garrow pointed to the far right of the screen. 'This is Lottie Rush over here.'

'Okay,' Georgie said. Even though the image was grainy there was no doubt it was Lottie.

'Now watch this,' Garrow said as he played it forward again.

As Georgie watched closely, she saw that Lottie was having what looked like an intense conversation with another woman. Their faces were very close.

Then Lottie leaned in and kissed the woman on the mouth for several seconds before giving a furtive glance back to see if anyone had spotted them. Then Lottie laughs and takes the woman's hand. It was virtually impossible to see the other woman as they were standing in the darkness of the marquee and the image quality was very poor.

'Bloody hell!' Georgie said. 'Any idea who that is with Lottie?'

'No,' Garrow said. 'But I know that Digital Forensics can have a go at cleaning it up for us.'

Georgie raised an eyebrow. 'Maybe Lottie and Jack weren't arguing about him having an affair on the morning of the wedding. Maybe they were arguing about her having one.'

CHAPTER 43

Ruth had called Nick to come down to meet with the officers from the NCA. The National Crime Agency was a UK-wide police unit that looked primarily into organised criminal gangs and the trafficking of drugs, weapons and people. Ruth wondered whether this was a visit about something outside of their investigation into Jack Rush's murder – or was it connected. She immediately thought of the Range Rover that had bumped them and followed her home. The Russian connection made her wonder whether the NCA were here in relation to that.

Ruth had told the duty sergeant to put the NCA officers in Interview Room 3. As she made her way through the ground floor of Llancastell nick, she saw Nick coming the other way.

'Any idea why the NCA are here?' Nick asked as he reached her.

She shook her head. 'The only thing I can think of is that it's related to the Range Rover and Russian owner.'

Nick gave her a nod. 'Yeah, I did wonder about that. Although I wasn't sure if that came under the remit of MI6?'

'We'll soon find out,' Ruth said.

They arrived at the door to Interview Room 3, opened it and went inside.

There were two officers sitting at the table. The older man – mixed race, forties, smart navy suit – got up as they entered. The woman – thirties – blonde, pinched features, glasses – gave them a half smile as she moved a small laptop on the table towards her.

'Hi, DI Ruth Hunter and DS Nick Evans,' Ruth said by way of an introduction as she went over and shook both their hands.

'DI Trevor Lett and DS Tracey Wilkinson,' Lett said in a friendly tone.

They all sat down.

Ruth gave Lett an enquiring look. 'And to what do we owe this pleasure?' she asked. 'Long way for you guys to travel?'

Wilkinson sat forward on her chair and pushed her glasses up the bridge of her nose. She wore a rather serious, even sour expression on her face in comparison to Lett. 'We're here to talk to you about the Jack Rush murder investigation.'

Right, so now we know, Ruth thought as Nick glanced over at her.

'Okay.' Ruth nodded. 'What do you need to know?'

Lett pulled his chair in and then picked up one of the folders that were on the table. 'Actually, I think it's us that need to bring you up to speed with an ongoing NCA operation that is directly relevant to your investigation,' he explained.

Ruth shot Nick a look. *Interesting.*

Wilkinson peered over the top of her glasses at them. 'We've had Jack Rush under our surveillance for eighteen months now.'

'What? What for?' Ruth asked, slightly thrown by the answer.

'Money laundering,' she said.

'Go on,' Nick said as he leaned forward over the table.

Lett opened his laptop, tapped a key and turned it to show them the screen. There was a surveillance photograph of Jack Rush shaking hands with a very sinister man in his sixties in a big overcoat. It's so cold that their breath is freezing in the image.

'Jack Rush has made three films in Russia and Budapest in the past five years,' Lett explained. 'And this man, Sergei Solonik, has co-financed all three films to the tune of one hundred and twenty-five million dollars.'

'Who is Sergei Solonik?' Nick asked.

'Solonik is the boss of one of the biggest Russian organised criminal gangs,' Lett explained. 'He's been connected to over a hundred murders in the past twenty years but nothing seems to stick. And, as you're probably aware, it's relatively easy to buy off officials and police officers in Russia these days.'

'We're not sure why Jack Rush got involved with Solonik but he's an incredibly dangerous man,' Wilkinson said. 'Our financial officers believe that Solonik was using the financing of these films to essentially launder his money and get it out of Russia. And Jack Rush was helping him do that.'

Ruth sat back in her chair and took a moment. The whole nature of the investigation might have just been turned on its head. She was already aware of how the Russian mafia had used London to launder their criminal money since the millennium. She'd had some dealings with it when she worked for the Met. The Laundromat scandal, as it became known, saw over £600 million unknowingly handled by UK banks such as Lloyds TSB, HSBC and even the Royal Family's exclusive bank,

Coutts. Worldwide, the scheme is supposed to have seen between £16 billion and £65 billion of Russian mafia money moved out of Russia. To do that, they were given a free rein by the Kremlin. It used to be a joke that so many Russians had bought property in West London – and a Premier League football club – that it was nicknamed 'Chelski'.

Ruth frowned. 'Do you think that Solonik might have a reason to kill Jack Rush?'

'Possibly.' Lett nodded. 'Our intel is that Rush and Solonik fell out over the deal that Rush was offering during the last film he made over there. They've just finished filming but we think that the dispute started about four months ago.'

'And we understand that you believe that Jack Rush was poisoned?' Wilkinson asked.

'Yes. Someone switched Rush's cocaine for potassium cyanide,' Nick explained.

Lett gave them a dark look. 'Of course, it's not unknown for Russians to use poison to assassinate those that have crossed them. In fact, it's almost become a cliché.'

Ruth nodded, remembering Alexander Litvinenko, a former Russian intelligence officer, who was killed with poison in London in 2006. And of course there were the infamous Salisbury Poisonings in 2018 when a former Russian military officer and double agent for British Intelligence, Sergei Skripal, and his daughter Yulia, were poisoned with the Novichok nerve agent.

'We've had a couple of incidents with a mystery Range Rover in the past few days,' Ruth said.

Nick looked at his notebook. 'Its plate is G247 YZ and it's registered to an Aleksandr Pitrov in Moscow.'

Lett and Wilkinson shared a knowing look.

'Yeah, we know Pitrov,' Lett said in serious tone. 'He does Solonik's dirty work. But we didn't know that he was in the UK. What happened?'

'Followed us and bumped the back of our car over near Abersoch,' Ruth explained. 'Then followed me home last night.'

Wilkinson pushed her glasses up the bridge of her nose again and sighed. 'Pitrov is just letting you know that he's around. He's used to intimidating or bribing police officers in Russia.'

Oh, good. Nothing to worry about then, Ruth thought sardonically to herself.

'What can you tell us about the lead up to Rush's murder?' Lett asked.

'Rush kept his cocaine in a drawer of his desk in his office which is on the first floor of the house. Rush usually kept the office locked and it was very rare for members of the family to go in there,' Ruth began to explain. 'His wife, Lottie, bought the cocaine for them both which was a regular thing. She claims that Jack used cocaine on the Thursday night with no adverse effect. So, we believe that the switch was made between late Thursday night and Saturday night, when Jack died.'

'So, a window of about forty-eight hours?' Lett asked, to clarify.

'Exactly,' Ruth agreed. 'We've interviewed all the family. Lottie says that the only time she went into the office was to give the cocaine to Jack on Thursday afternoon. Everyone else denies entering the office during that forty-eight-hour period.'

Nick looked over. 'But we do have a prime suspect, Charlie Huntington. His fingerprints were found all over the office, desk and drawers. Plus, we found a fibre from his jacket in the seal on the plastic bag that contained the cyanide.'

Lett raised an eyebrow. 'Does he have a motive?'

'Yes,' Nick replied. 'A prenup agreement that Jack Rush hadn't got around to signing. His death has made it invalid.'

'What's your hunch?' Lett asked.

Ruth took a moment. 'We're not sure yet. And to be fair, Rush's wife and his two sons all have a motive to kill him and were in the house at that time.'

Wilkinson frowned. 'Are you close to charging anyone yet?'

'Not really.' Ruth shook her head. 'We're still a distance from the CPS threshold for Huntington at the moment. But it could have been any of them unfortunately.'

'What about cleaners or anyone else that might have access to the house during that timeframe?' Lett asked.

Nick shook his head. 'We've checked and there is no one. And even if someone broke in unnoticed, Rush kept the doors of his office locked if he wasn't around.'

'The only person we're yet to speak to is an Amelia Wharton, who was Jack's Head of Development. We think she might have had a meeting with Jack on the Friday morning. And it may have been in Jack's office but we're not certain yet.'

Lett nodded thoughtfully. 'So, even if Pitrov did want to assassinate Rush, he would have had great difficulty in gaining access to his office?'

Ruth nodded. 'I think it would be virtually impossible.'

Nick rubbed his beard and asked, 'Why do you think Pitrov is in the area?'

'My assumption is that Rush owed Solonik money. And probably a lot of money. And he's not going to rest until he gets it back,' Wilkinson explained. 'I assume that Pitrov is here to keep on eye on the family, wait for the will to be read and see who inherits Rush's money.'

'And then what?' Ruth asked.

'And then I'd guess that Pitrov will make contact with that person and persuade them that they need to return Solonik's money,' Wilkinson replied.

Ruth exchanged a dark look with Nick. They didn't need Russian hitmen in North Wales trying to call in a debt.

CHAPTER 44

Ruth and Nick were approaching Bala. The sun was high and bright in a pure azure sky which looked like it could have been Mediterranean. As they slowed, the huge lake – *Llyn Tegid* – honed into view. It stretched for as far as the eye could see and was bordered by thick rows of towering conifer trees.

'Biggest natural lake in Wales,' Nick said gesturing over to it. 'One kilometre wide and five kilometres long.'

Ruth looked at him with a bemused smile. 'If you ever get kicked out of the police, you'd make a wonderful tour guide.'

Nick fumbled in his jacket for second. 'I've got something here for you, boss,' he grinned before pulling his hand and giving her the finger. 'Oh, here you go.'

Ruth shook her head. 'I'm pretty sure that you've done that joke on me before.'

'Killjoy,' Nick mumbled as they took a right-hand turn. They were heading for the cottage where Amelia Wharton was staying with her mother. 'You know the story behind the lake?'

'I don't,' Ruth said. 'Go on.'

'No,' Nick had second thoughts. 'You're just going to take the piss again.'

'I won't. I promise. Brownies' honour,' Ruth said doing some kind of three fingered salute.

'You were never a Brownie,' Nick scoffed.

'I went twice but Jennifer Flint, the local psycho, kicked me in the shins and pushed me over so I never went again,' Ruth admitted and then looked over at him. 'So, are you going to tell me the story, Nicholas, or what?'

'Keep your hair on,' he laughed as they drove uphill. 'There was this wicked prince called Tegid. And he held a party in Ancient Bala to celebrate the birth of his grandson. And he invited the most talented people from all around the area, including Landon, the greatest harpist in the whole of Wales. When Landon was playing at the party, he was distracted by a bird who told him that whatever he did, he must flee to the hills that night or die. So, Landon did what the bird had suggested and while everyone slept, he made his way up these very hills,' Nick said as he gestured either side of where they were driving. 'And he awoke the next morning to see that Ancient Bala had disappeared and the lake *Llyn Tegid* was now in its place.'

For a few seconds, Ruth frowned. Then she looked at Nick and shrugged. 'So what?'

'Sorry?' Nick said sounding offended.

'I don't mean to be rude, but every time you tell me one of these ancient Welsh myths, it has no point. No lesson to be learnt. No conclusion to be drawn,' Ruth sighed. 'What's the moral of the story? Always heed the warnings of a small bird and scarper?'

Nick looked annoyed. 'It's a mythical story not a fable.'

'Okay. But I still don't see the point,' Ruth said now worrying that she had really offended Nick.

'Well, that's the last time I tell you any Welsh myths while we're out and about,' Nick grumbled.

'Can I hold you to that?' Ruth joked.

'I'm officially offended so I'm going to ignore you,' he said and then pointed. 'Appleyard Cottage. This is it.'

'I apologise,' Ruth said as they parked outside the quaint, picture-postcard cottage.

Nick gave her a supercilious look. 'I'm still ignoring you.'

She knew that he was half joking.

They got out and Ruth popped on her sunglasses. The air was thick with the smell of freshly cut grass and the scent of daisies.

They walked up the neat garden path. The front garden was immaculate with box hedges and well-tended flower-beds. The lawn had been cut with neat stripes and there was washing that had been hung out on the line in perfect symmetry.

Ruth knocked on the door and took a step back. A hanging basket with lovely purple flowers that flowed over the edges swayed a little in the gentle summer breeze.

A few seconds later, a woman in her forties with red curly hair, piercing blue eyes and fashionable glasses came to the door. She wore expensive looking 'casual' clothes.

Ruth flashed her warrant card. 'DI Ruth Hunter and DS Nick Evans, Llancastell CID. We're looking for Amelia Wharton?'

'Hi there,' she said in a confident but friendly voice as she moved the glasses up to sit on her hair. 'That's me. My office rang to say that you were coming over.' Then she gestured. 'Please. Come in.'

'Thanks,' Ruth said as they went inside.

The hallway was nice and cool. There was a grand-father clock on the far side and a table with a vase full of dried flowers. The floor was dark, polished block wood with a red-patterned rug that was a little worn.

'Why don't you come through to the living room?' Amelia suggested casually. 'Can I get you anything?'

Nick shook his head. 'We're fine thanks.'

The living room was old-fashioned, neat and tidy. There was a small bookshelf in one corner and an upright piano that was stacked with yellowing sheet music in the other. The walls were adorned with watercolour paintings of the local countryside and a poster advertising a nearby art gallery.

Ruth and Nick sat down on a large comfy sofa opposite a big armchair where Amelia sat down slowly and crossed her long legs. She was wearing chestnut-coloured ankle boots.

'It's been such a shock,' Amelia said shaking her head. Whatever North Wales accent she might have had was now gone.

Ruth spotted a series of family photographs that had been lined up carefully across the top of the piano. There were a few of Amelia as a child, presumably with her mother, moustached father and a sister. There was also a single photo to one side of a woman in her twenties who was very attractive, who Ruth assumed was Amelia's sister.

Ruth nodded. 'We're very sorry for your loss,' she said gently getting her head back to detective inspector mode.

Nick took out his notepad and pen. 'There are just a few questions we'd like to ask. It won't take more than a few minutes.'

'Of course. Whatever I can do to help,' Amelia sighed sadly as she moved a long strand of red hair from her face. Then she looked intently at Ruth. 'Do you really think that someone actually killed Jack?'

Ruth nodded. 'I'm afraid so.'

'That's terrible,' Amelia said in a virtual whisper as she looked away. 'And poor Sofia. They were so incredibly close.' It was almost as if she was talking to herself.

Nick turned the page of his notebook and took out his pen. 'We understand that you and Jack had a meeting last Friday morning. Is that correct?'

'Yes,' Amelia replied calmly in a tone designed to demonstrate that she had nothing to hide.

'Can you tell us what that meeting was about?' Nick said.

'Just a bit of a catch-up,' Amelia said casually. 'I'd done some script notes on a couple of screenplays that we'd commissioned. I wanted to get Jack's thoughts on them. He's been out of the country a lot finishing off our latest film.'

'Can you remember what time you met on Friday?' Ruth asked.

'Early. It was a breakfast meeting, although we just had coffee,' Amelia said. 'Jack is usually up by five a.m. but I don't think I arrived until eight a.m.'

Nick looked over. 'And how long did your meeting last?'

'An hour. Maybe a bit longer.'

Ruth leant forward. 'Did you see anyone else while you were at the house?'

'I saw Lottie and we had a bit of catch-up downstairs first,' Amelia said. 'Then I saw Sofia and Charlie come back from a morning run on the beach.'

'Did you see any other members of the family?'

'No. That was it,' Amelia said.

'And how did Jack seem?' Ruth asked.

'Good. Fine,' Amelia said but there was something slightly 'off' about her response.

Ruth narrowed her eyes. She sensed that Amelia was hiding something.

'Are you sure?' Ruth asked.

Amelia thought for a few seconds. 'Jack had been diagnosed with cancer a while ago. We talked about that. He was concerned about the future.'

'Did he mention that he was dying?' Ruth asked tactfully.

'Not in so many words. But it didn't take a genius to work it out,' Amelia admitted quietly. 'And he'd told me that his illness had focused his mind on his estate and his family. He was in the process of changing his will because of it.'

'He told you that?' Ruth asked. It seemed quite a personal thing to tell an employee which implied that he trusted Amelia.

Nick gave Amelia a questioning look. 'Is there anyone that you can think of that might have wanted to harm him?'

'Where do I start!' Amelia gave a dry little laugh. 'I think there are plenty of people out there that would have liked to have *harmed* Jack. He was my friend but he was very confrontational in business. And ruthless. He'd made plenty of enemies in the business. But I'm not sure anyone would have gone as far as to... you know... kill him like that.'

'What about his family? Did he talk about them much?' Ruth asked.

'Not really.'

'What about his marriage to Lottie?' Nick said.

Amelia took a breath as she thought for a few seconds. 'Jack and Lottie's marriage was pretty volatile. But it was one of those marriages that also seemed to work despite all that.'

'What about his children?' Nick said. 'You must have formed an opinion about them?'

'He absolutely doted on Sofia. And little Jasmine,' Amelia replied. 'But his relationship with his sons was very strained. I think he wanted them to follow him into the family business. His dream was for one of them, or both of them, to take over Rush Pictures from him. He wanted to create a legacy. But neither of them showed any interest in that. But I know he was very hard on them so they just rebelled against him.'

'Did he talk about his son-in-law, Charlie?' Ruth said.

'Not really,' Amelia said. 'He said that he was a nice enough young man but I could see that Jack had reservations about Sofia marrying him. Jack was very controlling like that. And deeply suspicious.'

Ruth looked at Nick to signal that they'd got as much as they needed from Amelia and it was time to leave.

'Thank you for your time,' Ruth said as she stood up. 'And if you do think of anything else that might help us, please let us know.'

'Of course,' Amelia said. 'I'll see you out.'

CHAPTER 45

Garrow was sitting at his desk. Having finished trawling through the wedding video, he was now looking at the CCTV footage from the camera at the front of the house. He'd gone back to the Thursday night. They were working on a forty-eight-hour timeframe so he wanted to see who, if anyone, had visited the house in that time other than members of the immediate family and the housekeeper Gwyneth who had been interviewed.

He had noted that a woman, presumably Amelia Wharton, had arrived at the house at eight a.m. and left again just before ten a.m. What was now drawing his attention was a delivery van driver that had arrived at the house at three p.m. on Friday afternoon. There was something about the way the driver was acting that just seemed suspicious – as if he was there to suss the place out.

Garrow rewound the CCTV footage and watched his arrival again. The driver got out but before he went to the front door, he took a long look around the front of the house and clocked the CCTV camera. It was definitely suspicious. The driver then knocked on the front door. Lottie opened it, signed for the package and then went back inside. The driver walked over to his van but rather than getting straight in, he took out his phone and made a call that lasted about thirty seconds. Then he took another look around the house before getting into his van and driving away. Garrow zoomed in a little and saw that the van had *SMC Couriers – North Wales and the North West* printed on the side in red lettering with a logo.

Using Google, Garrow typed SMC Couriers in to see if he could find their website, telephone number or address.

Nothing.

That's weird, he thought to himself.

Logging into Companies House, Garrow did a quick search for SMC Couriers.

Still nothing.

Garrow sat back with a frown. As far as he could see, SMC Couriers didn't exist. So, who was the driver and what had he delivered to Lottie Rush on Friday afternoon?

A new email flashed up in the top right-hand corner of his screen.

It was from Digital Forensics. They had managed to clean up the wedding video footage of Lottie sharing a kiss with a female guest.

Clicking on the video file, Garrow watched the footage again. This time the woman's face was very clear.

Garrow zoomed in to have a closer look. He didn't recognise her.

'Jim, Jade and I are just going over to Abersoch to question Jasmine about those missing video files,' Georgie said as she came over. 'Is there anything else we need to ask her.'

'I don't think so,' Garrow said still looking at the screen.

Georgie's eyes widened as she spotted the image of Lottie kissing the female wedding guest on Garrow's computer. 'Is that the footage from the wedding video?'

'Yes. Why?' Garrow asked seeing her reaction.

'Because the person that Lottie Rush is kissing is Amelia Wharton, Jack Rush's Head of Development,' Georgie said.

'Are you sure?'

Georgie nodded. 'I've just seen her profile on the Rush Pictures website and that's definitely her.'

CHAPTER 46

Ruth and Nick were now about ten minutes outside Bala as they headed back to Llancastell nick. The sun dazzled angrily on the windscreen and Ruth put on her sunglasses. Then she reached over and put on the AC. She let the cool air blow over her face for a few seconds.

'My dad used to have this battered old Ford Cortina. It was a maroon colour,' Ruth said as she reached into her jacket to get a cigarette. 'When it was hot like today, it had what we called 'the blowers' which rattled and blew out luke warm air. And it had this fake leatherette on the seats that used to heat up in the sun so that it literally fried your skin when you sat down. I remember me and my brother Chris were both wearing shorts and refusing to get in as the seats were boiling hot.'

'Got to love a Ford Cortina,' Nick said with a smile. 'Although I always wanted a Ford Capri.'

'Boy racer,' Ruth joked.

'Guilty as charged,' Nick said.

'My cousin Gary had a Ford Capri. White with black trim. He was a right wide boy,' Ruth recalled. 'Even had some furry dice to go with it.'

'Classic,' Nick guffawed.

Ruth's phone buzzed. It was Garrow.

'Jim?' she said answering the phone.

'Boss,' Garrow said. 'While you were out, I found something on the wedding video. Lottie Rush was holding hands with a woman and kissing her. I had the footage cleaned up. The woman is Amelia Wharton.'

'What?' Ruth said, sounding surprised. 'When you say kissing…'

'They're talking and holding hands for about ten minutes. And then they kiss, you know, properly. They're definitely together,' Garrow explained.

'Okay. Thanks for letting me know,' Ruth said as she ended the call. Then she turned to Nick.

'Everything all right?' he asked with a quizzical frown.

'Not really. We need to turn around and go back to Bala,' Ruth said.

—

Georgie and Kennedy walked across the garden in the intense sunshine. When they'd arrived at the Rush's home in Abersoch, the Family Liaison Officer had told them that Jasmine had last been seen in her tree house over towards the orchard.

'Imagine growing up in a place like this,' Kennedy said as she popped on her sunglasses. 'Imagine having a pool, tennis courts and a bloody orchard.'

'Yeah,' Georgie agreed. 'That would have been nice. My grandmother had an old rusty swing.'

Kennedy laughed.

The air was thick with heat and the faint hum of honey bees.

Walking in the afternoon sun was really taking it out of Georgie and she could feel her ankles swelling by the second. 'I take it there weren't many orchards in Streatham?'

'Jesus,' she snorted. 'No. Our estate was definitely lacking in tennis courts and orchards. A couple of stolen cars up on piles of bricks. That was about it. And the nearest pool was Brockwell Lido. And on a day like today, you might just find a couple of feet of free cracked concrete to sit on.'

Georgie pulled a face. 'I was pretty lucky then. We had a lovely little garden although we weren't ever really allowed to play in it.'

'Why not?' Kennedy asked.

'Mum was a keen gardener and it was her pride and joy. If she saw any kind of game breaking out on the lawn she'd go nuts,' Georgie explained.

'Wow. She sounds like fun,' Kennedy joked.

'Yeah, I'm pretty sure that no one has ever used the word "fun" to describe either of my parents,' Georgie admitted and she felt a twinge of sadness about the fact that they showed such little interest in her, her baby or her life in general.

'There it is,' Kennedy said pointing over to an old wooden tree house up in the branches of an enormous oak tree. It had been painted in pastel pinks and blues. A rope ladder hung down from the platform.

'God, it looks like the sort of tree house you'd find in an Enid Blyton novel,' Georgie said as they approached.

The wind picked up and the cool sea breeze felt refreshing against Georgie's face as she took a deep breath. She blew out her cheeks and wiped the sweat from her forehead with the back of her hand.

They stopped under the tree house.

'Jasmine?' Georgie called up in a friendly voice.

Nothing.

There was a creak of wood as if someone was moving inside. Then it stopped.

Georgie looked at Kennedy and shrugged. Someone was definitely up there.

'Jasmine?' Georgie called again.

There was silence.

Then a face suddenly appeared.

'Oh, hello!' Jasmine said as she looked down at them with a pair of binoculars. 'I've been spying on you ever since you arrived.'

Kennedy gave her a wry smile. 'Have you now?'

Georgie put her hand up to shield her eyes from the sun. 'Hi, Jasmine. There's a couple of things that we'd like to talk to you about. Are you okay to come down here for me?'

Jasmine shrugged. 'Or you could come up here? It's very nice. I've got a blanket and some snacks.'

Georgie gestured to her bump. 'Yeah, I don't think it's very safe for me to be climbing up rope ladders in my condition. And I'd probably break it anyway.'

'Oh, yes.' Jasmine gave a little laugh. 'I'll come down.'

She then swung over the platform, grabbed the rope ladder and then dropped to the grass in a matter of seconds.

'Very impressive,' Kennedy said.

Jasmine gave them an interested look. 'How's the investigation going? I heard you arrested Charlie. My sister was crying.'

Georgie looked at her. 'We can't really talk about the case at the moment.'

'I understand.' Jasmine tapped the side of her nose. 'But you can tell me. It's not as if I'd tell anyone else,' she said in a conspiratorial tone.

Georgie couldn't help but admire her confidence. She wished she'd been that confident at twelve. 'Yeah, even though I'm sure you would keep it to yourself, Jasmine, we still can't tell you.'

Jasmine frowned. 'Don't you trust me?'

Kennedy glanced at Georgie as if to say that they weren't getting very far.

'Anyway,' Kennedy said. 'We…'

'You do know that if this was a book or a film, there would have been another murder by now,' Jasmine said.

That's a strange thing to say, Georgie thought to herself.

Kennedy raised an eyebrow. 'What makes you say that?'

Jasmine shrugged. 'That's how a story like this would play out. If it was fictional of course. I spend my life watching old movies. Hitchcock, Orson Welles, Tarantino. And someone would now be murdered because they knew too much. You know. All that Sherlock Holmes, Agatha Christie stuff.'

Georgie gave Jasmine a curious look. She was very eccentric. 'Jasmine, we'd like to talk to you about the wedding video that you made.'

'Okay,' Jasmine shrugged nonchalantly. 'Did you like it?'

'Erm, yes. But there is an issue. You went up to your bedroom to transfer the video files onto a memory stick that you then gave to me,' Georgie said.

'That's right,' Jasmine said. 'Is there a problem?'

Georgie nodded. 'Some of those original files have been deleted.'

'Have they?' Jasmine asked trying to appear surprised but failing. She was clearly lying.

'Come on, Jasmine,' Kennedy said gently. 'What happened to those files?'

'I've no idea,' she said sounding a little angry. 'How would I know?'

Georgie narrowed her eyes. 'Are you sure about that?'

'Are you calling me a liar?' Jasmine snapped. 'That's not very nice.'

'No, of course not,' Georgie reassured her. She then waited for a few seconds.

Jasmine's breathing was shallow as if she was anxious about something.

'Jasmine,' Georgie said quietly. 'If you decided to delete those files because you wanted to protect someone, then we'd understand.'

Jasmine frowned as she mulled over what Georgie had said. 'Protect someone? I don't know what you're talking about.'

'Are you're sure about that?' Kennedy asked dubiously. 'It just seems very strange that they're not there.'

'Well, I didn't do it,' Jasmine insisted curtly. 'And I'm not covering for anyone.'

Georgie nodded but she was certain that Jasmine was lying to them. She wondered what was on those files and why she'd got rid of them.

'Okay,' Georgie said as she reached into her jacket and pulled out a contact card. 'But if you do think of something. Or if you do remember anything about that video, this is my card and it's got all my contact details on it.'

Jasmine reached out to take it suspiciously. 'Does that mean I can go now?' she asked.

'Of course,' Georgie replied.

Jasmine turned and then jogged away in the direction of the orchard.

Georgie gave Kennedy a dubious look. Neither of them believed her.

CHAPTER 47

'You're in a relationship with Lottie?' Ruth asked, to clarify as she and Nick now sat opposite Amelia Wharton in the same positions in the living room as twenty minutes earlier.

'Yes,' Amelia said defensively.

'Did Jack know?' Ruth asked.

'Yes,' she replied.

'And how did he react to that?'

'He was absolutely furious.' Amelia shook her head with a withering sigh. 'It was utterly pathetic!'

Nick frowned. 'You don't think he should have been furious?'

'Of course not!' Amelia snorted as if this was a ridiculous suggestion. 'Jack has slept with dozens if not hundreds of women. This is a man who sexually assaulted a beautiful young actress, and then tried to force her to sign an NDA. And when she refused, he made sure she never worked again and she ended up taking her own life.' Amelia looked a little emotional as she said this. 'So, the idea that his fragile male ego and pride was hurt by Lottie and I having a relationship is frankly absurd.'

'Is this what you were talking about at your meeting?' Ruth asked.

Amelia took a few seconds to think.

'Amelia?' Ruth prompted her.

'Yes,' she said quietly.

'Your meeting with Jack on Friday morning wasn't about scripts or anything to do with Rush Pictures then?' Nick asked, to clarify.

'No,' Amelia reluctantly admitted. 'No, it wasn't.'

Ruth narrowed her eyes. 'Can you tell us what your meeting was about?'

Amelia sighed and ran her hands through her hair. She was clearly feeling awkward. 'I was summoned to the house so that Jack could fire me, if you must know.'

Nick frowned. 'Jack fired you from your job because of the affair that you were having with his wife?'

'I know. The hypocrisy of it is quite astounding,' Amelia said shaking her head. 'But Jack is… sorry… Jack *was* a very petty man with an enormous ego.'

Ruth was puzzled. 'But you attended the wedding the following day?'

Amelia nodded and slowly folded her arms. 'On the Friday, Jack told me that I wasn't welcome at Sofia's wedding. But Lottie went crazy and told him that I was coming as her guest and he couldn't stop that happening. I think they argued about it for the next twenty-four hours.'

Ruth realised that the rows between Jack and Lottie that had been reported to them by the family weren't about Jack's latest affair as they had assumed. They had been about Lottie's relationship with Amelia and her attendance at Sofia's wedding.

'I assume it must have been very awkward at the wedding?' Ruth said.

'Not really,' Amelia said calmly. 'Jack ignored me. And I just had a lovely time with Lottie. I had a great time actually.'

Ruth took a few seconds to process all this. 'Let's go back to the fact that Jack fired you from your job at Rush Pictures. Did you know that's what he was going to do when he asked you to come to the house in Abersoch?'

'Oh, I see what you're doing.' Amelia gave them a wry smile. 'You're wondering if I knew that I was going to get sacked prior to meeting with Jack. And therefore was I involved in somehow planting this poison in his office.'

Ruth was struck by how calm and assured Amelia was in her answer.

'You didn't actually answer the question,' Ruth pointed out.

'I know.' Amelia said. 'The answer is yes. I did have a very good idea that Jack was going to fire me on Friday morning.'

Nick looked over at her. 'When did Jack contact you to ask you to come to the house?'

'On the Wednesday,' Amelia replied. 'And now you're thinking that I had plenty of time to plan Jack's murder and buy whatever it was that killed him and plant it in his office.'

Ruth gave her a quizzical look. 'And did you?'

'No. Of course not!' Amelia gave a little laugh. 'For starters, I'm not a psychopath. And the whole thing sounds like a plot from some Victorian melodrama.'

'But you do understand how suspicious it looks?' Ruth stated. 'You know that you're going to be sacked from a very good job by a man who has a history of infidelity. You're having an affair with his wife. You have a very strong motive to want to kill him and you have the perfect opportunity to do it.'

'That's all true,' Amelia admitted. 'But I didn't do it. And if you had a shred of evidence that I had murdered him, other than your flimsy hypothesis, you would have arrested me and taken me to your police station for questioning.'

Ruth shared a look with Nick. It was frustrating but what she'd said was correct.

'So, unless you are going to arrest me, there is nothing else I can tell you except that I didn't kill Jack,' Amelia said as she stood up. 'And I'd like you to leave now.'

CHAPTER 48

It was late afternoon when Garrow went outside for another clandestine meeting with Lucy. He was getting hooked on the thrill of their little rendezvous. Glancing up, he spotted that a suspicious gathering of grey clouds had now covered the sun and the blue sky. As the wind picked up, he could feel a chill in the air. He was surprised as it had been so hot in the middle of the day.

Getting to the car, he opened the door and sat down in the passenger seat. Then he glanced over at Lucy who had a knowing smile on her face as she offered him a plastic box.

'No wig?'

'Flapjack?' she asked, ignoring him.

Garrow frowned. 'What's in them?'

'Oats, raspberries, nuts, seeds and honey,' she replied. 'Very healthy actually.'

Garrow went to take one and then stopped himself.

'God, are you really so suspicious of me that you think this is some horrible game of culinary Russian roulette?' she laughed.

'Yes,' he admitted.

'What do you think I've put in there?' she snorted. 'Rat poison with strychnine? Cyanide?'

Garrow reacted.

Lucy narrowed her eyes. 'Ooh, is that what the killer used on Jack Rush? Swapped his cocaine for something white and powdery? Cyanide?'

Garrow took a moment but then nodded.

'Wow. Cyanide. Classic,' Lucy said triumphantly. 'Old-fashioned, classy. And very nasty.'

'Oh, you know your poisons, do you?' Garrow sighed.

'Of course,' she said. Then she theatrically put the palm of her hand over her eyes, waved her hand around and then randomly took a flapjack from the half a dozen or so that were in the box. She took a big bite, chewed and swallowed. 'See?'

Garrow rolled his eyes. 'You're not going to do that whole fake gurgling, dying thing again, are you?'

'Oh. Well, I was going to,' Lucy grinned. 'But seeing as you don't think it's funny...'

Garrow took a flapjack, bit into it and chewed.

'Good, isn't it?' she asked expectantly.

'Yes. Excellent,' Garrow admitted. 'And this is all great but I am kind of busy and in the middle of a murder investigation. You messaged me to say that you've got something that might help?'

Lucy frowned and pulled a face of mock indignation. 'Oh, Jim. I thought you came out to see me and sample one of my flapjacks. I'm hurt.'

'No, you're not,' Garrow groaned. 'What is it?'

'Ever heard of Elizabeth Davies?' Lucy asked.

Garrow nodded. 'Yes, her name came up. The actress that alleged she'd been raped by Jack Rush and then took her own life back in 2001. Why?'

Lucy looked at him. 'Jack Rush's murder wasn't a crime of passion. It wasn't a sudden explosion of overwhelming fury. It was a cold, calculated plan to kill him in the most excruciatingly painful way possible.'

'Okay,' Garrow agreed. 'What does that tell us?'

'It tells us that the killer had been biding their time,' Lucy said. 'I did some digging around. Elizabeth Davies had a sister, Lucinda Rathbone. She was an actress too. She wrote an article about her sister in a Sunday newspaper after she died. And when Lucinda was questioned about her sister's death, she said that one day she was going to avenge her sister.'

Garrow shook his head. 'Thing is, Lucinda Rathbone hasn't registered on our radar once yet. There's no evidence that she's ever been anywhere near Jack Rush or the house. No one mentioned her. So, I take your point but our focus is on the immediate family.'

Lucy shrugged as she took another bite of her flapjack. 'Okay,' she said with her mouth full. 'Just trying to help and throw around some ideas. You're being incredibly ungrateful of my input.'

CHAPTER 49

It was dark outside by the time Ruth left her office to conduct an evening briefing and bring all the members of the Llancastell CID team up to speed with the case. The temperature seemed to have dropped suddenly and it felt as if the first hint of autumn was in the air. It was the beginning of September after all.

'Right, guys,' Ruth said raising her voice. 'If we can settle down, please. Then we can start to think about going home.' She sipped from a bottle of water as she approached the scene boards which were now jam-packed with information. 'As most of you know, this is a fast-moving case so even though we met this morning, I wanted us all to pool what intel and developments we've got so everyone is up to speed. We have now had to release Charlie Huntington, who remains our main suspect. But until we find more evidence, the CPS have said that we haven't reached the threshold of charging him with Jack Rush's murder. What about phone records, bank statements, social media?'

Garrow looked over. 'Nothing suspicious, boss.'

Ruth gave a frustrated sigh. 'Okay, thanks Jim. Where are we at with James and Ed Rush?'

Nick sat forward in his chair. 'No further developments. Ed was angry that Jack was pulling the plug on the property company. James was annoyed that he wouldn't

229

pay for him to go to Paris. And we know that over the years, Jack had been a bully, controlling and psychologically abusive towards them. Whether separately or together, they have means, motive and opportunity. But we have no concrete evidence against either of them.'

'I've asked for some stuff on Sofia and Jasmine Rush. Anything yet?' Ruth said.

Kennedy signalled with her pen. 'Sofia doesn't have a criminal record. She works as an associate producer for Rush Pictures.'

Ruth frowned. 'What's an associate producer?'

'No idea, boss,' Kennedy admitted. 'We have requested some stuff on Jasmine but because of her age, it's taking a while to come through.'

'Okay. Thanks, Jade,' Ruth said as she pointed to a photo. 'Our major development today has been Amelia Wharton, Jack's Head of Development. We've discovered that she has been having an affair with Lottie Rush. Jack knew about the affair and had called Amelia to his office in the house to sack her. All this gives Amelia motive. Obviously, we have no idea if Jack left Amelia in his office for any period of time where she could have switched the cocaine. But other than that, we have no concrete evidence.' Ruth sat down on the edge of the desk and looked at the team. 'I can definitely say that in nearly thirty years as a police officer, I've never worked a case with so many possible suspects and so little concrete evidence. Frustrating doesn't come into it.'

'This is a long shot, boss,' Garrow said. 'But we haven't really looked into Lucinda Rathbone. She was the sister of Elizabeth Davies, the young actress who made allegations of rape against Jack Rush and then took her own life.'

'Okay,' Ruth said a little confused. 'And why do we need to look at her?'

'She made several public comments that she was going to avenge her sister's death and that Jack Rush would regret what he'd done,' Garrow explained.

'Okay,' Ruth nodded. 'But we've had no suggestion that this Lucinda Rathbone has made any more threats recently or had any contact with Jack Rush?'

'No. But given that she did make death threats,' Garrow stated, 'I thought we should at least have that conversation.'

'Good point,' Ruth said with a half smile. 'Just what we need, Jim. Another suspect to add to our list.'

There were a few tired chortles from the assembled team.

Garrow gave a self-effacing smile. At least he could see the funny side of it, Ruth thought.

'I'm joking, Jim,' Ruth reassured him. 'Do you know where she is?'

Garrow shook his head. 'That's the thing. I did the basic checks. Council tax, HMRC, social media. Nothing. I can't seem to find her anywhere.'

Even though it was a long shot, Ruth didn't like the fact that she couldn't be traced.

'Okay, do some more digging and see what you can find, Jim,' Ruth said. 'Anyone got anything else?'

'We have the Russians,' Nick pointed out.

'Oh, yes, the Russians, of course,' Ruth said in slightly sarcastic tone. 'Mustn't forget them. They wanted to assassinate Jack because he stole laundered money from them.'

Georgie looked over. 'Not forgetting that poison is the Russians' favourite MO,' she reminded everyone.

'Boss,' Garrow said. 'Bit of strange one that I haven't managed to run past you. But it might be relevant to this. I've got a video of a delivery driver acting very suspiciously. You should probably have a look.'

Ruth pointed to the screen on the wall. 'Can you put it up there?'

'Of course,' Garrow said as he turned to his computer and began to tap away.

A few seconds later the CCTV footage of the driver from SMC Couriers was up on the large screen. The delivery driver arrived, gave Lottie Rush a package which she signed for. He 'cased' the house and where the CCTV was located, and eventually got back into the van and drove away.

'Bloody hell,' Kennedy said. 'I don't think he could have acted any more suspiciously if he tried, could he?'

'No,' Ruth agreed. 'Who are SMC Couriers?' she asked.

Garrow pulled a face. 'As far as I can see, they don't exist.'

Ruth raised an eyebrow. 'How do you mean?'

'Type them into Google and nothing comes up,' Garrow explained. 'So, I did a check at Companies House. Nothing.'

'That's very weird,' Kennedy said.

'Sounds pretty dodgy to me,' Georgie agreed.

Nick rubbed his beard as he looked at the screen. 'And it was Lottie Rush who received and signed for that package. And we know that she buys cocaine for herself and Jack.'

'Do we think that SMC Couriers is just a front for drug dealers then?' Ruth asked rhetorically.

Garrow shrugged. 'Has to be worth asking her what she signed for. It's definitely very suspicious.'

Ruth nodded in agreement and then glanced down at her watch. 'Right, home time, people. Thank you for all your hard work today. Get some food and some sleep. Back here at six a.m. sharp, please.'

CHAPTER 50

Closing the front door behind her, Ruth kicked off her shoes and gave an audible sigh. She was exhausted and her legs ached.

She could hear the sound of the television. Sarah must still be up which was lovely.

Padding down the hallway, Ruth poked her head through the door.

'Hello?' she said with a smile.

Sarah looked over and then frowned. 'Ooh, you look tired.'

'Oh, charming,' Ruth laughed. 'Nice to see you too.'

Sarah ignored her and pointed to an open bottle of red wine. There was an empty glass beside it. Sarah was holding her own glass of wine.

'I've got a Merlot on the go,' she explained.

'Have you now?' Ruth said with a wry smile as she walked over and poured a glass for herself.

'Foot massage?' Sarah asked.

'Oh, my God, I love you,' Ruth groaned as she flopped at the other end of the sofa. 'Maybe you can have a go at my calves as well.'

Putting down her wine, Sarah began to massage her feet. 'Yeah, don't push your luck, sunshine.'

Ruth winced. 'Ow, you're meant to be massaging them, not doing some kind of dark Guantanamo Bay torture routine.'

Sarah pulled a face. 'You're very grouchy. What's the matter with you?'

'Never mind that,' Ruth said as she pointed to the television. 'What are we watching?'

'They're showing lots of Jack Rush films on Channel 4 as a tribute,' Sarah explained. 'Did you know that he made a lot of films in Eastern Europe and Bulgaria?'

'I did actually,' Ruth replied. 'I can tell you a funny story about that.'

'Funny amusing? Or funny dark?' Sarah asked.

'Funny, he laundered millions of dollars for Russian gangsters through those films, stole some of it and they wanted to kill him,' Ruth said.

'Oh, right. Not funny at all then?'

'No,' Ruth said with a sigh.

'It was Russians that killed him?' Sarah asked.

'We're not sure,' Ruth admitted.

'Explains the poison I guess,' Sarah said. 'Love a bit of poison, the Russkies.'

'Erm, I don't think you can use the term "Russkies" any more,' Ruth pointed out.

'Why not?' Sarah asked.

'I think it's derogatory or offensive,' Ruth sighed. 'Probably some Gen Z bullshit.'

'I thought it was the millennials who were woke or snowflakes?'

'God knows,' Ruth groaned. 'All I do know is that it makes me feel very, very old.'

'That's because you are.'

'Oi,' Ruth laughed. Then she looked at the screen as the next film started.

It was called *Beyond The Church Gate*.

Soft classical music played as the opening credits came onto the screen.

Executive Producer – Jack Rush.

As the credits continued to run, the opening scene showed a quiet English village in what looked like the 1920s.

'Isn't this the film with Elizabeth Davies?' Ruth asked, realising the connection to the case.

'That's right,' Sarah said.

'I always thought that this was a Merchant Ivory film with Helena Bonham Carter,' Ruth said.

'That's *A Room with a View*, stupid,' Sarah chortled. 'We can turn it off if you want? It's getting late.'

Ruth held up her hand. 'Erm, no, it's okay. I'd like to watch the first few minutes actually.'

Ruth wanted to see the actress that had alleged that Jack Rush had raped her during the making of this very film.

Then the names of the cast started to appear on the screen. Somehow it seemed disrespectful to turn it off now.

The cast credits continued.

Elizabeth Davies.

A few others appeared and then Ruth saw the name *Lucinda Rathbone*.

For a second, Ruth couldn't remember why she knew that name. Then she remembered.

'Lucinda Rathbone? That was Elizabeth Davies's sister, wasn't it?' Ruth asked pointing to the screen.

'That's right,' Sarah nodded. 'She was an actress. She was married to that British actor Lawrence Rathbone who was meant to be the new Hugh Grant about twenty years ago. I haven't seen either of them in anything for ages.'

'So, Lucinda Rathbone was an actress?' Ruth asked.

'Yes. Why?' Sarah asked turning to look Ruth.

'It's just that Lucinda wrote an article about her sister Elizabeth for a Sunday paper,' Ruth explained. 'I suppose it exposed all the stuff that eventually came out with Weinstein and #MeToo. But she also said that she was going to avenge her sister's death.'

Sarah frowned. 'And she was talking about Jack Rush?'

'Yes, she must have been,' Ruth nodded as she watched the film begin.

A beautiful young woman in her twenties rode a bicycle through the village as the music played. She was clearly the central character.

'That's Elizabeth Davies,' Sarah said pointing at the screen.

The beautiful young woman arrives at a picturesque country cottage, rests her bike up against the wall and goes in through a back door into a kitchen.

A woman who is slightly older and wearing a pinafore comes out of the pantry to talk to her.

The older woman has curly red hair and piercing blue eyes.

'And that's Lucinda Rathbone,' Sarah said. 'As I said, I haven't seen her in very much recently. I guess what happened to her sister must have really affected her.'

But Ruth wasn't listening. She grabbed the remote control roughly from Sarah and paused the image on the screen.

'Sorry,' Ruth said as she stared intently at the image.

'Are you okay?' Sarah asked pulling a face.

The face of Lucinda Rathbone filled the screen.

Except it was the face of Amelia Wharton.

'Jesus Christ!' Ruth gasped with surprise.

'Ruth?' Sarah said with concern.

'Sorry it's just…' Ruth said blinking. 'We've been talking to a woman called Amelia Wharton all day. She was Jack Rush's Head of Development until he sacked her for having an affair with his wife.'

Sarah frowned. 'I'm really lost now.'

Ruth points to the screen. 'The only problem is that Amelia Wharton is actually Lucinda Rathbone.'

'Bloody hell,' Sarah said her eyes widening.

Ruth grabbed her phone. She took a photo of the screen and then dialled Nick's number.

'Boss?' he said as he answered. 'Everything all right?'

'Not really,' she admitted. 'I need you to pick me up. We're going to Bala to arrest Amelia Wharton.'

'Because?' Nick asked.

CHAPTER 51

It was three a.m. by the time Ruth and Nick had travelled to Bala, arrested Amelia Wharton and brought her back to Llancastell nick under caution. On the journey, Ruth hadn't divulged what she had discovered about Amelia's true identity. She didn't want to play that hand until they interviewed her under caution so they could see her reaction.

They were now sitting in an interview room at Llancastell nick.

Ruth pressed the button on the recording equipment and said, 'Interview conducted with Amelia Wharton, 3:06 a.m., Interview Room 1, Llancastell Police Station. Present are Amelia Wharton, Detective Sergeant Nick Evans, solicitor Johnathan Miles, and myself, Detective Inspector Ruth Hunter.'

Ruth then waited for a few seconds, moved a folder over so that it was in front of her and looked over at Amelia. She was as cool as a cucumber. She had been since they'd arrested her.

'For the purposes of this interview, could you state your full name, please,' Ruth asked.

Amelia turned her head casually. 'Amelia Wharton.'

'Have you ever been known by any other name?' Ruth asked in a casual tone so as not to draw attention to the trap she was laying.

'No,' Amelia replied.

'For the purposes of the recording, I'm going to show the suspect Item Reference 378N,' Ruth said as she took her phone, pulled up the image of the actress Lucinda Rathbone that she had taken from her television and turned the screen to show her. 'Can you tell me what you can see on this phone screen, please?'

Amelia peered over but didn't react at all when she saw the photo.

'Amelia? Could you answer the question, please?' Ruth said.

Amelia's eyes stayed focused and unblinking on the phone screen until Ruth moved it away.

'Let me put this another way,' Ruth said. 'Is that you in the image on the phone screen?'

'Yes,' she said defiantly as if it was a stupid question.

'So, your name is not Amelia Wharton?' Ruth asked.

'No,' she gave a little derisive snort. 'You know full well that's it not. That's why I'm here. There's little point in us playing games, is there?'

Ruth looked directly at her. 'I don't think that it's us who have been playing games, do you?'

Amelia smiled. 'It's been a long and difficult road.'

Nick sat forward. 'Can we establish that you are Lucinda Rathbone and that you were at one point an actress?'

'Lucinda Davies,' she corrected him. 'If you'd done your research, you'd have seen that I divorced that pompous little man in 2008. But yes, I was an actress for a while.'

'And Elizabeth Davies was your sister?' Ruth stated.

'Yes. She was,' Amelia said taking a deep breath to steady herself. It was the first time that she had shown any emotion since they'd met her.

'And you blamed Jack Rush for your sister's death, is that right?' Nick asked sensitively.

'I don't *blame* him.' Amelia narrowed her eyes. 'He raped my little sister and then made sure she never worked again. He murdered her. There's no other way of looking at it.'

'But you changed your name and I'm assuming your identity?' Ruth asked.

'How else was I going to make my way through the film business and end up working for that monster?' Amelia asked.

'That was the plan all along?' Nick said.

'Yes. Of course,' she shrugged. 'But I couldn't be the woman whose famous actress sister had killed herself, could I? I had to change that for anyone to take me seriously.'

'And to eventually get a job at Rush Pictures,' Nick added.

'Precisely,' she said coldly.

'Can you tell me what happened when you visited Jack Rush in his office at his home last Friday morning,' Ruth said.

Amelia rolled her eyes. 'I've already told you. Jack fired me.'

'You see, I'm pretty sure that you must have been waiting for nearly twenty years to get your revenge on Jack Rush,' Ruth said. 'You publicly made threats against him and said that you would one day avenge your sister's death.'

Amelia shrugged. 'So what?'

'Come on, Amelia,' Ruth said in a tone that bordered on friendly. 'You can't tell me that it's a complete and utter coincidence that you visited Jack on Friday in his office and then thirty hours later he died in there.'

'What can I tell you?' Amelia sighed. 'It was a very happy coincidence, luckily for me. But coincidence it was. Of course, I wish it had been me that did it.'

Ruth narrowed her eyes. 'I've been a police officer for nearly thirty years. I don't believe in coincidences. They just don't exist.'

'Haven't you already arrested someone for Jack's murder?' Amelia scoffed. 'It's about time you made your mind up who you think killed him.'

Nick looked over at Amelia. 'What was the purpose of getting a job at Rush Pictures?'

'My grand masterplan you mean?' Amelia said sarcastically.

Nick shrugged a nod.

'I wanted to see what Jack was like up close and personal,' Amelia stated. 'Before I took him down.'

'You mean kill him?' Nick said.

Amelia thought for a few seconds. 'Although I've lied about who I am and I've managed to ingratiate myself into Jack Rush's life, I don't think you have any evidence against me, do you?'

Ruth pulled her chair in slightly. 'What was the affair with Lottie about?'

'Actually, it started as a way of hurting Jack,' Amelia replied. 'But then it actually became a true love affair.'

'Can you tell us when you switched the bag of cocaine on Friday morning?' Ruth asked.

'Okay, okay.' Amelia laughed. 'If we're going to do this properly then let me take you back a couple of days, shall I?'

Ruth wasn't quite sure what Amelia was talking about but she nodded to encourage her to continue.

'I was pottering around in my dear old mother's garden shed, trying to tidy things up now my dad has passed,' Amelia explained. 'And, if I'm honest, I knew that Jack was going to fire me because of my affair with Lottie. It was very stupid on my part. I'd worked so hard to get to be right in the middle of the Rush empire. But, as they say, we are most alive when we are in love.'

'You knew you were running out of time?' Ruth suggested.

'Exactly,' Amelia agreed and looked at Nick. 'She's very good, isn't she? I knew that I was about to be banished from the Rush empire forever. I had to act quickly. But I couldn't very well take a knife into Jack's office and stab him in cold blood. I needed something with some kind of delay. And that's where we come back to my little story about my mother's shed. I knocked over a black tin and saw that it said rat poison on the side. It looked very old. And that's when I noticed that the poison was a white powder. It looked like cocaine to me. That got me thinking of course.'

'When did you swap it then?' Nick asked.

'Jack left me alone for a few minutes,' Amelia explained. 'He has the bladder of a kitten these days. I knew we were building up to the grand sacking. And while he was out, I just took the cocaine from Jack's desk.'

'How did you know where to find it?' Ruth asked.

'I've been to the house before. Several times,' Amelia said. 'I've taken cocaine with Jack off that very desk. I know where he keeps it. It was just a matter of swapping a bag of rat poison for the cocaine before he got back from taking a piss. It took all of thirty seconds. It was very easy, to be honest.'

Ruth looked at Nick with relief. Amelia had confessed to murdering Jack.

'Lucinda Davies,' Ruth said as she fixed her with a stare. 'I'm arresting and charging you with the murder of Jack Rush. You do not have to say anything, but anything you do say will be taken down and used in a court of law.'

CHAPTER 52

Ruth opened her eyes slowly and realised that she'd been sleeping in the chair in her DI's office. She glanced at her watch and saw that it as 6:30 a.m. She and Nick had finally wrapped things up with Amelia – now Lucinda Davies – at four a.m. with the custody sergeant. Lucinda would be kept in one of the custody cells before being taken before a judge at Mold Crown Court later that morning. Assuming that Lucinda continued to admit to her guilt, there would be no trial and she would be sentenced at a later date.

'Coffee?' asked a voice.

It was Nick. He looked as fresh as a daisy.

'Where did you end up sleeping and why do you look so well rested?' Ruth groaned as she stretched and yawned.

'In the car. Put the seat back, put on some music and I was well away,' Nick explained.

Ruth took a long swig of coffee and sighed, 'Bloody hell, I needed that.'

Nick sat down opposite her with his black coffee. 'We got a result,' he said.

'We did,' Ruth nodded. 'I've got to admit that I didn't see that coming. But this case has been very strange from the start.'

'Yeah, definitely not one to forget in a hurry,' Nick agreed.

Looking past Nick, Ruth could see that most of the CID team were already in.

'Bloody hell, Nick,' she groaned. 'I can't believe most of that lot are in and you left me sleeping here.'

Nick grinned. 'Ah, well you looked so cute, with your feet on the desk, snoring.'

'I don't snore,' she protested.

'Wanna bet?' he laughed.

'Come on,' Ruth said as she slipped on her shoes. 'Let's start to wind things up.'

As Ruth walked out of her office, there was applause and some whistling which was customary when an investigation finally got their man – or in this case – woman.

'Thank you, yeah, yeah,' Ruth said uncomfortably as she waved her hands to settle everyone down. 'As you're all aware, Amelia Wharton, who we now know was in fact Lucinda Davies, confessed to deliberately poisoning Jack Rush in an interview with Nick and I in the early hours of this morning. She has also written and signed a confession to that effect.'

'Saves us going to trial, boss,' Georgie said with a smile.

'And thank God for that,' Kennedy agreed.

The atmosphere in the CID office was buoyant.

'And just so you know, I'll be standing at the bar at the Red Lion from 5:30 p.m. and drinks will be on me,' Ruth said with a grin. 'I'm incredibly proud to lead this CID team and thank you all for your hard work on this case. I know it's been very complicated.'

There were cheers and applause.

'But we do need to tie this all up properly,' Ruth said. 'I want officers over at Amelia's mother's house in Bala today. Go through her belongings and her car. Let's get her phone records, bank statements, social media posts, the lot. If she turns around at some point and decides to plead not guilty, I don't want us to have taken our eye off the ball. I want as much evidence against her as we can get. And I don't want the CPS banging on my door demanding to know why we've not done a thorough job. So, I'll be in my office if anyone needs me.'

Georgie came over. 'You're going to the reading of Jack Rush's will in Chester later today, aren't you?'

Ruth nodded. 'I am. Thank you for reminding me.'

'Mind if I tag along?' Georgie asked.

Ruth smiled at her. 'Of course I don't mind.'

CHAPTER 53

Ruth sat at the far end of the enormous meeting room at Karan Patel's law firm in Chester. The whole of Jack Rush's family were seated around the table for the reading of Jack's will. Ruth had already received several glares from Lottie. She assumed that was because of what had happened with Amelia Wharton aka Lucinda Davies. Ed and James Rush sat together looking sullen. Charlie was talking in a hushed voice to Sofia. Ruth assumed that he was now a very relieved man since they'd charged Amelia with Jack's murder. Jasmine was sitting nearby looking at something on her phone.

Karan sat at the near end of the table as he sorted through various documents. He then put on his reading glasses and looked at the family.

'Okay, everybody,' Karan said as he cleared his throat. 'Obviously this is a very sad occasion for all of us. I'd been Jack's lawyer for the past twenty years. But I also counted him as a friend and I will miss him greatly.'

No one seemed to react to Karan's sentiment. Jasmine looked up from her phone and Sofia signalled for her to put it away.

'It is incumbent on me to inform you that Jack changed his will about a month ago,' Karan explained. 'As you all know, Jack had been suffering from health issues and he told me it had clarified a few things in his mind about the future. And the future of this family.'

Lottie narrowed her eyes as Karan was talking.

'However, I don't think there is anything that is particularly complicated here. Jack's assets included the house in Abersoch,' Karan said as he looked at the will. 'Multiple properties in Chester, London, New York and Los Angeles. A villa in Ibiza. Various stocks, shares, investments, pension fund. And Rush Pictures, of course. The estimated value of Jack's estate is £78 million.'

Ruth scanned the various members of the family but no one seemed to react to the vast sum of Jack's net worth. She assumed that they all knew he was an extremely wealthy man.

'So, I'm going to read you Jack's will now,' Karan said as he took the document in his hands. 'I, Jack David Rush, being of sound mind and body, leave the entirety of my estate to my daughters, Sofia and Jasmine. I have instructed my lawyer to set up a trust fund for Jasmine and her inheritance will be available to her on her eighteenth birthday.'

Silence.

Sofia looked over at Jasmine who hadn't reacted at all.

'As I said,' Karan stated. 'All very straightforward.'

Ed sat forward with a sarcastic grin and began to clap his hands loudly. 'Brilliant, Dad. That is fucking hilarious.'

James scowled at Sofia and shook his head. 'He wasn't even your real father.'

Lottie got up from her chair and stormed out of the room.

'Okay, everyone,' Karan said calmly. 'That concludes our business here.' He then got up as the members of the family talked in angry voices.

Ruth stood up, walked across the room and followed Karan out into the corridor.

'That seems to have ruffled a few feathers,' Ruth said.

'I don't think any of them can be that surprised,' Karan said in a withering tone. 'Jack had been grooming Sofia to be his heir for years. And she might not be his daughter biologically, but Sofia is more like Jack than any of his actual children.'

'Really?' Ruth asked with a dubious expression. 'That's not the impression I got at all.'

'She's very good at masking it. But Sofia is going to be just as cold and ruthless in running Rush Pictures as her father. You mark my words,' Karan said.

'I thought they might have fallen out over the prenuptial agreement,' Ruth said.

'Why?' Karan snorted. 'That was Sofia's idea, not Jack's. She was the one that wanted to make sure Charlie couldn't just waltz off with the family money. Very shrewd.'

Ruth was very surprised.

Karan pointed to his office at the end of the corridor. 'Anyway, I must get on.'

'Of course.' Ruth nodded and made her way back to reception. She was still trying to process what Karan had told her about Sofia. It was such a contrast to the young woman that Ruth had encountered in recent days.

Ruth came out of the offices and looked around. Georgie was sitting over on a bench on the pavement, drinking coffee. She gave Ruth a little wave.

'How did it go?' she asked.

'Everything went to Sofia and Jasmine,' Ruth said.

Georgie's eyes widened. 'Really? That must have gone down well with the others.'

'Lottie stormed out.'

'I saw her leave,' Georgie said but looked distracted as Sofia came out of the building. 'Better go and have a word.'

Ruth nodded as Georgie got up from the bench.

'Sofia?' Georgie called.

Sofia looked at Ruth and Georgie as if she was debating whether or not to talk to them. Then she came over.

'Do you want to sit down again?' Sofia said gesturing to the bench.

Georgie gave a wry smile. 'Now I've stood up, I'm actually feeling a bit dizzy.'

Ruth took her arm and helped her as Georgie sat down again.

'That's better,' Georgie sighed and then gestured for Sofia to sit down next to her which she did.

'Did you know the stipulations of your father's will?' Georgie asked.

'Yes.' Sofia nodded. 'Or at least I had a good idea that's what he'd done,' she admitted. 'He'd spent the last few years teaching me how to run his empire if anything ever happened to him. He talked about retiring and handing me the reins but I couldn't see that ever happening.'

'But it's all yours,' Ruth said, watching Sofia closely. The whole little girl lost act seemed to have vanished and it had been replaced by a steely confidence.

'That's right. And Jasmine's of course,' Sofia said.

'I'm sorry that we've had to meet under these circumstances,' Georgie said.

'Me too,' Sofia said as she looked up and a black Mercedes pulled up on the road beside them. She got up and put a reassuring hand on Georgie's shoulder. 'Good luck with everything. Let me know how it goes, okay?'

'I will do,' Georgie said.

For a moment, they watched Sofia waltz away, get in the car and speed off.

Ruth looked at Georgie with a suspicious frown. 'You ever get a nagging feeling that not only is someone hiding something, but they have a much darker side that you've never seen before.'

'Sofia?'

Ruth nodded. 'I don't know why, but my instinct is telling me to have another look at her.'

Before they could say anything else, Georgie winced in pain. 'Wow, that really hurt.'

'Contraction?'

'Something like that.'

'Are you okay?' Ruth asked with concern.

'It's fine,' Georgie reassured her and then she pulled a face. 'Actually, I think my waters just broke.'

CHAPTER 54

Ruth sat at Georgie's bedside in the Llancastell University Hospital maternity ward. Georgie winced again in pain and Ruth took her hand. Then Georgie relaxed again. She was starting to have contractions.

'You do know that they're probably going to send me home now,' Georgie said.

Ruth frowned. 'I wouldn't be so sure about that.'

'But I haven't got any of my stuff from home,' Georgie said looking a little panicked. 'I can't stay here. I've got stuff to do.'

'If they tell you to stay, then you're staying,' Ruth said, aware that she sounded like Georgie's mother. 'Have you got your hospital bag packed at home?'

'Yes. It's a small pink bag to the right of my bed,' Georgie explained but she looked worried.

'You can give me your keys and I can pop and get it,' Ruth said trying to reassure her.

'Thank you,' Georgie said and then frowned. 'What did you think about what Sofia said outside the lawyers?'

'She's definitely not the young woman I thought she was,' Ruth admitted. 'You know Karan told me that it was Sofia that pushed for the prenup, not Jack.'

'What? That's not what she told us?'

'No. Karan described her as cold and ruthless,' Ruth said with a frown. 'I didn't get any of that from our conversations.'

'Maybe that was all a big act,' Georgie suggested.

'But why?' Ruth asked. 'If she didn't have anything to hide, why did she feel the need to not just be herself? What was she hiding?'

'I don't know, but it is definitely a strange one,' Georgie sighed. 'And her comment that Jack was unlikely to retire and hand the company over to her, despite grooming her to take over.'

Ruth nodded in agreement. 'Can you remember when Jack and Lottie married?'

'It was the year before Jasmine was born,' Georgie stated. 'So, 2009?'

'And Sofia would have been twelve or thirteen,' Ruth said thinking out loud.

Georgie narrowed her eyes. 'What are you thinking?'

'I'm thinking that it seems strange that Jack identified Sofia as the one to groom to take over the family business,' Ruth said. 'Biologically she's not his daughter.'

'Maybe he just realised that his two sons just weren't up to the job and that Sofia was,' Georgie suggested.

'Maybe,' Ruth said but she wasn't entirely convinced.

Before they could continue, a midwife came over.

'Hi, Georgie,' the midwife – blonde, late forties, smiley – said in a calm, friendly voice. She had a badge that read *Bethan Williams*. 'Okay, I'm going to examine you again. But your waters have broken and you are in the early stages of labour now.'

'Can I go home?' Georgie asked.

Bethan gave her a smile. 'Let me just examine you and we can see.'

Bethan put on her disposable light blue gloves and examined Georgie for a few seconds.

'Okay,' Bethan said. 'Well, you're close to being four centimetres dilated so I don't think it's a good idea for you to go home now.' Bethan looked at Ruth. 'Have you got anyone that can go home and get you everything you need?'

'That's me,' Ruth said raising her hand a little.

'Aw, that's great,' the midwife said. 'Is your mum going to be staying with you the whole time you're in here?'

Georgie smiled. 'She's not actually my mum,' she explained. 'But she's a very good friend.'

'Oh, I'm sorry.' Bethan gave a little laugh.

'How long before…?' Georgie asked.

'Before "baby" arrives?' Bethan said. 'Oh, it's going to be quite a while.'

Ruth nodded. 'It took Ella nearly thirty-six hours to appear.'

'Thirty-six hours! Bloody hell,' Georgie groaned.

Bethan smiled. 'Don't worry. Just relax. You're here now. Do you want me to get you anything. Cup of tea? Water?'

'Water would be good,' Georgie replied as she read-justed her pillows.

Bethan wandered away.

'Right,' Ruth said decisively. 'Let me have your keys. I'll go and get your bag and then pop into the shop to pick up some things.'

'Wine gums. I really fancy wine gums.'

'Wine gums? We can do wine gums. And you're going to need to eat something more substantial than that even if you don't feel like it.'

'Thanks, Mum,' Georgie joked as she reached into her bag and handed Ruth her keys.

CHAPTER 55

Nick sat at his desk and glanced over at a framed photograph of Amanda and Caitlin that had been taken at Chester Zoo the year before. He'd just checked in with Amanda who was sounding a lot brighter and more positive than she was this morning. She'd spent much needed time with her sponsor.

Amanda's relapse had brought into sharp focus how much she meant to Nick. He didn't know what he'd do without her and seeing her so upset had really rattled him. It had also reminded him that they were both alcoholics and if they didn't work at their recovery, it could all go wrong. And they had their daughter Caitlin toyou think of.

Nick knew someone in AA who had been twenty-four years sober. He had eventually drifted away from meetings and stopped working his twelve-step recovery programme. One day he told his wife that he was going to join her in a glass of white wine. When she protested, he reassured her that he was no longer an alcoholic and only went to the occasional meeting to help new members. He was sure that after nearly a quarter of a century of not drinking alcohol, he could now drink safely. He drank the glass of white wine and proceeded to drink three more over the evening. As far as he was concerned, he was now cured. The next day, he went to the pub, drank four pints and came home. It was a miracle. The weekend came and he went out with all his friends. They were amazed to see him drinking. But when they all wanted to go home, he was having none of it. He was staying out no matter what. Waking up in urine-soaked trousers in a police cell the following morning, he was informed that he had assaulted a police officer the night before. He was sent to prison for six months. Nick reminded himself of this story when he got complacent. He would always be an alcoholic and there was no cure.

Nick's phone buzzed, breaking his train of thought.

'DS Evans,' he said answering his phone.

'Sarge,' said a female voice at the other end of the line. 'It's DC Vicky Conway from Digital Forensics.'

Nick had known Vicky since she was a probationer. She'd always struck him as sharp and intelligent so it was good to see her now over in Forensics.

'Hi, Vicky,' he said in a friendly voice.

'You guys were looking for some video files that had been deleted from a computer owned by Jasmine Rush.'

'That's right,' Nick replied. However, now that Amelia Wharton / Lucinda Davies had made a full confession to Jack's murder, the files of Jasmine Rush's wedding video seemed far less important.

'We've managed to find them,' she said. 'They were automatically saved to the cloud.'

'Oh, right. Great. Can you get them over to us to have a look at some point?' Nick asked. He didn't want to tell her that they may no longer be relevant to the case.

'They've been encrypted so we've got to change them to a format that you can read on your computers,' she explained. 'But I've had a look at one of them. I think you should probably come over here now and take a look.'

'That sounds ominous,' Nick said.

'I don't know all the ins and outs of the investigation,' Vicky said. 'And I know that you've already charged someone with Jack Rush's murder. But there's stuff on here that you should see sooner rather than later.'

'Okay, I'm on my way,' Nick said as he ended the call. He was now concerned as to what they'd found.

Getting up from his desk, Nick looked over at Garrow. 'Jim, they've found those deleted video files from Jasmine Rush's computer. Want to come over to Digital Forensics to have a quick look? They seem to think there's stuff on there that we need to see.'

Garrow nodded. 'Definitely.'

Grabbing his jacket, Nick and Garrow headed towards the doors that led out of CID and made their way downstairs.

CHAPTER 56

Ruth marched along the corridor with Georgie's hospital bag from her home and a supermarket bag full of food, drink — and wine gums. Entering the maternity ward, Ruth saw Georgie and went over.

'Got it,' Ruth said with a smile as she sat down next to the bed.

Georgie pointed to the supermarket bag. 'I'm about to give birth. That looks like a weekly shop.'

Ruth shrugged. 'I didn't know what you'd fancy apart from wine gums. I remember craving prawn cocktail crisps and Irn-Bru. Normally I don't like either of them.'

Georgie took a breath and blinked. She didn't look quite right.

'You okay?' Ruth asked.

'Bit dizzy. And I feel very sick,' Georgie said with a frown.

'Okay,' Ruth said calmly. 'I'll get the midwife.'

'No, it's fine.' Georgie shook her head. 'I don't want to cause a fuss.'

'Don't be silly.'

Ruth stood up and gave Bethan a little wave.

'Ruth!' Georgie sighed.

Bethan wandered over. 'Hi, how are you doing Georgie?'

'I'm very dizzy. And I feel sick,' Georgie admitted. She was starting to look pale.

Bethan nodded. 'I'll come back in a minute and just check that everything is okay.'

'Thank you,' Ruth said as her phone rang. It was Nick.

'Hi, Nick,' she said as she answered. 'Don't panic, but I'm with Georgie in the hospital. Her waters have broken and she's starting to have contractions.'

'Is she okay?' Nick asked sounding concerned.

'Yes, she's fine,' Ruth reassured him. 'I'm sitting with her now.'

'Oh, good.' Nick sounded relieved. 'We've had a call from Digital Forensics. They've found those deleted video files that were on Jasmine Rush's computer. They've asked me to go over as a matter of urgency. It seems that whatever is on them, they want us to see them right away.'

Bethan arrived and began to take Georgie's obs – pulse, blood pressure, etc.

'Okay,' Ruth said looking puzzled. 'But they didn't say what?'

'No. Jim and I are heading there now,' Nick explained.

'Right, let me know when you've had a look,' Ruth said.

'Will do. And send my love to Georgie,' Nick said as he ended the phone call.

Ruth went to pass the message on but Georgie was now looking very unwell.

'Georgie?' Ruth said sounding concerned.

Bethan was finishing taking Georgie blood pressure. As she looked at the monitor, she blinked thoughtfully.

'Okay, Georgie,' Bethan said in a calm but serious voice. 'Your blood pressure has fallen quite dramatically in the past hour, so I'm going to get a doctor to come and look at you. Okay?'

Georgie nodded and then glanced at Ruth. She looked frightened.

Ruth reached over and took her hand. 'It's okay. Don't worry. They're just being on the safe side.'

CHAPTER 57

DC Vicky Conway – thirties, jet-black hair, ruddy face – pointed to the screen that they were looking at. 'So, this is the first file that we managed to get from the cloud,' she explained. 'As I said, it's going to take a while to get it all transferred into the right format.'

'But you thought we needed to have a look?' Nick asked.

Vicky nodded with a serious expression. 'I thought so. I'll show you.'

She pressed play.

A handheld camera POV could be seen on the monitor.

Nick recognised it as the main staircase at the Rush mansion.

'*And welcome to our crib,*' said a voice that Nick recognised to be Jasmine Rush. '*I'm going to show you around today.*'

The camera POV started to go up the stairs. '*Notice the designer glass stairs. Okay, they're very dangerous and I've nearly fallen down them a few times, but they do look cool,*' Jasmine said as she continued to walk up the stairs to the top.

'*And this is the upstairs of the house. This is where most of the weird stuff happens around here,*' Jasmine said as she walked along the landing. '*But that's a different story.*' She gave a little laugh.

The camera then turned to the left to show a huge en suite bedroom that was fashionably decorated.

'*Here we have the master bedroom where Mummy and Daddy sleep,*' Jasmine narrated in a mock presenter's voice. '*Although Daddy does have to sleep in the spare bedroom when Mummy is angry with him. And that's quite a lot of the time.*'

The camera came back and continued down the landing.

At the end, there were a pair of double doors open.

Nick recognised that they were the doors that led to Jack Rush's office.

'*Ooh,*' Jasmine said. '*Now that's very interesting indeed. Daddy has left the doors to his office open. He doesn't usually do that. Shall we go and have a look inside?*'

The camera moved down the landing, through the double doors and into Jack's office. It then moved over to his desk and showed his various film awards.

'*And there's his Oscar. It's incredible, isn't it daaarling?*' Jasmine said, but she sounded as if she was being sarcastic. The camera then went over to the desk, turned, and then Jasmine clearly sat down in the big office chair. '*I wonder what he hides in here?*'

The camera POV showed Jasmine's free hand as she opened all the drawers, before she saw a silver box in the bottom drawer. Taking it out, she put it on the desk.

'*What a beautiful little box,*' Jasmine exclaimed as she reached out and opened the box. '*What does he keep inside here?*' Then she pulled out a small bag of white powder – cocaine. '*Oops. I should probably put that back.*'

The camera POV showed Jasmine putting the cocaine back into the box, closing the lid and placing the silver box back in the drawer.

Nick exchanged a concerned look with Garrow. It was making for uncomfortable viewing.

Jasmine then knocked a small hole punch off the desk and it dropped to the floor.

'*Oh, dear, hold on,*' Jasmine narrated as she propped the camera on the desk so she could use both hands to retrieve the hole punch.

For the first time, Jasmine's face appeared on the screen and she gave a little wave. '*Hello everyone!*' she said with a cheeky grin.

Jasmine disappeared out of sight for a moment. '*Oh, what's this?*' she said in her 'narrator's voice' as she came back into the shot with the hole punch and a large A4 folder.

Jasmine looked straight at the camera. '*Now this was stuck under the desk which is very suspicious don't you think?*'

Jasmine then opened the folder and began to pull out a huge stack of photos.

Her expression completely changed to one of horror.

As she put the photos out on the desk, it is clear that all of the photos are of Sofia.

Sofia naked in the shower.

Sofia getting dressed with no top on.

Sofia sunbathing in the garden.

It's clear that they had all been taken without Sofia's knowledge.

'Jesus,' Nick said under his breath.

'That's seriously creepy,' Garrow said in a virtual whisper.

'It gets worse,' Vicky said with a dark expression.

Jasmine shuffled through the photos with an increasingly disgusted look on her face.

The photos were now of Sofia in her early teens. And she was naked or in her underwear in all of them.

Off camera, there's a voice.

'*What are you doing, Jas?*' asked a female voice.

It was Sofia.

Jasmine looked up. '*I found these under Dad's desk. What the actual fuck!*' she said quietly. '*I feel sick looking at them.*'

'*You need to put them back,*' Sofia said desperately, out of shot.

'*Why?*' Jasmine demanded angrily.

'*Please, Jas,*' Sofia pleaded. '*It doesn't matter.*'

'*Yes, it does,*' Jasmine snapped. '*He's sick. It's disgusting. Did you know he was doing this?*'

'*Jas. Please, before he comes back and finds us in here,*' Sofia said.

Then Jasmine's expression changed. '*Has he… Has he ever touched you or anything?*'

Silence for a few seconds.

'*Sofia? Tell me. Has he ever made you do stuff with him?*'

There is a long silence.

Then, '*Oh, my God, is that bloody thing recording? Turn it off, Jas!*'

The screen went black.

Nick looked over at Garrow and then at Vicky. They were all in complete shock.

CHAPTER 58

Ruth was now sitting waiting. Georgie had been moved into a single room so that she could be monitored more carefully. The doctor had said that Georgie was suffering from maternal hypotension. It could be fatal for both mother and child during birth if it wasn't managed very carefully. They were going to administer intravenous fluids to see if they could increase her blood volume and therefore raise her blood pressure. If that didn't work, they would administer phenylephrine, a medication that would hopefully do the same thing. The main objective was to stop the baby going into distress in the womb due to the lack of blood.

Biting her cuticles, Ruth was gasping for a cigarette but she daren't leave the maternity ward. Her stomach was tight with nerves.

Looking up, she saw Nick hurrying towards her. He sat down, a little out of breath.

'I got your message. How's she doing?' Nick asked softly.

Ruth pulled a face. 'They're just monitoring her very closely. But I'm sure she'll be okay.' Ruth wasn't sure about that at all but it wasn't worth worrying Nick as well. 'You going somewhere?'

'Abersoch,' he said with a dark look.

'Why?' Ruth asked, wondering why he looked so stern.

'Those deleted videos Forensics retrieved,' he said. 'There's a video that Jasmine made at the house. She goes into Jack Rush's office and starts to snoop around. First of all she finds his cocaine in the drawer.'

'Jesus,' Ruth whispered.

'And then she found a folder that Jack had hidden under his desk,' Nick explained. 'Secret photos of Sofia in the shower, getting dressed, lying on the bed naked. They go all the way back to when she first moved in when she was about twelve.'

'Oh, God, that's horrible.' Ruth groaned. 'How the hell did the SOCO team miss that?'

'He must have moved them... Sofia came in to find Jasmine looking at them all,' Nick continued. 'But she told her to put them back. That it didn't matter. It was very strange. As if Sofia already knew they were there. Then Jasmine asked her if Jack had ever touched her but before she says anything else, Sofia sees the camera is on and the recording stops.'

'Bloody hell,' Ruth sighed. 'That's horrendous. But we've got Amelia Wharton's confession.'

'I know.' Nick nodded. 'But I think we owe it to Sofia and the whole family for the truth to come out, don't you?'

'We need to tread very carefully,' Ruth said. 'I think you should talk to Sofia and Jasmine. If there was some kind of abuse, Sofia is going to need all the help and support she can get. And I'd like to know what Lottie knew about it, if anything.'

Nick nodded. 'Jasmine is obviously going to need an appropriate adult at the station. And clearly, neither of them have done anything wrong. But we have a duty of care to make sure that both Jasmine and Sofia are safe going forward.'

'I agree,' Ruth said as Nick got up. 'Keep me posted.'

CHAPTER 59

An hour later, Nick and Garrow drove through the gates leading to the Rush mansion. Most of the camera crews and journalists had now left the area. The story was starting to become old news and it wouldn't surface again until Amelia Wharton / Lucinda Davies was sentenced for Jack Rush's murder.

As they pulled up onto the huge driveway, Nick spotted a white Porsche.

Inside was Sofia sitting in the driving seat with Jasmine in the passenger seat.

'Looks like we're just in time to talk to them,' Garrow said as Nick stopped the car and they got out.

They approached the Porsche and Nick gave Sofia a signal that he wanted to talk to her.

Sofia buzzed her window down and gave Nick a suspicious look. 'Can I help?'

Nick glanced over at Jasmine. 'Yes. We wanted you and Jasmine to come back to the station with us actually. Nothing to worry about, just some routine stuff but it is important.'

'No. I don't think so.' Sofia scowled at him. 'I'm taking Jas out for lunch. We've been cooped up in this house for too long. And now you've arrested that woman, I don't see why you need to speak to us.'

Garrow moved around the car slowly.

Nick took a moment to think. 'It's just that we've now seen the videos that Jasmine deleted from her computer. And we would really like to talk to you both about what's been going on there. We'll obviously let Lottie know too.'

'You had no right to do that!' Jasmine snapped angrily.

'I'm not going to let you take us to a police station,' Sofia said as she started the car's engine.

'Sofia, I'm going to need you to turn off the engine,' Nick said calmly. 'There's no implication that you or Jasmine have done anything wrong. We just want you to explain what we've seen.'

'No.' Sofia ignored him and pulled the car forward.

'Woah, woah!' Nick shouted. 'What are you doing, Sofia?'

'If you want us to come with you,' she growled. '…then you can talk to my lawyers.'

Garrow came back to where Nick was standing and then looked at Sofia. 'You're not going to be driving anywhere today, I'm afraid. You've got a very flat tyre at the back. It's not safe for you to drive.'

'What?' Sofia groaned angrily.

Nick reached down and opened the driver's door. 'Come on. This won't take long and we'll drop you straight back afterwards.'

CHAPTER 60

Nick was sitting opposite Sofia in Interview Room 2. There was no need for anyone else to be present as Sofia wasn't being interviewed for anything that she'd done wrong or a crime that she'd committed.

Nick looked at her with an empathetic expression. 'Sure you don't want something to drink?'

Sofia shook her head angrily. 'I want to clear all this up and get me and my sister out of here.'

Nick nodded. 'We saw a video that Jasmine had recorded in Jack's office. And we also saw the photos that Jack had kept hidden under his desk.'

Silence.

Sofia's face fell as she took a breath to compose herself. 'Well, I wish that Jasmine had never seen them,' she whispered.

'Had you any idea they were there?' Nick asked.

Sofia took a few seconds to think. 'I knew that he took photos of me.'

Nick looked shocked. 'And you thought that was ok?'

'No, of course not. I thought it was scary and creepy,' Sofia replied.

Nick narrowed his eyes. 'Why didn't you say something?'

'Mum and I had had a pretty rough time before she met Jack. And he gave us both everything we could have ever dreamed of,' Sofia admitted. 'Mum was happy. So what if my stepfather was madly in love with me.'

'Did Lottie know about this?'

'She's not an idiot. I think it was pretty obvious how Jack felt about me from the time we moved in with him.'

'But she never said or did anything?' Nick said.

'She couldn't, could she?' Sofia replied. 'Jack gave her an incredible life and she didn't want to rock the boat. So, she just looked the other way and pretended it wasn't happening.'

'Didn't that make things deeply uncomfortable for you?' Nick asked.

'Sometimes,' Sofia admitted. 'But it also made me the centre of Jack's world for the past decade. And I liked the attention. My real father wanted nothing to do with me.'

Nick frowned. 'Jack never tried to touch you or anything like that?'

'God, no,' Sofia snorted. 'That wasn't his style. He just wanted to watch me at a distance. I knew that he was never going to act on his feelings.'

'And he never said anything inappropriate to you?' Nick asked with a curious expression.

'No, of course not,' Sofia sighed. 'His love for me wasn't grubby. He just saw me as this perfect being. He didn't want to touch me but he didn't want anyone else to either. That's why he hated Charlie so much.'

Nick looked at her. 'And you just allowed it to continue?'

'I was being lined up to be one of the most powerful film producers in the world,' Sofia explained. 'If Jack wanted to be in love with me and take photos of me, that was fine. I knew I was safe. And in return, he was going to give me a life and career beyong my wildest dreams. But I don't expect you to understand.'

CHAPTER 61

'Jasmine,' Garrow said gently. 'I'd like to talk to you about the videos that you deleted. The ones that you had on your computer.'

Jasmine was sitting opposite Garrow and Kennedy in Interview Room 2. Beside her was a woman in her fifties who was acting as Jasmine's 'appropriate adult' as she was under the age of eighteen.

'Okay,' Jasmine shrugged nonchalantly. 'Which video would you like to talk about first?'

'Well, we saw the video where you went into your father's study and found the photos of Sofia,' Garrow said quietly. 'That must have been very upsetting for you?'

'Yes, it was. It was disgusting,' Jasmine replied, her nostrils flaring with anger. 'It made me hate him so much.'

'And we saw that Sofia came in and found you looking through those photos,' Garrow said.

'Yes.' Jasmine nodded. 'And she told me to put them away.'

Kennedy looked at her. 'So you did put them back?'

Jasmine nodded. 'I told her that we should call the police and get him arrested.'

'What did Sofia say to that?' Garrow asked.

'She said we couldn't do that,' Jasmine replied. 'That we'd lose everything if Jack was arrested. I didn't under-stand what she was talking about. And even though Sofia said that my father never touched her, I could see that she was lying to protect him. He was a monster.' Jasmine looked directly at Garrow. 'And of course, that's why I did it. I needed to protect my sister from him before he did it again.'

Garrow took a few seconds to process what she'd said. He looked at Kennedy who had a concerned expression.

'Sorry, Jasmine, you said "that's why I did it"?' Garrow said. 'What exactly do you mean by that?'

Jasmine gave him a withering look. 'That's why I killed him. What did you think I meant?'

Jesus.

Garrow took a breath. He'd had no idea this is what was going to happen during this conversation.

'Jasmine, I'm just going to put this machine on, so we can record what we're talking about, okay?' Kennedy said gently.

'Yes, of course. That's why I'm here, isn't?' she said as if Garrow was being stupid.

Kennedy leaned over and pressed the red record button on the machine. There was a long electronic beep.

'Interview conducted with Jasmine Rush at Llancastell Police Station. Present are Jasmine, Helen Rose from social services, DS James Garrow and myself, DC Jade Kennedy.'

Garrow could feel his pulse quicken. 'Okay, Jasmine. Can you tell me what happened?'

'I knew that I had to put a stop to what my father was doing to her,' Jasmine said very calmly. 'And of course you've seen the video that I made?'

Garrow nodded.

Jasmine pulled out her phone and tapped it so that a video played. 'You see I knew that my father kept cocaine in his drawer after I'd found the silver box. And I'd seen some very old wasp-killing powder in the garden shed. I did some research online and it said that it was fatal to humans. And it's white powder so that's how I got the idea.'

Jasmine tilted her phone to show Garrow a video of Jasmine, wearing rubber gloves, carefully using a tiny spoon to deposit the poison into a small, clear plastic bag.

'Can you tell me why you filmed this?' Garrow asked, realising that the video she was showing him might still be being reformatted by the Digital Forensics team.

'It's obvious, isn't it?' Jasmine said in a condescending tone.

'Not really,' Kennedy said.

'I'm a twelve-year-old girl. And I'm killing my father to stop him abusing my sister,' Jasmine explained. 'No judge or jury is going to send me to prison for doing that, are they?'

'We found a fibre from Charlie Huntington's jacket in the seal of the bag,' Kennedy said.

Jasmine nodded. 'I thought Charlie was the most obvious person to frame. But I knew you'd probably find out it was me eventually.'

Garrow's heart sank. Jasmine really did believe that what she'd done wouldn't be punishable by law.

'Jasmine, I'm afraid that I'm going to have to read you your rights,' Garrow explained.

Jasmine smiled. 'Of course. I understand that. You're just doing your job.'

CHAPTER 62

Ruth glanced down at her phone. She had been exchanging messages with Sarah to tell her about Georgie. It had been nearly an hour since Ruth had spoken to Bethan or any of the medical staff on the maternity ward. Maybe no news was good news, but it certainly didn't feel that way.

Sensing that someone was approaching, Ruth looked up and saw that it was Adam, the paramedic that Georgie had just started to date. He was still wearing his bright green paramedic uniform and wore a heavy expression on his face.

'Hey,' Ruth said looking up at him.

'I came as soon as I finished my shift,' Adam said quietly as he sat down next to her. 'What's happening?'

'I'm not sure,' Ruth admitted. 'Falling blood pressure seems to be the issue. They've taken her to a single room down there but no one has told me anything for a while. I'll go and ask in a minute.'

Adam looked at her. 'Thank you for keeping me updated.'

'Of course,' Ruth said. 'I know it's early days but I also know how fond she is of you.'

Ruth's phone buzzed. It was Nick.

'Sorry, but I've got to take this,' Ruth said as she gestured to her phone, got up and wandered to a deserted part of the ward. 'Nick? Everything all right?'

'Erm, not really,' he said. 'Are you sitting down?'

'No,' Ruth replied, concerned by Nick's tone. 'What's going on?'

'Okay. Very briefly. Jasmine Rush discovered secret photos that Jack Rush had been taking of Sofia ever since she and Lottie first moved into the house in Abersoch. They're pretty grim. Sofia knew that Jack was completely infatuated with her but didn't do anything about it. However, Jasmine convinced herself that Jack had been abusing her sister, so she poisoned him to protect Sofia. We've got a video of Jasmine spooning wasp poison into a bag. And pre-1980, wasp poison contained potassium cyanide. She's made a full confession.'

'Jesus Christ, Nick!' Ruth hissed under her breath. 'What about Amelia Wharton?'

'I've no idea,' Nick replied. 'But I'm ninety-nine per cent sure that she's innocent. We're meeting with the CPS in a minute but we are going to have to bring Amelia back here for questioning again.'

Silence. Ruth's head was now whirring with thoughts as she tried to process what Nick had just told her.

'Boss?' he said.

'Yeah, I'm still here,' Ruth told him. 'I know that Georgie needs me but I'm SIO on this investigation. I feel like I should be there too.'

'No. You're in the right place,' Nick reassured her. 'I've got this. And I'll keep you posted. Any news on Georgie?'

'Still waiting,' Ruth sighed.

'Okay, well I'll speak to you in a bit,' Nick said ending the call.

Ruth let out an audible sigh as she wandered back to the seats.

'You okay?' Adam asked with a frown.

'If I told you, you wouldn't believe me,' Ruth said quietly. Then she spotted the midwife Bethan coming over.

'Hi there.' Bethan had a serious look on her face. 'I've just spoken to the obstetrician about Georgie.'

'Okay,' Ruth said now panicking. 'What is it? Is she okay?'

CHAPTER 63

Nick sat down opposite Jane Hickson, the lawyer with the Crown Prosecution Service that Ruth had met two days earlier. Nick thought that she looked more like a librarian than a lawyer.

Hickson shook her head as she read Jasmine Rush's statement of what she had done and how she had poisoned her father. 'I don't think I've ever read anything quite like this before. And I've been doing this job for thirty years.'

Nick nodded in agreement. 'Yeah, I've never been involved in an investigation like this before either. And when we have encountered twelve-year-olds who have been involved in major crime, it's usually county lines or knife crime. Certainly not this. It's straight out of an old murder mystery novel.'

Hickson scratched her head as she sat back in her chair. 'The tragedy is that Jasmine really thought that she was protecting Sofia when she didn't need protecting.'

'And she just assumed that because of that, and because of her age, she wouldn't be convicted,' Nick sighed sadly.

'Her defence will probably enter a plea for manslaughter,' Hickson suggested. 'But given the planning and the video evidence, it's going to be very difficult to convince a jury that she didn't murder her father.'

'And given her privileged upbringing, she's going to find being in a youth detention centre pretty grim,' Nick stated.

Hickson nodded in agreement. 'I take it you now have all the videos that Jasmine deleted from her computer?'

'Yes,' Nick replied. 'Digital Forensics have downloaded them all now.'

There was a knock at the door and Kennedy poked her head in.

'Sarge, I need a word when you're finished, please,' she said with an urgent tone.

Nick moved his chair and glanced over at Hickson. 'I think we're pretty much finished for today?'

Hickson nodded as she stood up and put her folders into her smart leather briefcase. 'Yes. I've got a mountain of paperwork to do now. But I think that's it.'

Nick reached over, shook her hand and then followed Kennedy outside.

'Everything okay?' Nick asked.

'We've got Lottie and Sofia down at reception demanding to see Jasmine. Lottie is causing a bit of a fuss,' Kennedy explained.

'Okay,' Nick said thinking. 'Can you go and get Jasmine from custody and put her in the main meeting room? I'll go and get Lottie and Sofia and take them over to see her.'

'Will do, sarge,' Kennedy said as she turned to walk away.

CHAPTER 64

Ruth watched in horror as the maternity crash team wheeled Georgie out of her single room at speed. She was unconscious and had an oxygen mask attached to her face.

'Georgie,' Ruth said as the bed came past. She looked so pale and so vulnerable.

Adam was standing nearby, looking concerned.

Bethan hurried over. 'Okay, so we're taking Georgie into theatre right now. And we're performing an emergency C-section as her baby is showing signs of distress. And Georgie has lost consciousness due to her blood pressure.'

Ruth felt sick with worry. 'Is she going to be okay?'

'She's in good hands,' Bethan said but she hadn't actually answered Ruth's question which was worrying.

'Do we just wait here?' Ruth asked.

'You can come into theatre with us,' Bethan said.

Ruth frowned. 'Really?'

'I'm assuming that you're Georgie's birthing partner?' Bethan said knowingly.

'Yes, of course I am.' Ruth nodded but her heart was pounding against her chest.

'You're going to need to put on scrubs before you come into theatre,' Bethan explained and then gestured. 'Do you want to follow me?'

Ruth glanced back at Adam. 'It's okay. They're going to be fine,' she reassured him.

Then she hurried down the corridor as she followed Bethan towards the operating theatre.

CHAPTER 65

Nick walked along the corridor with Lottie and Sofia following behind. Lottie seemed to have calmed down and stopped threatening legal action.

They arrived at the main meeting room and Nick opened the door. Jasmine was sitting at the table and Kennedy was standing to one side.

Lottie and Sofia raced across the room to embrace Jasmine.

'Oh, my God,' Lottie sobbed. 'You poor, poor darling. Don't worry, we're going to sort all this out.'

Sofia crouched down beside Jasmine, her eyes full of tears. 'This is all my fault,' she wept. 'I can't believe that this has happened.'

Grabbing a chair, Lottie sat next to Jasmine and took her hand. 'Listen to me. It's going to be fine. We're going to get you the best lawyers and barristers in the country. I promise you.'

Jasmine nodded but she just looked overwhelmed.

Sofia dragged a chair over. 'And I don't want you saying anything else to the police unless you have our lawyer present,' she said as she gave Nick a hostile glare.

'Are you okay, darling,' Lottie said moving a strand of hair from Jasmine's face and then stroking her hair. 'Where are they keeping you?'

'In a cell down there,' Jasmine said as she pointed towards custody.

'In a cell!' Lottie exclaimed with a pained expression. Then she scowled at Nick. 'You can't keep her in a cell. She's twelve years old, for God's sake! You'll have to keep her in here.'

Nick looked over. 'I'm afraid that won't be possible. Jasmine has been charged with a serious offence and she will need to stay in custody until there is an initial hearing.'

'And when will that be?' Sofia asked angrily.

'It won't be until tomorrow morning,' Nick explained calmly.

'She can't stay here overnight,' Lottie snapped.

There was a knock at the door.

Nick opened it and saw Garrow who gave him a dark look.

'You okay in here?' Nick asked Kennedy as Lottie and Sofia continued to fuss around Jasmine.

'Yes, sarge,' Kennedy said giving him a knowing look.

Nick looked at Garrow. 'Everything okay?'

Garrow pulled a face. 'We've had a phone call from HMP Styal.'

Nick was concerned as he knew that was where Amelia Wharton had been taken on remand until she was taken to court to be sentenced.

'What is it?' he asked.

'Lucinda Davies hanged herself in her cell. They found her this morning,' Garrow sighed. 'She's dead.'

'Jesus,' Nick groaned. 'How the hell did they let that happen?'

'They didn't see her as a vulnerable prisoner,' Garrow replied. 'But she left a note.'

Nick frowned. 'Any idea what the note said?'

'Yes,' Garrow said. 'The Prison Governor has sent us a photo of it. But the gist of it is that she admitted that she'd lied about murdering Jack Rush. She wished she had done it more than anything in the world. But someone very lucky had beat her to it.'

CHAPTER 66

It was early evening and Nick and Amanda were making their way along the corridor towards the maternity ward. Nick had received a garbled message from Ruth to come to hospital but the rest of her message had been virtually inaudible.

Reaching out to hold Amanda's hand, Nick could feel the anxiety in his stomach as they pushed through the doors to the maternity ward. Glancing around nervously, Nick couldn't see anyone.

'Where's Ruth?' Amanda asked with a frown.

Nick moved swiftly towards the nurses station. 'Hi. I'm trying to find out some information about Georgie Wild. She was brought in early this afternoon?'

The nurse nodded and then gestured. 'Do you want to go and wait in her room. It's that single room over there.'

Nick frowned. 'Can't you tell me if she's okay?'

The nurse didn't react. 'If you can go into that room, then I'll get someone to come and talk to you in a minute.'

Nick looked uneasily at Amanda. He couldn't tell from the nurse's response what was going on but he felt physically sick.

Walking across the maternity ward, Nick and Amanda went into the empty room.

'Where's Adam?' Amanda asked as she sat down on a chair.

'I don't know but I thought he'd be here,' Nick said as he paced around the room nervously.

'Do you want to sit down?' Amanda asked pointing to a chair.

'No, I don't think I can,' Nick said trying to take a breath to steady himself.

Then his attention was drawn to the door as it started to open.

Nick held his breath. He just prayed that whoever was coming in was going to have good news about Georgie.

The door banged and then Nick spotted the front of a wheelchair.

What's going on?

As the door opened fully, he saw Georgie sitting in the wheelchair. She was holding a baby in her arms, wrapped in a soft white blanket.

Behind her, Ruth was pushing the wheelchair with a beaming Adam behind her.

'Oh, my God,' Nick sighed with relief as he went over.

'Oh, hello,' Georgie said with a beaming smile. 'This is Sylvie.'

'Aww, hello Sylvie,' Nick said as he peered down at Georgie's daughter. 'She's beautiful.'

'Thank you,' Georgie said.

'And that's a beautiful name,' Amanda sighed as she came over too.

'It was my grandmother's name,' Georgie explained.

'Right, we need to get you into bed,' Ruth said as she came around to help her.

Georgie looked up at Nick. 'Are you okay to hold her while I stand up?'

'Of course,' Nick said feeling a little overwhelmed.

Ruth and Adam helped Georgie into the bed. 'This one had us all a bit worried there for a while,' Ruth said as she pulled the sheets and green blanket over Georgie.

'A bit worried!' Adam snorted.

'Emergency C-section,' Georgie said by way of an explanation. 'Not that I can remember much about it.'

There was a knock at the door and it began to open.

It was Kennedy. She was holding a huge pink teddy bear.

'Hey, congratulations!' Kennedy said as she came over and kissed Georgie.

Nick came over with Sylvie in his arms. 'Here she is. This is Sylvie.'

'Aww,' Kennedy said. 'She's adorable.'

'Where's Jim?' Ruth asked.

'He sends his apologies,' Kennedy said. 'He said that he had something he couldn't get out of.'

The door opened again.

Sarah and Daniel walked in.

'Hi,' Sarah said as she went over to Georgie.

Daniel was holding a bunch of flowers which he then gave to Georgie while looking a little awkward.

'Here you go,' Daniel said quietly. 'Congratulations.'

'Thank you, Daniel.'

Your FREE book is waiting for you NOW

THE THEATRE STREET KILLING PREQUEL

South London 1995. A brutal murder.

Find out about Ruth Hunter and her move from Uniform to being a detective in CID.

Get your free prequel at

http://www.simonmccleave.com/vip-email-club

and join my VIP Email Club.

CANELOCRIME

Do you love crime fiction and are always on the lookout for brilliant authors?

Canelo Crime is home to some of the most exciting novels around. Thousands of readers are already enjoying our compulsive stories. Are you ready to find your new favourite writer?

Find out more and sign up to our newsletter at canelocrime.com